VAMPIRES & A REASONABLE DICTIONARY

VAMPIRES

&

A REASONABLE DICTIONARY

Žarko Radaković and Scott Abbott

punctum books * brooklyn, ny

First published in 2014 by
punctum books
Brooklyn, New York
http://punctumbooks.com

ISBN-13: 978-0692022238
ISBN-10: 0692022236

Library of Congress Cataloging Data is available from the Library of Congress.

Cover artwork by Nina Pops, with permission of the artist.

Facing-page drawing by Heather Masciandaro

Creative-Editorial Team: Sarah George, Christy Koester, Natalie Lapacek, and Mary McCormick

Since the country in which I was born has disintegrated, and since it is still in the jaws of a machine that cuts it and shapes it, I live like a being with a broken memory.

Žarko Radaković, *Vampires*

It's done. The divorce. I've cut my moorings. I'm adrift and nervous as hell. I think I'll be okay, unless the International Monetary Fund or the U.N.'s International Tribunal for the Former Yugoslavia or the Federation of Concerned Mountain Bikers decides to take a hand in molding my character.

Scott Abbott, *A Reasonable Dictionary*

TABLE OF CONTENTS

BOOK 1: VAMPIRES
Žarko Radaković

BRIDGE

Žarko Radaković and Scott Abbott

// 97

BOOK 2: A REASONABLE DICTIONARY

Scott Abbott

A REASONABLE DICTIONARY

// 103

BIOGRAPHIES & ACKNOWLEDGMENT

// 169

VAMPIRES

Žarko Radaković

translated by Alice Copple-Tošić

§

to no one

§

SUMMARY

Listen, narcissists are always convinced that they are right and nothing can disprove them, not even torture! Of course, narcissists are asocial. Of course, they go from one misunderstanding to another. And that's painful. And since they never admit that they are wrong, all that's left is bitterness. Narcissists end up in isolation and embitterment.

Ottmar Kontzen, in conversation at a psychotherapy session

One summer at the end of the 20th century, a man in his forties accompanied by a younger female traveling companion, ten years younger, spends a short vacation in the south of a neighboring country. They sleep in a different place every night. They walk through the landscape, wander through city streets, leisurely sit in the gardens of empty houses. They have long meals in half-empty restaurants . . . One night in a hotel on the seashore, after a late television broadcast of the film *Fog*, the man calls a friend in his homeland. During the brief conversation, he finds out that seven years after their divorce, his ex-wife has been put into a mental institution . . . During the night the man talks to his mother on the phone and finds out that another friend has tried to commit suicide and is currently "in a serious state," "lying in a hospital" . . . On the way home the man runs over a cat and then loses control of the car. When it happens he is listening to Bill Frisell on the radio . . . Once he gets home the man experiences numerous changes . . . He "hooks up" with a much younger woman who tries to bite his neck during sex, after which he turns rough . . . He attends the meetings of a "secret organization" . . . He does not sleep at night . . . Walking through town he breaks the window of an apartment where the light is turned on . . . He decides to change his place of residence . . . One night he goes to the movies and sees *Vampires*. It strikes him that this is one of the most important events in his life, which is already quite shaken up. That same evening he makes an important acquaintance; there are exciting adventures; long hours of talking, arguing and fistfights . . . Absorbed in images from daydreams . . . Battling with insects . . . Attacking a gas station . . . Nocturnal noises in the hotel . . . Orgies . . . Pallor . . . Bleeding gums . . . The man calls his mother and tells her he is going back to his hometown . . . After a raid in a restaurant in the center of town, he injects himself with a medicinal serum . . . He spends some time in a village where a pig is slaughtered at a celebration, he confronts substantial changes . . . He meets enemies . . . He meets friends . . . Long conversations . . . A battle for details.

§1: THE SUNRAYS WERE ALREADY SLANTED

The sunrays were already slanted when we climbed to the village on a rise above a gorge. The house where I was given some honey (or rather, bought it) was like a Protestant church: not too gloomy but narrow, decorated with bouquets of flowers, equipped with a "solid" sound system. The woman in the house (like a den or hen-house) was a priestess of my time: tall; attractive; slightly long nose; hair pulled back and tied in a firm knot; wearing tight, bright green panties; bare, pointed, rather small breasts; wireless ear phones in her ears and a navy blue belt around her waist where an empty knife holster dangled; she stood in the frame of the kitchen door; on the floor were brown Nike sandals, slightly apart. When I asked for a glass of water, she brought a pitcher, of course, from the kitchen; I sat in an arm-chair for a while and read the newspaper; she kneeled on the floor and polished the doorknob on the bedroom door; it was terribly hot outside, the cicadas were making an indescribable racket.

Not long afterward, a man came into the room wearing Bermuda shorts. I looked at him discreetly over my reading glasses. His shoulder fell with a jerk. The woman was in the bedroom sorting men's underwear on the bed: underpants, short socks, undershirts, knee socks. The sound of a spinning washing machine drum came from the bathroom. The rotor had just moved to centrifuge. The noise in the kitchen was louder, too: the kettle started to whistle.

I crossed my legs.

Later, I saw the man on a bench in front of a telephone booth on a plateau above a broad field. He was the personification of a monk of our times: barefoot; torn pants; bloody eyes staring blearily into the distance; requisitely bald; a revolver stuck in his belt; with a half-empty bottle of local wine; a wedding ring on each finger of his left hand; a t-shirt with the coat of arms of the national football team; a cell phone on the bench next to him of course, the eyes of "that guy" were caressing the gentle slope of a nearby hill; of course, there is a mountain bike leaning against a tree next to the bench; at one point the man licks a clearing on the slope; combs his fingers through the crowns of the chestnut trees; slips his tongue through the top of a tree and sticks the tip into the crack of a nutshell; silence; holy peace; the monk of our times starts to whistle; a fly lands on his knee poking out of his torn peasant trousers; the monk spits; the compact spittle flies a good two meters and then falls on a tree stump with a slap and a dozen flies land on it immediately.

Later, in the early evening, a crazy ride through the desert. With the last rays of the day, the blood-red sun scratches rough spots on the skin of god-fearing earth. The stubble fields glisten in the last spasms of the evening orgasm.

Spectacular nature.

The road leads to a magnificent gorge with a face of its own: full of pimples, full of wrinkles, acne, wounds, pockmarks and claw scars; this face is roaring with laughter: a raspy voice calls from the abyss of a crater. Down at the bottom of the cirque (in the well-known tourist village of Navacelles) is a protestant church, of course, with several houses around it, close together in a herd. Tourists are gathered on restaurant terraces. Illuminated by the last sunrays, each one manifests a perverse being: the first breaks matches between his fingers; the second stares with blinking eyelids; the third caresses the table leg; the fourth chews without letup; the fifth is silent; the sixth yawns; the seventh is reading a book; the eighth gratifies himself with a fork over an empty plate; the ninth is drinking beer; the tenth looks over the eleventh's shoulder; the eleventh is writing a postcard, etc. . . .

This sight frightened me, of course. I wanted to vanish into thin air. "As far away as possible from religious and ideological indoctrination!" "As far away as possible from ethic cleansing!"

The uphill road had dangerous hairpin turns. It was a menacing and truly unpleasant wasteland. The earth below was dark and the sky threatened flames. The drive became that of a rider of the apocalypse. The hotels along the way looked like hospitals or prisons. "As far away from here as possible!" I shouted!

And then I ran out of gas (I thought).

It was right in front of a house in the shadow of a plane tree right at the entrance to a village; a group (herd?) of houses in a gorge where the rapids (in panic?) were running from the river (where?).

"A hotel," I said.

"An *auberge*," I heard.

For a while I stared into the pitch-black night through the fly-spattered windshield. I sat still behind the steering wheel and pretended to drive. As I lowered my hand to the gearshift, I felt a resistance in the clutch that immediately reminded me of the rear-view mirror where I seemed to see a police patrol car which, of course, only increased the need to turn on the windshield wipers, and then the left blinker, and then after a while I started to press the brake pedal, and that, of course, brought the desire to change to the other lane and hit the gas, so I had to make a childish "prrrrrrrr" and I had already turned onto a dark street, my high beams were already illuminating the half-naked body of a hitchhiker, blond (no, light-brown hair), a woman with dark eyes. I could not move away from the steering wheel. "Prrrrr" I repeated. The car had stopped long ago, the lights turned off. A nightingale was singing outside.

For as long as I can remember, I can't, all at once, get out of the rut I'm in. It's not that I'm afraid the movement might continue fictively and all of that mass, with me at the head, might crash into some wall blocking the way. I have trouble finding the point behind a resistance movement. The moment I feel a rebellion could turn into a group uprising, I stop believing in people. Didn't I feel like the hero of the movie *They Live, We Sleep*? I felt the need to be an "invisible man." I was sitting, or standing, immobile, and staring at my memories. The images were amazingly palpable. But instead of squeezing the juice out of my memories and throwing away the skin, for a long time all I did was take in the color of the material. I even went over the pores of the skin on my hand, noting its shine or roughness and the tightness between the bulging veins. Since the country in which I was born has disintegrated, and since it is still in the jaws of a machine that cuts it and shapes it, I live like a being with a broken memory. It's not that I have lost my criteria or am no longer able to read between the lines. But the evil movements of less and less individually recognizable phenomena on the planet seem to me to be the distant reflections of gradually fading essence. Childhood no longer exists. Marriages have fallen apart. Parents are six feet under. Children grow up alone, like nettles, weeds, or wild cactuses. No one addresses anyone else with what is inside them. As if there is nothing there anymore. But I see a chance for humankind in that very emptiness of being. "Possibilities lie in the unsatisfied need for a new language that will be close to silence." My problem is that I still have one foot in the past. No one has yet to give me a vampire bite. I still have not been injected with a drop of "new reality." I still move outside the fishbowl. I really feel ice flows as being cold and not just a decoration. Not long ago, I stood at length in front of a mirror and truly recognized my face, and admired it. I do indeed distinguish day from night. I do indeed distinguish penis from clitoris. I still have breakfast, lunch and dinner, and sometimes even a snack. I did not ascribe my recent failure at work to being overly sensitive. And my complex relationship with my parents did not weigh me down. On the one hand, I felt the need to laugh; on the other, I analyzed everything incessantly. Of course, I looked for a way out in traveling. My battle for geography was the same as a drowning man clutching at a straw. And what do I meet along the way? Hordes, packs, herds, groups of individuals infected with the vampire virus. Jaded eyes looking nowhere. Smoothly combed hair and even more smoothly shaved heads. In the street those neo-beings wash, dry and polish already clean cars for the umpteenth time a day. They all wear sunglasses. There is not a single bit of litter on the sidewalk. In the apartment a cleaning lady, naked to the waist, listens to the latest hit, wipes dust off a computer screen. Sexual relations are reduced to dry licking and biting the long ago lifeless genital body of a partner who only becomes aroused when tickled. There is nothing in the garbage can. In the underbrush of a creeper on the wall of a house, thousands of sparrows are flocked together like tame and obedient cockroaches. And it is only under bridges or in the corners of parks or in the ruins of abandoned factories, or in the reserves of disintegrated countries or in the collection camps of refugees from the civil wars of torn-apart countries, that they group together, those whose bodies still tremble and swell under the weight of the atmosphere, the sun, the rain, hunger and healthy diseases. But there are fewer and fewer of them. The teeth of male and female vampires are already clacking toward fresh, bloody flesh. The epidemic is spreading at breakneck speed. And I think I am only holding my ground thanks to my endless stupidity, reduced to curiously observing it all. Yes, I am terrifically stupid. And I promise the readers of this chronicle that I will keep that stupidity under wraps until the very end.

It was wonderful on the terrace of the *auberge*.

The three-horned crown of the old plane tree. The nocturnal fragrance of fig leaves. In the darkness, neighboring houses slowly materialize like benign horses in a darkened stable, through the molasses of the darkness. The eternal murmur of turbulent water in the wild stream at the bottom of the gorge.

And just when I began to love myself again (no one else was supposed to be there), something moved ominously into the darkness from the hotel entrance. A fat ugly dog appeared in outline. It was like a monster from one of (otherwise esteemed) John Carpenter's recent films. "Here is the source of the disease," I said in a half-whisper. "Monument to contagion," I wrote down. The murmur turned into a whiz. Three cyclists whizzed through the night. They were wearing different phosphorescent colors like team jerseys. The dog moved in slow-motion, as in a dream. I remembered writing the story *Under the Stone Bridge* in the book *Repetitions*.[1] There was supposed to be a description of the cellar in a monastery. I gave up on the undertaking because of the rush and wanting to write about love. Of course, times are different here, now. At one point the dog turned around. It was at the end of a dark hall. The owner of the *auberge* appeared out of the moonlight: she was a short, middle-aged woman, thin, wearing black-and-white striped pants. Her face was truly ugly. "There's the monster!" Broken nose. Pointed eyeteeth. One front tooth knocked out, the other one broken. Eyes filled with the passionate, crazy desire to carry out her intentions, and to vanquish.

During the night, images of the hotel personnel slipped into my dream along with the sounds of chirping crickets and bubbling water in the stream and the roaring laughter of the last customers in the restaurant. Two women (the owner and a maid), a man (the cook, an amiable young man, homosexual) and the dog (now with two different heads). All four of them are ripping me apart, torturing me. The view out the bedroom window is like a conduit to the sky. But it is too far away. In addition, the plane tree branches are too dense for any clear picture . . .

That's how it was, dear reader, at one point in the town of Gornies in the French mountains of Cevennes. The place was magnificent in the morning, which will be the subject of another story. But let's see where this story takes us, and let's see what it's like!

---

[1] Scott Abbott and Žarko Radaković, *Ponavljanje* (Belgrade: Vreme knjige, 1994); reprinted as *Repetitions* (Brooklyn: punctum books, 2013).

I wrote a letter to my friend in Ganges:

"Dear Peter, after significant setbacks to my health, here I am walking in the mountains of Cevennes. It is amazingly similar to the area around the Drina River. This increases my anger even more at the disintegration of our country and at our people being thrown into disgrace. And then in the village of Lasalle, when I saw a young Dutchman wearing the Croatian national football team's jersey, a feeling of injustice stirred inside me . . . Football is where you have to win . . . That's the way it is here, dear fellow."

That was also when I began to experience events as comparative images. Suddenly instead of a eucalyptus tree I was looking at the tall top of a poplar. Suddenly instead of grapevines I saw the branches of a cherry tree. Clumps of lavender turned into stalks of plantain crowded together. I even saw rosemary bushes as blades of spurge. Where poppies spread as far as the eye could see, I saw endless cornfields. And every Mediterranean oak tree immediately reminded me of willow rods in the marshes of Vojvodina.

Later, lunch: in a tiny garden on a truly amusing street. What was it that I ate? Chicken in crayfish sauce. And the whole time I was thinking of the snack I had in Bešenovački Prnjavor on the slopes of Fruška Gora, the Ruma side, i.e. from the south. I truly did think of those bacon slices and pieces of salty pickled onion.

As I walked through the wilderness in the area around Saint-Guilhem-le-Desert, imagining the pleasant slopes of that same Fruška Gora mountain, but now from the Karlovac side—i.e. the north—I saw a dog, there (in the region of Saint-Guilhem-le-Desert) in the remote, ravaged bastion of goat breeders. I immediately perceived the animal as a fellow writer entrenched in a newly founded but already insolvent publishing house, located at first in a new building right in the center of town that very quickly turned unto a neglected, dilapidated, musty building, its basement filled with roiling waves of an army of rats and its attic with rafters where several thousand bats hung like cruise missiles aimed at everyone inside and outside the house—ready to fly. "The harbingers of evil," I thought. "Town criers of epidemics, ruination and bombing." Not even the dog was an ordinary mammal anymore, I saw. It barked not only as I walked by, mundane and warm-blooded, but at my every thought as well. A vampire mutant, I thought. "A degenerated four-legged ex-two-legged animal!" An anti-creature that immediately interrupts any thought of the present, past, and even the future. If there was anything acceptable in that prelude to horror, it was the fact that I was embarrassed by every one of my previous thoughts, not because of possible error, but because of the cheap, kitschy structural units of thought. Yes, that dog was the beginning of a derangement that would later, in all likelihood, give rise to rebellion.

◯ SETE, 6 AUGUST 1998

I was deranged as well during my usual afternoon hike. Today it was in the region of Saint-Guilhem-le-Desert. The whole time I had the town of Sete on my mind and it seemed to be the focus of my trip. This happened on August 6, 1998, the hot day of this story.

The fatigue of the previous days' travelling (and storytelling) had now moved from my body (and soul) to my mind. I ran out of water during the hike. The desert heat was at an unprecedented level. I felt a heavy, acrid, almost suffocating thirst (as well as a suffocating, heavy and almost bitter fear). My mouth was dry (and my chest, too). The wind from the west that was now heading north, where it would then blow with all its force to the south, brought restlessness to my body that spread to every cell in my brain. Suddenly I was frightened of the stones underfoot that I trod with increasing uncertainty. Suddenly I glimpsed my feet on the ground as heroes of the unknown tale of a fugitive. I panted, gasped, coughed. Did I cry? Only with the last twitches of my breathless thoughts did I become aware of this other, quite different story. Driven by panic caused by what was now the compulsion to stay in the same story, I foolishly rushed "nowhere."

The path wound through wasteland covered with underbrush. The mountain wreath (no longer resembling the Fruška Gora chain or any other hill in the former or the current Yugoslavia) looked different to the hiker with every step. At times it was a vast slab without beginning or end, placed on its side. At times it was a giant hedge, dense and close by. At times it was the picture of a beautiful landscape made inaccessible by the chasm between the viewer's eye and the picture frame. "Where is this path heading?" is a question I am unable to answer even today, in the hot, lively, sometimes even chaotic little town of Sete, where I have blundered into this memory of my Knifer (Julije Knifer, the main character of my previous and all my future tales), someone who truly denotes the coordinates of experiences in the south of this country.

We did not reach Sete until the early evening. It had been a slow ride along a winding road down the slopes of the last, southernmost hills of Languedoc. The wind and slanting sunrays disconcerted the driver so much that in his indecision regarding all the wine stores along the way, he ended up not buying that wondrous, calming elixir. The colors went from bloody-reddish-yellow to yellowish-purple. The early evening was a true rampage of color. Everything was in flames. The earth, sky, creatures, the road and the cars. Those were moments of the pure madness of forms thrusting into each other with screams. And every puncture of one form into another was like a snakebite or the kiss of a nymph. Their bodies spread the lecherous poison. The driver's skin was suddenly covered by multicolored bruises. Sete, the town of Julije Knifer, shellfish, and boats, was like the mouth of a volcano that I willingly entered that evening, freed of my fear of change. These were the natural phenomena of every moment of time, advancing at breakneck speed. Finally, the evening that had now fallen with a heavy thud, as though detached, did not inject any sort of calming agent into the lifeblood of the town; rather it shook even the last Undecided out of their slumber. As though a button had been pushed, the town started working in overdrive. Life appeared in all its fullness.

We spent the night in a hotel on a busy street in the pedestrian zone, crossed by a main street with cars that burst into my dreams all night long, breaking up the story of an amorous couple in a forbidden embrace. And they were lying on a bed, dressed, timidly touching the parts of each other's body, slipping hands through the openings of unbuttoned shirts and under the lifted ends of clothing. It was not sweltering on that night of the story about sin. But it was noisy. Every touch of an aroused body was followed by a thud from the end of the street. It was the sound of boards being thrown on hard ground. Later, in the deepest recesses of the night, garbage trucks: they produced the sound of civilization being ravaged. (In the meantime, the lovers were completely naked, liberated, covered by scratches and bruises.)

Morning in the café in front of the entrance to the indoor market. All the men are wearing perfectly ironed shirts. The eyes of the young woman sitting at a table with her legs crossed, staring proudly at a stall selling woven bags, are as wet as the puddle of spilled beer on the table top, which the waiter will immediately clean with an even wetter rag, and as misted as the glass in which Perrier water is bubbling, and as dark (deep) as the coffee that has just arrived.

Around noon eyes are focused on a soup plate on the table in a restaurant on the canal. Earth colors prevail. The bouillabaisse truly tasted of the quintessence of this area. (As though I had eaten an overcooked brick removed from the wall of the prettiest house, the mansion on the square with the town hall.)

The waiter was wearing shorts. His legs were covered with curly fuzz that perfectly imitated the noodles in the liquid in the soup plate into which he resolutely, now quite free of any complexes, threw several small pieces of toast spread with saffron mayonnaise, where they floated like logs. I watched them float as I carefully listened to the blows of a fisherman on a small boat, down below, right next to the restaurant railing, killing an octopus. And it was as slimy as melted grated cheese adhering to a floating gull, now completely melted and like a sponge in a sink.

Later, a plate full of small pieces of octopus in tomato sauce, rice with saffron, and shellfish filled with ground meat spiced with local herbs.

The view across the table and the canal with anchored fishing boats was imposing. Fishermen on the decks, as though following the beat of the town's heart, were killing octopuses with wooden sticks as they swam in buckets of seawater, then prepared them to be cooked, fried, marinated, and so on.

The meat on my plate tasted like the smell of a fisherman's skin. And the sauce on my face smelled like the color of the tiles on the town hall to the right of the brick mansion (from the previously eaten soup).

The plate from which I was eating with true pleasure and quite slowly was like the marble plaque on the façade of the building where Paul Valery was brought into the world (French writer, born on October 20, 1871 in Sete). Smooth, large, wide and solid, it was like a basin in which grains of rice, set in motion by the long slender fork, rolled like marbles on a children's marble field. And those fanciful bits of truth were wondrously put together as a letter from the poet. And even more wondrously, by putting sauce over these masses of verse, a thick substance was produced that then, all by itself, formed (why, of course!) a meander by Julije Knifer (Yugoslav . . . No, now only a Croatian painter, who lived and worked in Sete in 1993). And later, in the afternoon, lunch had an essentially calming effect on the body that, stimulated by the additional influence of wine (locally made) and coffee (short) (the color of the dark eyes of the woman I turned to look at), liberated, went through some not yet investigated parts of town: the harbor, canals and hilly slopes of Mont St. Claire. Of course, it would be unfair not to mention the warm, "fuck-me," numbing effect of the custard covered with caramel sauce. (I did not have any cognac; but I changed my underwear in the bathroom. I put on swimming trunks.)

I reached the beach after a long bus (or train) ride on the road (or rails) along the sandy coast (or marshy isthmus).

It was early afternoon (or late morning). The sun had just passed its zenith (or was just approaching its zenith). And it was not all that hot (or it was really too hot). Through the half-open window of the car (or train), the wind ruffled the hair of a weeping (or smiling) young (or old) woman. And I blinked (or closed my eyes). And it was like (or really was) turning off the daylight.

Beach (Shore.) Sea (Sand.) And so (on).

Evening on the top of Mont St. Claire. Eyes zigzagging over slopes and the plain spreading far to the four corners of the earth, turning into images of the land and the vast sea. And only one boat was anchored, immobile, withstanding the power of the water. It looked like a toy. It was funny. And magnificent at the same time. And mysterious. And ridiculous.

As soon as the first streetlights went on, the mosquitoes started to bite. First the lighthouse at the entrance to the yacht harbor sounded with a blinking green beam.

The wind picked up.

I moved my hand: I lowered it from my knee to my foot. I stuck my chin in my left hand. My fingers held onto the drunken view. It was rocking over the now blue-red horizon. The sky separated from earth like a frontline. When all the lighthouses within sight turned on their beams, I wanted to rise up and lower myself gently on the waves of the sea where the fish were waking from their daily slumber and getting ready for the nocturnal hunt for insects, plants, people, animals, towns, villages (villages above all!) and, of course, boats on which the unconscious consignment awaited execution.

During that time the lighthouses blinked rhythmically. They released different colored lights that were like a local painter's streaks shaping the panorama of the town's evening and the surroundings in which living and nonliving things plunged into each other to the rhythm of carefree coitus. This lasted quite some time. It continued when new streetlights were lighted in the picture. My hand was now hanging from the edge of my field of vision, touching the highway above the coast (toward nearby Montpellier) where the high beams of a car rushed by, illuminating the veins, nerve cells, heart and brain of the viewer who, tickled by the blinking lights on the town streets, burst into roaring laughter. Of course, the gulls took flight into the now seemingly deepened and extended and expanded sky. Of course, cats jumped toward house windows, falling upon each other in the panicked fear that day was returning. And a tremendous cat war began, prompted by the populace in the form of two rock-throwing, cursing, laughing and spitting young boys.

Later, in the empty restaurant next to the market, a man at the bar with a glass of beer on the counter. The waiter, leaning on a spigot that dispenses drinks into glasses, is singing loudly to music on the radio. Several customers at a table in front of the entrance to the place are rocking to the music's rhythm. An empty table on the edge of the sidewalk: the daily newspaper with a short report on events in Kosovo, a long article on the Lewinsky/Clinton affair and a really long report on the Sete-Montpellier football game. (Did the game end without a winner?)

Drunken stumbling through empty, now sleeping streets. Winding, stopping short. Breaking off. Disappearing forever.

There was a faucet on a square. I turned it on. And immediately turned it off. The water, of course, flowed briefly. Of course, that splash echoed like an exploding bomb.

Glistening in the night on the shaved heads of two black guys. They were sitting on a low wall, exchanging excerpts from their unwritten biographies. They were smoking cigarettes and their white teeth gleamed.

On the train to Agde I sniffed the fruit in a plastic bag on my lap.

The station in Agde, in a flashing jerk of memory, turned into the smell of the station in Inđija.

Agde.

I clearly saw a boy poke his head out the window of a house on a narrow street and throw an open container of yogurt at the rails. He missed them by a hair.

On the banks of the Eros River, I experienced the height of Beauty. (I cried for joy.) (I was ingesting wine like a pump.) With a three-meter-long tongue I licked the breasts of a young woman at the table next to me in the restaurant. The water was so close. (I remembered the dinner at "Crocodile Bay" on the banks of the Paraiba River.) Schools of fish darted around a piece of bread (that floated beaming with joy). ("Above all else I love the mouths of rivers, the shore where freshwater enters the salty sea.")

I ordered a drink made of anise. (Ricard. Ricard.) It smelled of lovers' sweat.

(And I saw Julije Knifer again. He was standing in front of a fishmonger's stall. His glance scaled a surmullet's little body.)

I saw a car in the harbor that reminded me of Germany. The sound of the motor took me back to the late 1960s. In the water, I saw the face of Raša Livada, my first-grade classmate from elementary school in Zemun (Yugoslavia).

I saw a sausage in a plate on the table of a restaurant I passed. It was curling around pieces of roasted potato.

⟋ COLOGNE, 13 AUGUST 1998

More heads—friends and family—were floating in a sunken boat, not as faces but names, like symbols of people.

The façade of the house that I stared at for hours looked like lace.

Julije came out of a café by the market. He stopped at the entrance to the market building.

A cooling wind from the east brings a change of events. It raises the few faded leaves and the blades of grass scorched by the previous days' searing heat. The sidewalk where the wind whirls the remains of life in late summer is particularly clean today.

I saw my female colleague B. on the crosswalk of a broad street next to the Radio Deutsche Welle building. Her face reflected the more striking parts of the city's morning picture: a truck that has just turned around in the middle of the street, a conductor waiting nervously at the half-empty bus station for a victim in the next bus, a man with an umbrella in front of the entrance to a store selling sports equipment (medicine balls, shot puts, high-jump poles and, of course, weights).

The sun scratches my cheek with its slanted morning rays. Black coffee poured out of the cut. (Roaring laughter . . .).

The doctor's waiting room was as quiet as a church. (The local cathedral was celebrating its jubilee that day.) People were sitting (on simply constructed, comfortable wooden chairs) with crossed legs. The soft, barely audible music (from speakers in the corners of the room) reduced the tension of patients waiting for their moment of truth.

Željka (or Živana) once again had pain in her lower back. Nenad (or Conrad) was suffering from fat deposits around his waist (it quivered like bacon in aspic). Maksimović (or Radaković) was rheumatic again today. Bojić (or Šević) could not see well. Dijana (or Mirjana) had whooping cough. They all suffered from hormone disorders: the women have facial hair and the men's nipples have broadened with wide concentric circles. I was suffering from several weeks of insomnia: I was hallucinating. One morning instead of a coffee cup I saw the vagina of my fourth, long since ex-wife. I immediately hurled an ashtray through a closed window. The neighbors on my street were wakened (by the porcelain hitting the windshield of a parked car).

🖘 17 AUGUST 1998

(I don't smoke!)
I went shopping.
(More wind.)
A Vespa was parked at the entrance to a café.
A gentle afternoon. Warm smells. A truck was parked on Wormser Street.
Again I felt unsure of myself before the stern faces of the passersby.
The dog on a leash held by my neighbor was quite well-fed and heavy.
We moved. We changed everything: apartments, furniture, looks, moods, characters, souls.
The car was already on its last legs. The bed linen was torn too. The pillow-case, for example, was ripped open. Its insides stank of the present.
One evening I was sitting in a bar in the western part of town, slowing drinking rum. Rhythmic music was blaring from the corners of the room. The group *Us3* was playing. I had been following their music for years. I first got to know their music through my young friend Ivan. He almost looked like the rapper of the group, KCB. At the time, I was particularly interested in *Broadway & 52ⁿᵈ*—hot off the press. The sixth piece on the disk, "I'm Thinking about Your Body," was my cult favorite. I was sitting in the room of the old apartment on Hertha Street, staring dully at my picture on the wall, letting the powerful, deep tones and blows on the electric keyboard break parts of the furniture, twist the position of my body, and even slice through my thoughts in their crazy attempts to reach the south of the continent with them. The rapper was Shabaam Sahdeeq. He

sent me straight to the west. Shabaam Sahdeeq's voice was a lot softer than KCB's and his unusually gentle spoken-narrative tirades were more like negations of Ivan. Listening to that musical storytelling accompanied by the sad and slightly oriental wailing of Ed Jones' soprano saxophone, backed by the unusually precise, brilliant and simple piano music of Tim Vine, I saw my boss's face almost the whole time, reproaching me for my long phone calls in a soft voice and gentle words. It was not until I was in my new apartment (on Alteburger Street) that *Broadway & 52nd* became ultimately important to me—even though it was mannered in all respects compared to the truly, objectively, and officially more important disk *Hand on the Torch* by *Us3*, with the cult version "Cantaloupe" (*Flip Fantasia*) of the classical piece by Herbie Hancock, already older today but still potent. From the first day in my new residence, I listened for hours to the music of *Broadway & 52nd*: for example "Snakes," a melody that sent me, not even I know why, to a scene from the movie *Escape from New York*; or the number "Come On Everybody (Get Down)" where I suddenly saw Zoran, Jadran and Jan, their arms around each other in "manly" fashion, dancing a quiet kolo with slow and simple steps, their faces serious, eyes closed, in a dignified trance; or "Soul Brother," a melody that wore me down to tears and took me exhausted to the bed of my colleague's wife, debauched, but truly unhappy, where I not only gave myself to her ardently but also rose to the role of a priest who preaches and forgives, and admonishes, and kisses; or "Doin' a Crime," a number I listened to those days along with the energetic brush strokes of Dušan the painter who slowly, for days and months, painted the walls of my new apartment, creating, probably, with this slowness and frequent repetitions of one and the same, and then again with his elusive working hours—for example, he would say he was coming at eight in the morning and then came at two-thirty in the afternoon—a unique work of art in which I was signed on not only as the obedient assistant but also as someone who had truly (creatively) gone mad, not showing (creative) nervousness, in the (creative) uncertainty of how long that incomeprehensible work would last. Painting to the music of *Us3*, my impatience and Dušan's unpredictable coming and not coming to work turned into a unique and unforgettable performance.

I was not thinking of anything specific. I wanted to forget my setback with the previous landlady. She would not take me as her future tenant. She felt I was not sincere enough. Even though I had a serious expression on my face the whole time, even though I always looked to the side, even though I followed her obediently, I did not appear infatuated enough with the apartment that she showed with great pride. In the large, bright, airy living room she placed her hand very gently on the rough white wall and suddenly breathed deeply with the body of the house, that festive day (the city cathedral's jubilee), dressed its best. I did not turn giddy at the colors that spread and glistened when the evening sunrays dashed against the doorjamb to the next room in which, somewhat later, the landlady moved like a mature gazelle. Without speaking, she gazed about the quiet, and thereby pleasing and so delightful room. I looked at her kerchief, tied decoratively over her long pulled-back hair (Was it a knot?) as she talked about waterproofing the soft-wood floor and in its cracks I saw the earth of my country ("far away and foreign"), without once mentioning that I wanted to turn that coquettish room into a study and workshop to process all my dreams. The woman did not even notice the spark of excitement I hid in the kitchen, perceived as a marvelous playground, promenade, or clearing under milk wood, in-to which the hall, stairs and vestibule entered like byways, detours and shortcuts. Suddenly I felt enlightened. It happened when I looked at the dishwasher. (It was shining as though on a meadow lighted and heated by the sun after rain.) (It was like a pregnant woman on a bench in the park in late afternoon.) And as the landlady calculated the additional costs in the total rent out loud, in the gas line on the heater I saw a tendon of my now tired body, its movement uncertain, that appeared vague to the landlady, and because of the stiffness of my posture, even repulsive. I felt that I was engaging when I tripped on the threshold into the bathroom, when I hit my head on the doorjamb to the bedroom, and when I stumbled over the flowerpot in the corner of the living room when I went back to have another look out the window. Nevertheless, in the hallway when I told her I liked the apartment, judging by the expression on my face, the woman took this to be mild criticism. I did not stutter, because I did not say anything. Like I was waiting for her to throw me out. And the woman was so modest and dignified. In spite of her clumsiness in dealing with people, she was nice.

Later, in the street, I felt like going back to the apartment and crying in the vestibule. It seemed like a lost homeland.

↺ 18 August 1998

One evening, I was sitting in an empty bar in my (then) favorite western part of town. The place was exceptionally quiet. There were just a few isolated customers. They gazed blankly out the window at the sidewalk and the infrequent, sauntering pedestrians. Sounds were muffled by the clear picture and intense colors of the early evening. It was at its peak. It folded over all existence. The forms of things were simply engulfed by the fiery interior of the sunset. There seemed no need, or desire, to breathe in that solarium of the dying day. It truly went from one state to another. It truly was a moment of perceiving one's true self. My sitting there quietly at the table (over such a distinct bottle of mineral water on the table) and my being engrossed in writing a text in an open notebook (today truly resembling a wanton woman) was part of the scenario. I wrote and wrote, writing myself wholeheartedly into the sunset, into turning on the artificial lights in the street and in store windows, drowning in the picture of the early evening story.

Of course, this was a love story. The heroes are gentle, good, and nameless. And just when I wanted to start a (forbidden) affair with one of my heroines (as befits all my stories), someone outside the story looked at me askance.

It was a young woman, tall and slender, muscular, with smooth skin. She was sitting, legs crossed, her quiet, steady gaze (over my head) (out the window) looking in the distance along the sidewalk and further down the empty street. There was truly something angelic in that woman's expression. There was truly something beguiling in her eyes: the picture of someone in constant observation with unobtrusive curiosity hiding behind it.

I must say that in those moments of pleasant frustration, I was torn between the need to sleep and the desire to go out into reality. Those were moments on the borderline. My own truth was both the subject of the story and the target of the unknown woman's observation.

I felt the need to talk. I felt the desire for intrigues. Like looking through the ends of a conduit (at once I am reminded of it by the story I am telling right now) and seeing a new world in which everything exists as two, one facing the other, without barriers, but with numerous questions that need to be answered slowly.

"What are you writing about?" asked the woman after I had waved my hand invitingly and she, with a smile, came up to the table and sat on the chair, which was wanton as well.

I saw at once that the woman was a vision that was constantly breaking up. There was not only movement but also incessant vibration. Her words came out of her body. They gushed from the pores of her skin. And they seemed sensual. And rasping. At times moist, at times pleasant to the ear, at times warm, at times dry, at times cold, and, of course, always audible.

"This is a story about someone who keeps coming and going. But it's not just about movement. This is a story in which there truly could be no beginning or end. Because everything appeared out of the blue. A story like eyes drawn to what is *accidentally seen* that does not become a signal because it is constantly moving away," I said.

I must admit that the woman looked at me amorously. She also seemed to fidget on the chair. And the muscles under the smooth skin on her arm trembled with the thrill. And the ghost of a smile inconspicuously hid the spark of passion. Once again only her voice remained, like a being on a picture where the outlines of narration are already visible (which, of course, as befits my stories, should be done away with at once).

"Storytelling has long been for me just the transmission of my own self," I said.

"You mean your experiences," she said, right after a shy, deep, bottomless smile, dark eyes that suddenly shone with surreal beauty mixed with a warmth in which I recognized the past.

"No," I said. "Storytelling has long been for me just plain Watching. Observation has long been for me something before and beyond the picture. Words, if they are spoken, are not written down, either as subtitles under sketches or as the uttered words of those who are in the picture as shadows. Words are only coordinate points in which geometric feelings are conceived. There is no location. No plot. No tempo. Rhythm is out of the question here. Development must be broken at once by layers of color. Speech must be smothered and must dry up. Visible, everything must be visible. Even the unimaginable."

The woman moved almost imperceptibly. A shake of the head that stretched the hair on her neck like whips. The curls on her forehead were like magnificent, royal, silky pubic hairs.

"Talk," she said.

"Look," I said.

"I'm listening," she said.

"I'm silent," I said.

And, drumming my fingers on the tabletop, I followed (for myself) the sound of the music by guitarist Bill Frisell who has become so dear to me recently.

The landlady lived in the northern part of town in a house with a bright, narrow façade between buildings dating from the late 19th century. Each of the buildings in that part of town had its own character. The street resembled the counter in a bar and the houses were customers. Each one looked different in terms of height, age, and race. Each one was wearing different clothes. Each one was drinking a different drink. It seemed to me that the only thing these extremely controlled, half-drunk beings had in common was their gaze. Their eyes were on the bartender, a heavyset bald man with a trim beard. Was he holding a sawed-off shotgun? He watched the movements of each individual customer. As soon as someone took a sip of their drink, he reached for the pencil tucked behind his ear and with a sudden movement of his hand made a mark on the cardboard coaster in front of the customer. "What's your name?" he asked the unknown customer, looking the stranger knowingly in the eyes, then wrote down his name on the coaster. Did he also give the order, "Drink"? Then his dull, bleary eyes looked over the customer's head illuminated by a very bright light on the ceiling that made the different drinks in the different glasses tremble silently from the power in the compressed atmosphere. I seemed to see a speck in one of those glasses, a tall crystal one filled with yellowish liquid. It resembled a tiny double of the customer at the bar, emerging from the very depths of the surface. A sudden change in the pressure caused bloody puss to flow through his nostrils from his inflamed sinuses. The surface of the liquid in the glass was a slimy mass that gave way under the weight of the ceiling light like a plank floor bending under the weight of a bully's steps. And just as I was thinking, "Now the floor's going to crack," the customer at the bar, as though at the command of the stocky bartender who already had the pencil in his hairy hand, leaned over the glass, touched the still clean crystal of the glass with his thin, nimble, waxy fingers, raised it to his lips and knocked back the contents: the drink, a cocktail of bloody puss on the surface of the liquid, plank flooring seen through the lens of the cut glass and the unconscious tiny double (seen through the cut glass). And the sound of that heavy gulp coincided with the creaking tip of the bartender's pencil as he made a mark on the coaster in front of the customer. Was a shot then heard from the sawed-off shotgun; did the bartender curse the customer's "mother"?

The street cut through a lively neighborhood of the city, coursing without any specific purpose: it did not connect "important" "places," neither was it busy nor did it have a memorable name. It seemed like a vestige of force, shattered somewhere in the middle of town. As if a ("local") Bigwig personally, himself, had crashed down and his weight had smashed and pulverized everything. Of course, there were victims. "Once again before a Tyrant with fuzzy features!" Of course, the masses rushed out of the restaurants, apartments, offices, churches, stores, doctors' offices, garages, companies and saunas. The ruins were quickly removed. (At the bartender's command?) The street, like everything in the city, had an air of the Lord's brief appearance. The street was thought to be named after one of His fold in a time before "genesis," thus in the period of revolutionary chaos. It was reminiscent of historical secret meetings in out-of-the-way basements; of ("local") diversions at railway stations; of fateful speeches in half-empty auditoriums; of banned books published "abroad"; of historical orgies in hospital rooms; or of prominent parties at night in the buildings of future institutions, later in lecture halls, packing plants, factory offices, gymnasiums and Internet cafes. The Almighty was present everywhere. But no one ever saw Him with the naked eye. He would only appear rarely—when half-asleep, weary, in a lovers' embrace, during a fight in cold storage among the sides of beef, when visiting a patient in the intensive care ward of the nearby hospital, when turning to look at a shamelessly dressed woman wearing torn stockings, or when sitting for a long time on a toilet seat. With an unusually soft breath, light touch, uncommon smell and unearthly voice ("whisper!"). Woe unto you if you did not believe in His coming. Woe unto you if you smiled at Him. Woe unto you if you did not tremble before the honor of His imponderability during that dramatic moment of His coming. Woe unto you if you wanted a picture: His picture, a neighbor's picture, your boss's pictures, your lover's picture, a picture of yourself, a picture of anyone at all.

The street stretched from north to south on a line between west and east, winding like a drunkard or drug addict or starving scarecrow or enthusiast. The street lurched, shifting its weight from the foot of one passer-by to another, from one house to another, from one corner to another, longingly seeking the south that got lost in the mist of the dust cloud of a construction site, a factory chimney, vehicle exhaust pipes and, of course, evaporation from the boiling cauldrons of beer in breweries with that essential drink of the inhabitants of the northern part of the town, the so-called "northerners" who made up the majority in the neighborhoods where they lived. It was a real army of beer drinkers. They also drank pure water in glasses the size of beer-mugs. Their thoughts were measured by percentages of alcohol. And they lived in kegs, warehouses and on conveyer belts. At forums. At parties. In movie theaters. In cabaret dives. In bars, of course. In groups, of course. Even if they were different, everything was devoted to One: the common Lord. Covens of witches. Diesel car buffs. Teachers in love with Africans. Bowlers. Heart patients. Flea market aficionados. Avid smokers of cigarettes they rolled themselves. The association of shaved heads. Aficionados of Cuba's northern shores. The society to protect the rights of "singles." Each on a solo mission. All together.

From the second floor of the house the apartment looked like a shooting stand in an unctuous early evening forest. Like the observation post of wild boar hunters. The tiny balcony looked over the winding street. There was a good view of the building on the other side of the street from that vantage point. And it had an inconspicuous square shape, lamellar, built in the 1930s during social, ideological, and religious disintegration. No one at the time suspected the contents and rhetoric of history that would hold for the next hundred years. No one even dreamed that what held true at the time would become the subject of negative discussions at party meetings. History seemed like soft sourdough. You made the dough and baked the bread and ate it. You fed yourself with (dough) or (history). And the more poisonous the ingredients of the dough, the fatter you got. You lived off events. You ingested historical facts, digested them, and built the world on them. That world expanded like a jellyfish. It spread like cancer to everything that was innocent, one's own, and sincere. The city devoured its surroundings with its history. Forests, fields, meadows, and clearings withdrew far into the interior of the country. The mountains were already crowded with fleeing plants, insects, animals and ne'er-do-wells. The rivers of refugees ran uphill. They made their way to freedom with great difficulty. There was less and less of it. History sowed death triumphantly. Urban dwellers' faces were paler and paler. Urban dwellers' teeth, particularly their eyeteeth, were longer and sharper.

Even though seen out the wide open window (today), the street was empty and it seemed like no one was passing by, since it resembled a building site on Sunday afternoon, the houses seemed (not only today) like the walls of an enormous swimming pool of the past in which the dense, viscous, mass of history (last revised in 1968) pressed with all its weight on the bottom (in this case the sidewalk and pavement).

There were no trees on the street. Instead of tree trunks, there were rows of diagonally parked cars. They were evenly placed with an equal distance between them. Even though everything was so relaxed and even melancholy and cloyingly agreeable, never for a minute (looking down from the window on the second floor of house number 113) could you imagine that under such a carefully parked car there might be a cat, for example. The cats, it seemed, were napping in apartments. So the rooms were like lairs. (So the apartments were cages.) And the grease spots on the parking places did not reflect the life of the owners of the (until recently parked) cars. They merely reflected the dullness of the asphalt where something organic suddenly shined brightly, although no one wanted to step in it.

The owner of building number 113 on that street was a woman in her early fifties with a southern dialect, feline physique, with a stained but carefully parked look, greasy voice, and always calm movements of the hand that at one (truly dramatic) moment resembled the levers of history (last revised in 1968).

(That was the moment of looking out the window.)

✍ 20 August 1998

This evening in the late summer of the same year, our heroine is sitting in an armchair in the middle of the living room, very brightly illuminated by the early evening sunrays. Legs crossed, head thrown back, arms raised above her head and hands resting on her smoothly combed crown, she feels the trembling of her seething body. This is transmitted, by telephone, of course, to another nearby part of the city to a room already shaded by the setting sun in a garret apartment in which a man (younger than the woman), naked to the waist, hands placed on the edge of an enormous flowerpot with an oleander that finally blossomed this summer, almost uninterested in talking, articulates his replies to his collocutor with the words, "yes," "no," "aha," "of course," "sort of," and "it isn't." The words, "how do I know," in reply to her "why," too soft for his hard and cold body, sounded in the vestibule like the dull blows of a meat-axe into the flesh of a creature that was already put to death several times and never really wanted to live. And no one next door to either of our collocutors even suspected the difference in the energetic power of the spoken words. And they were not talking about anything specific. The subject of the conversation was sighs, several sobs, laughter, coughing and at one moment aggressive swearing, immediately dampened by silence.

Silence was some sort of refuge for the household members who, in the last rays of the sun, appeared to be members of an enormous family in which no one ever really heard anyone else. And each one functioned impeccably in the community. One went to the market, the second took out the trash, the third did the cooking, the fourth cleaned the rooms. Every neighborhood in that part of town was like the headquarters of a strong organization and a strictly controlled group, even if at first glance everything seemed to be so breezy, relaxed and leisurely. Something nonliving could be felt in the air. As though they were not apartments but sheds and the tenants living in them were not humans but anti-humans. The person telling this story does not mean anything negative regarding the paradigm "anti-." No! Here the prefix denotes a phenomenon that we are not yet able to explain. But that is not our goal. Everything still boils down to perception. That is sufficient for the time being. Everything still finds refuge in perception: the longer and longer faces of our fellow townsmen, the ever darker circles under our neighbor's eyes, the emptier and emptier eyes of the newspaper vendor, the paler and paler skin of the woman next door, the deeper and deeper bite marks on the neck of our beloved, the increasingly voluptuous walk of the salesgirl at the bakery, the pharmacist's lower and lower neckline, the butcher's sharper and sharper teeth and the thicker and thicker foam on the lips of the sweating bartender holding the sawed-off shotgun, with a pencil tucked behind his ear.

The landlady lived on the fifth floor of the building. In an apartment that, together with the garret above it, looked like a control tower. Everything could be seen from there: the clouds that brought rain, night, and debauchery; the seat made of soft calfskin in the window of the bicycle shop on the next street; underpants soiled with menstrual blood on the floor of the second-floor neighbor's bathroom; a child in painful convulsions under the wheel of a car that dashed out of a side street; drops of sperm on the butcher block in the butcher's shop on the neighboring square; a grinning man, his shirt unbuttoned under an elegant jacket, as he reads a newspaper with a photographic detail of the closest battlefield. Refuse in trash cans was also visible from that control tower apartment: potato peelings in the bag of the man living on the third floor, cabbage ribs in the bag of the man living on the fourth floor, bits of fat ("aha!") in the bag of the woman living on the second floor, an empty beer can ("whose is it!"), a broken wine bottle ("mine?"). That inspection made solitude feel good. It also warmed the icy soul. It also was a substitute for socializing. It really brought tranquility.

"I've always been bothered by that communal television antenna. We've repaired it several times. The wind knocks it down again every time," said the landlady.

"I don't have a bed. I don't have dishes. I don't even have a vacuum cleaner," I said.

"Even so, don't buy the kitchen from your predecessor," she said. And in that useful and well-intended advice I saw the calming calico of a cat staring indifferently at the blank television screen.

"We don't have mice in the house," she said.

"The cat sleeps most of the time," she said.

"See, I don't have hanging fixtures in the kitchen," she said.

"Hey, why do you need a carpet-sweeper," she said.

"Do you have a piano?" she asked.

✎ 22 August 1998

For as long as I can remember, housing for me has meant spreading the nest of the creative cosmos. Furniture really was part of the books. And kitchen appliances were most certainly decorative. The voices of the household members always came to me from a distance. I received them like a cook. Dirty laundry, often thrown all around the apartment, was to me like words that I put together every day into a lengthy text about someone energetically showing off.

I listened to a lot of music by guitarist Bill Frisell those days. He was one of the rare artists of my time that I took to heart. In 1990 (right after moving to this city; it was on the eve of war in Yugoslavia), saxophonist John Zorn's group was playing in a place in (my then favorite) western part of town. Bill played the guitar in Zorn's "combo" at the time. I knew something about the musician but not much about his music.

At the time I was looking for a hero for my new story that was to encapsulate events from the 1980s. The story was supposed to be open to everything that might happen later in that country in the 1990s as compared to the eastern and southeastern part of the continent. I was actually working on a story about the painter (and friend) Julije Knifer. I needed the right kind of musical underpinning for a more eye-catching representation of the artist's otherwise variable, rhythmic repetition of forms in the opus about so-called *Meanders* (the hero of Julije's stories). (I wanted to get out of the world of writing. I wanted to expand my media horizons. The literary story had long ago become a laborious, closed and confined space. Storytelling to me had become the wailing, pessimistic and maniacal sticking to often false or long-dead historical facts. I thus experienced writers as drowning people desperately grasping for stories that floated aimlessly on the surface of a stormy sea.) Through textual simulation, I wanted to convert the musical underpinning of Julije's "meandering" into a background story-line or backdrop on which Knifer's *Meanders* would develop like the "tree of my life." So I was looking for a musician who would be willing to compose for my "literating."

Negotiations with Sarajevo composer Goran (Bregović) fell through because the musician did not want, for my proposal, to deviate from his folkloric, historic, quite mythical-autochthonous "group mentality," and in my opinion, overly circular audio storytelling.

David had already left the country: he had gone solo abroad as an interpreter; in the 1980s he had composed so successfully in the minimalistic manner; and could have been highly useful to my undertaking; too bad!

Mika was too busy; he was teaching at the Academy of Music; too bad (!), because the intimacy of his picturesque tone was very suitable to my undertaking!

Mileta had less and less to do with art; he was writing his memoirs; and his tones, measures, particularly his cadence, were so visual; too bad!

Drinka had retired; she was only active as a social worker, as a fighter for human rights; too bad for my undertaking, because her music was physically passionate and seductive!

I could no longer count on the collaboration of magnificent Vukašin; he no longer made music. He had become a teacher.

Marina, interesting and always fresh, had also changed professsions: she was working (profitably!) in tourism.

Wonderful and always congenial Dragan had become an inveterate loner, uninterested in symbiosis. I could understand that. I respected it.

Perhaps the most interesting and striking person on the musical scene of the 1980s was Professor Z, an excellent composer, theoretician and educator; in the early 1990s she unexpectedly but successfully turned to theoretical physics and nothing could be done to change it; she refused to return to the arts, considering the times in which we lived "wrong for art." (She works at the Institute for Theoretical Physics in Dortmund.) Too bad for my project!

At that time I had the offer of an accordion player and I must admit excellent singer known by the name of Basara (from the town of Preševo in southeastern present-day Serbia). At first glance he was ideal for my artistic enterprise: he was into subversive ethno-minimalism. You might say: "That's what I was looking for!" But at the time it was hard for me to accept Basara's overly fractured panoptic music. Even though Basara, I must admit (even today), is an artist to my liking (and even more to the liking of my third wife)—he is vain, controlled, intentionally destructive and inclined to subversion, which is so important to me—Basara's overemphasized Orthodox motifs turn me off: perhaps they are subconsciously charged with ideology. It's like listening to indoctrinated anti-Communist canonizing, broken, disrupted by Old Church Slavonic tones, medieval mysticism, and a satirical accordion melody always directed against everything ingrained in his own music. Regional and turned within on the one hand, quite international and turned against himself, on the other, I would say. Basara's otherwise good sound seemed to me like a dirge of burning politics and the hurried application of current, newly manufactured historical facts. And I had to remove any doubts about the direct, inartistic historicity of my undertaking. Consequently, I rejected Basara's enticing score. Too bad! (I might use it later; perhaps in my story about Handke, planned for the first decade of the next century.)

Finally, not even Knifer's *Meanders* were part of the political platform, even though my teacher, Professor P., saw signs of anti-Leninism in the *Meanders*, making his case with the biographical facts of Knifer's teacher Tiljak, who was indeed a student of Kandinsky and Malevich, but had clearly developed Knifer's affinity for quiet resistance to all things ideological. That is what attracted me to Julije. All of a sudden I felt the need to defend Knifer from the dogmatists.

In those bestially restless final years of the dying century that shook all levels of history like a death rattle, I sought refuge in repose: reading the prose (terrific!) of Robert Walser, listening to the music of (forgotten!) Jean-Baptiste Lully and contemplating Julije Knifer's *Meanders*. What contemplating, what listening, and what reading!

Those were three paramount, all-inclusive, calming activities, and at the same time so sensorial, that, in spite of the unhappy times and in spite of the daily ravages of the soul, they could be coupled together with kindness (greatly needed by all) and truly encourage a creative attitude toward reality which, amazingly enough, had still not become virtual.

It is relevant to note, however, that Walser and Lully on the whole were inspiring, yet insufficiently tangible for my modernity. Knifer, who was Everything for me, thus an instance above the temporal and verbal, needed a new complement, I thought. And I had it, I always had it! In the Supra-Written, in the *above all handwritten* P.H. Later P.H. developed them, periodically in my presence, into a succession of "those" essential steps on "those" joint "historical" trips (that I will write about in the next century). For me that was the true beginning of "non-narrative storytelling," writing in which I saw myself as a missionary. "In search of the motive, the forms, the rhythm and music of storytelling!" as though hearing the Master's command. And I searched—not only for the forms of myself and my modernity but also for the specificities and modernity of form.

Encouragement came from P.H. himself. He wrote: "Your text on the trip to Bratunac is worthy of Crnjansk! [2] Impetuous, sensitive, infantile, it strikes at the pith of life."[3]

Encouragement came from Knifer too. He wrote: "Žarko, buddy, you've got to freak out!"

Encouragement came from Miloje as well: "Shut up and work," he wrote.[4]

And I got down to work. I imagined, however, that music was the foundation of non-narrative writing. But, with regard to sound, I was unable to overcome the longing for silence, and that did not suit the blaring sound of the time.

In the meantime, a manager from New York (Edward Ned Humphrey; otherwise originally from Boston; we met during our studies in Tübingen) suggested that I meet the American composer Steve

---

[2] Miloš Crnjanski (1893-1977), one of the preeminent 20th century Serbian writers. He spent a considerable part of his life as an émigré.

[3] The text on the trip to Bratunac entitled *Ausland: Eine Reise mit Peter Handke* was published in the book *Noch einmal für Jugoslavien: Peter Handke* (Frankfurt am Main: Suhrkamp Verlag, 1999).

[4] Miloje Radaković (born in 1954), Serbian writer and filmmaker, living as an émigré.

Reich. I accepted the idea at once. Enthusiastically. "Reich is really a good solution," said Knifer, too. I kept him informed about my hesitations, and even though he said that it was "all the same" to him, he perked up immediately at the mention of Reich.

That same evening we met in the garret of Kemmler's studios in Tübingen (Knifer was there working on one of the most important series of his *Meanders*). I brought a crate of beer, a cassette player, a camera and tapes with Reich's music. A sacredly quiet evening. ("The Dacić's were on vacation!") Christmas Eve atmosphere. Knifer was applying "white paint" to a white canvas, "livelier with every daub." An amazing harmony between the movements of the artist's hand and the rhythm of Reich's music.

Then at the height of silence, when Knifer said warmly, "That's IT," and that a painting for him, like music for Reich, was "only rhythm," I decided to call Ned in New York that same evening. The conversation cost me double. I was drunk. Ned was "smashed" as well. We talked at length about the garden we shared in Hauser Street in Tübingen. We laughed, of course. When Ned asked, "Whatever happened to Sabina Schneider?"[5] I asked him laconically what he had had "for dinner." And right then in that part of the conversation we suddenly toned down the conversation, like putting out a cigarette in a bowl of water; and we started to talk about "Steve Reich."

I got together with Reich in a hotel room not far from the National Art Gallery in Stuttgart, where the composer was giving a series of lectures on Balinese rhythms. I must say that I was surprised by the nervousness of a man whose music instilled peace of mind. He "jiggled his foot" nervously the entire time, tapping the bottom of his shoe on the parquet floor. Sometimes he sat on the bed ("in total disorder!"), sometimes he stood in front of the window (with greasy spots on the panes!) and looked outside in alarm ("as though expecting the police to arrive!"). He had never heard of Knifer, he said. That discouraged me at once. Before I even made my proposal, he started talking—extremely distraught, almost incoherent—about his work on *Different Trains*. I was certain that I did not make any mistake in that conversation. I controlled myself. Every single attempt to show him the monograph about Knifer was interrupted by his interjections about émigrés scattered about the world.

My meeting with Steve Reich ended in a debacle. I was miserable. Shattered. That evening I almost wanted to shelve the book on Kni-

---

[5] See the beginning of my book *Tübingen* (Belgrade: Pan Dušicki, 1990).

fer's art. On the phone with Mladen (Stilinović),[6] he said, "What's wrong with you?" "Calm down." "Steve was probably in a bad mood." In order to get me going again, Dragan announced that (in his book *Hamsin*[7]) he would publish some excerpts from my letters to him and finally get the desired symbiosis started. I felt bad for days. My family greeted me with, "You've lost weight. Are you sick?" The only thing that kept me alive was the longing for change. I wanted to move.

🖎 24 AUGUST 1998

The apartment was in the northern part of town, in zone B, on street A, house number 290. That street is one of the inconspicuous connective threads in the town. It winds through extremely different neighborhoods, parallel to the main thoroughfares. That street is a "world unto itself," quiet compared to the "asymmetrical" streets along the way, always "self-immanent." Only visible on satellite pictures. Or from its own sidewalk. But some parts are always deserted. The rare, never accidental passers-by on those parts of the street seem like dogs that are not taken out but sent out on their mandatory daily walk. Dogs, moreover, on the small square on the part of the street through zone Y, seem like policemen standing in front of the darkened pharmacy store window. No one talks to anyone else in front of the entrance to the *Sole Mio* restaurant: neither the woman who goes briefly into the street and then right back inside; nor the man who suddenly rushes out onto the sidewalk, staggering, and then disappears "like a shadow" into the gloom; nor the two men, holding hands, who stride confidently through the door only to be swallowed up by the interior of the restaurant, quite mysteriously for someone standing outside, someone who, otherwise, had not gone anywhere that night either.

Apartment number 27 was on the tenth floor of building number 290.

The elevator was not very stuffy. (Here again, as in my book *Pogled* (*View*), the elevator was made by the Schindler Company.)

The view from the living room balcony provided a convincing "pan" that ended, as in a dream, with the image of "a cathedral in the

---

[6] Knifer's and my common friend from Zagreb. A painter. See my book *Knifer* (Belgrade: Radio B92, 1994).

[7] Dragan Velikič, *Hamsin* (Belgrade: Vreme Knjige, 1993).

mist."

I opened the door to the bathroom. It was spacious and well lit. And I had a nice view of my satisfaction in the enormous wall mirror.

I almost did not want to leave the bedroom. (The landlord proposed that we move to the dining room.) I said I wanted to buy the china cabinet. The landlord offered me a chair. I took off my shoes. "I don't smoke," I said.

Outside through the wide-open terrace door, we saw a pigeon on the window ledges of the building next door. It was standing stock-still. It shat.

The sun was setting. It is hard to describe what I still feel today about the apartment's smell. I looked in silence. The landlord nodded his head. He was smiling, but he examined my hands quite probingly. "Yes," I said after he asked me whether I had a car.

It started to rain outside.

Late, really late summer. And it was no longer hot.

I turned to look at a woman in a short, tight skirt and clunky leather shoes. The rhythm of her energetic pace was almost a call to join her. This is what I saw after several hesitant steps in her direction: two men with the tops of their heads shaven, and a woman with no hair, a deep décolleté on her tight t-shirt, and barefoot, holding her sandals. They were standing in front of a BMW convertible. Of course, the car was black.

I stood in front of a drugstore for a while and, beside myself, so to speak, stared at a box with bars of soap falling out of it. They were all the same "pink" and were all "Provençal." Just the thought of that pleasant, unobtrusive smell of soap made me want to lick and nibble them. It was a calming feeling. And also a feeling of warmth.

Then, when a mother holding a child came out of the entrance to a building on the curve of a street that was so quiet that evening, I wanted to talk.

Instead of going to a see a friend who lived in the neighborhood, I went to the movies in the northernmost, distant, not my favorite part of town. The weather seemed to be different there. Like it was much, much colder. And it was truly dark there. Not a single streetlight was on in the street. All the blinds were lowered on all the windows of all the houses. Only one place in that part of town was lit. Making it all the more conspicuous. When I got close to it, it reminded me of the mouth of a fiery volcano just before it erupted. Even though every detail was unmistakable owing to the bright lights, the excessive energy of the individual sources made it impossible to connect the details.

"Connection impossible," I said as I entered the movie theater. "Could not make the connection," I wrote in the notepad on the knee of my body's leg reclining in the comfortable seat on one of the rows in the packed movie theater.

I felt like I was in prison.

I cannot say it was unpleasant.

The last woman to enter the theater, the last one before the beginning of the show, and who happened to sit on the last empty seat, right next to me, and who I happened to sleep with that night after the movie, right in her apartment not far from the theater, addressed me with the words, "You look awful. Do you feel all right?" During the movie we innocently held hands. At one point I wanted to light a cigarette. Everyone in the theater was staring at the screen. It figures. The picture was of a room with a window on a courtyard. I kept trying to make out the details beyond the windowpane. Without success. At one point I wanted to leave the movie theater, "to take a walk." Later, after the movie, after the wild lovemaking in that woman's apartment, and during the "typical" post-coital intimacy in bed, she said that when she came up to the seat in the movie theater, I looked "awful."

◯ 25 AUGUST 1998

There was a thriving composer in Belgrade in the second half of the 20th century, and I was particularly fond of her as a person: Radmila (Ra). Her light operas were impressive in those years. In the 1980s, background music was popular at get-togethers, celebrations, parties and saint's day festivities in Belgrade, Zemun and Surčin. The selection of seemingly light music was such that with just a slight shift of your attention you could get your whole body into it, and completely tune out your surroundings. Monotonous rhythms. The quiet vibrations of most often a single note. Then barely perceptible transitions to a two-note development of the musical story line. Perhaps it was this barely perceptible musical storytelling—developing without approaching a climax, so the body of the story acted like an onion, without a pit, without pith, without an interior—that drove me away from the idea of using Radmila's music as a backdrop to my work on Knifer. (It was not because Knifer complained about my demonstrations of Radmila's music! I was completely detached from Knifer's reactions!) I liked Radmila's "universality" and her comprehensive, physical surrendering to the sonorous reception of reality. "As her breasts gave rhythm to the quiet, heavy, comprehensive, vital being of the immobile stomach of life as a resonator of fertility, tranquillity, connection to the ground as the basis of reality," I wrote (and, of course, did not tell Julije). "Tantra tones," I then wrote. "Nevertheless, wasn't that substantial sound too strong for Knifer's gentle *Meanders*?" I wondered. Wasn't that emphatically stated tone overemphasized, too nomadic and homeless for Julije Knifer's *Meanders* that are beyond-time, beyond-place and beyond-story, thus acting beyond every intention?" I said. So I rejected Radmila's proposals for the musical background to Knifer's *Meanders*, or rather I put them aside. "I will probably use them in my piece on the furniture in the office of Deutsche Welle radio," I said to myself. I also did it because Radmila's work lacked conceptuality. ("My art is conceptual," Knifer once said.) ("Radmila's art is not conceptual," I said.) In addition, Ra had the habit (I thought) of dressing in "other people's clothes," at times without the slightest consideration for the authenticity of the "clothes," leaving them on herself even as "a mistake." As she said, "Those clothes should be worn, used up." But: it was like the person who had put on the clothes didn't like them. ("Like they were in disguise because of the clothes and not because of themselves," I thought.) ("Well, they can't like the clothes, since they don't belong to them," I thought.) (I had similar thoughts about the relationship between Tarkovski the filmmaker and the Tuscan landscape where the director moved after leaving his homeland, the Soviet Union, or just Russia which, I suddenly thought, "had never truly been his, and that might be why he never truly loved it.") Radmila's music was "used up" all the faster (it seemed to me). It broke up into component parts (I would say now), into parts (I would say), "immediately swallowed up by the musician herself who then digested them like raw ground meat," she had "selected," rejected and stylized ("Legitimately, but . . . ," I thought).

Nevertheless, the recalcitrant and soft, wildly monotonous "insolent" mimicking music was Something for me ("Unlike the adolescent songs of B.S.!") ("Unlike the eager, tribunal singing of N.P., N.B., N.D., P.D. and D.I. And even P.R!") (That's why I put Radmila's score aside.) (That's why I did not use Radmila's music composition book as a coaster for beer bottles on the coffee table in the living room.) (That's why I postponed my poeticizing to Radmila's music.) The music Radmila made was the total reflection of a "strong personality." Thus, recognizable. (Unlike, for example, the music of N.D., a secret electrician who was depressed and suffering from "illusions of grandeur," convinced he had "mind-boggling power." "I'm going to bring down Milošević," he rambled drunkenly one evening, which I, also drunk, did not take seriously.) Radmila's sound is truly the reflection of a purebred musician. Even if she were to appear before the public with an impersonal, archaic smile, in a casually unbuttoned coat, or with the left and right sides of her face wearing different makeup, she would come across as "Someone." (Unlike N.D. who, even though he is always dressed "to the nines" in a bow tie, tweed jacket and polished "flashy" shoes from the department store, most often stumbles over his words, waves his hands hysterically, twitches the left side of his face, struts about and constantly interrupts his interlocutor. I already wrote about N.D. in the book *Emigracija* (*Emigration*). He is described under the name Žan (Gene). So I won't go into more detail here about this otherwise very important hero in my books. I will postpone his story. More details about him will be forthcoming in the story about Handke, which I will undertake at the beginning of the next millennium.) Listening to Radmila's background destructiveness was just like the experience of undressing: myself, the surroundings, the very objects in a room that became increasingly denuded with every beat. (Unlike the melodic elements of N.D.—a depressed and indescribable musical erotomaniac who, instead of lust, emanated the desire to compare himself with musicians from the established bourgeoisie: Luigi Nono, for example, or John Cage, or Alfred Schnittke, or John Lennon, or David Byrne, or Phil Kokoska, or Vladmimr Goati.) Ra with her anti-beats descended to the very depths of hearing (*à la* Sid Vicious, Fuday Musa Suso, Aki Takase or Frederick Tseler and, of course, Miles Davis).

Just thinking of N.D.'s trip to Salt Lake City. N.D. lived in a small town close to the city. It was autumn. Mist. The farmers were fertilizing the fields. It smelled like manure. N.D. was a city kid and drunk that night as usual and was, of course, in despair as he staggered home along the road from the bar at the local gas station where he had drunk five shots of cheap whiskey and six beers ("Bud"). He threw up every ten steps. At home, in the house of an esteemed colleague, he (N.D.) grabbed the phone and called the numbers of the brothels in the nearby towns. He wanted to have sex with a "Taiwanese" that night! He could not explain to himself how he managed to call my apartment in Cologne, Germany, instead of the local brothels. At the time I was still in living on Hertha Street. As soon as I picked up the receiver, I smelled stables. From the background came the stench of evaporating alcohol. I cheered up. But instead of the dear voice of my "friend," the sound of mooing cows came from the darkness. Instead of the artist's words, I made out the cackling of hens on their way to roost. That cheered me up. I was living alone those years. My wife had left me for another man. My pet had died, "kicked the bucket." Stevan Tontić had been living in another country for ages. The heating wasn't working in my modest apartment. Emigration had become a wasteland. I was fated to telephone calls. N.D., however, made inarticulate sounds that were not at all soothing. The only clear word was "Taiwanese." When I think about that today—and it is a known fact that I am not normal and only have grotesque thoughts—suddenly all of N.D.'s art seems like his voice over the phone: just the mentally deranged churning out of familiar tones, I thought. The artist made them sound unusual by pushing his, most often, defective instruments, I thought. "Amortized measures, rhythms out of sync and confused harmonies are thrown out at random." "It is like listening to a symphony of coughing, sneezing, burping and moaning." "Most often it is aggressively interrupting someone, so they cannot even put one sentence together, let alone listen to the other person's complete thought." "And then distressful crying was heard (what for?), without any specific reason, like venting frustration for world suffering." "Then furiously and narcissistically showing off." "Then again the operetta-like, moralizing crying for the world." "And suddenly in that truly kitschy and mournful wailing of the sick, drunk or seriously injured artist, you feel compassion." "And that was the only contribution of the person listening to that ugly music in which the artist showed his originality and singularity by stealing and deforming something from someone else."—It's a known fact that I am not normal—"Repetition without the slightest participation!" "Insipid elaboration of nothing!" "It rings of emptiness," I once said to Branka (Arsić)[8]—She knew I was not normal.—"A man in trousers with legs that are too short and limp" and "a guy in a tie wearing someone else's clothes that hang on him, of course!" she said) . . . Ra was a purebred musician. Unbridled in a quiet way. Liberated. She had something to say . . . Although, if I had to choose in that genre of crushing late-operatic Yugo-disintegration music in the second half of the 20th century, I would immediately

---

[8] Serbian philosopher, emigrated from Belgrade to New York through Budapest. See her book *Razum i ludilo* (*Reason and Madness*) (Belgrade: Stubovi kulture, 1997).

choose the authentic, imaginative, substantial and more than refined Miodrag Vuković. That composer of pithy miniatures had been silent for a long time. Was he preoccupied? Did he want to be alone? Did he often not reply to letters? Had he taken a trip somewhere?[9]

✍ 27 August 1998

That same day I spent noontime at a pastry shop in the southern part of town. I was sitting at a round table (the only one in the room) (was I feeling rejected?), busy with the latte I had ordered (I was staring at the smooth surface of the liquid), my thoughts full of Professor P. (he often drank lattes at café-bars). I was convinced that my professor did not approve of Julije Knifer's art. I was also convinced that Professor P. had not delved sufficiently into Basar's music either. He certainly must have been impressed by the anti-communist tones. (The Professor was an anti-communist.) But did he feel Basara's or even Radmila's art at all? If he were a member of a jury awarding an annual prize for contributions to music, would he vote for Basara's chef-d'oeuvre *Mars*, a soap opera with elements of ballet and sleight-of-hand, or for Radmila's brilliant raga-miniature *De Vampiribus*? And those were compositions that we all, Dragan and Stevan and Miroslav (Mandić)[10] and I and Dinko (Tucaković)[11] and Mitar Dub-ljević[12] "devoured" those difficult, arid and hungry Yugo-years. Basara himself gave me a tape recording of his operetta. It was in the apartment of our common friend P. R. We were drunk, as we always were at P.R.'s saint's day parties. Basara stuck the tape in my jacket pocket. I would not even have noticed if he hadn't brushed it against the shoulder of a young woman (I don't remember if it was the critic

---

[9] Miodrag Vuković was born in 1947 in Cetinje, Montenegro. He was one of the most remarkable literary writers in the Serbo-Croatian language in the second half of the 20th century. He did not emigrate. I would note that his book *Krug, soba* (*Circle, Room*) (Belgrade: Knjizevna omladina Srbije, 1978) was one of the most crucial books of my time.

[10] Mandić was a nomad. From 1991 to 2001, he walked "for poetry," "for Europe" (!), because of "the erotica of wandering," because of "the wisdom of the road," because of that "warm, cloudy day" on Stražilov Hill on April 7, 1998. See *Ruža lutanja I-X* (*The Rose of Wandering I-X*) (Belgrade: Društvo prijatelja, 1992).

[11] Director of the Yugoslav Film Archives program in Belgrade. He stayed in Belgrade. He made a film during the bombing of Belgrade in 1999.

[12] Main hero of the book *Krug, soba* (*Circle, Room*) by Miodrag Vuković.

I. M.) who was sitting half-naked on the armrest of the armchair next to me, whipping herself with the ends of her unruly hair and shaking her half-drunk head and sagging breasts to the beat of Radmila's music coming from a dark corner of the room. P.R., who knew parts of that warm background music by heart, was humming softly "to the music" . . . . There were several typical "local" people in the apartment. D.K., S.S., E.M., T.K., T.T., P.M., R.U., S and N.D. They were all like heroes from a new Hong Kong soap opera. M.P., for example, was wearing a white "nylon" shirt. A.J. had a shaved head and an intentionally "freshly" broken front tooth. D.L. had put on two different shoes; he was sitting in an armchair, sprawling like a pregnant woman; he too was humming softly to parts of Radmila's opera. The music (Radmla's) from the radio was too loud, I thought. I looked at the woman behind the bar: legs like pillars; house slippers; like she was taking money to pay the bills and doing it like she was hanging laundry. ("That was not Z.B.") At one point I thought I was in the attic. "What's this?" I said under my breath to the woman who shyly took out her breast and silenced the screaming infant in her arms with the nipple of her swollen, milk-filled breast. ("That was not J.T.!") In the sudden silence that reigned all that was heard was the ticking of a man's wristwatch (M.P.!). Fingers gripped the pencil feverishly. Tears fell on the letters on the page. The clattering of a garbage truck was heard in the distance. And once again staring dully without breathing. Again pictures without titles. Words rain down on the table like balls from the broken housing of a ball bearing . . . "I love Belgrade!" I wrote.

The night with the woman from the movies was actually boring. It was, in a sense, like repeating one of the scenes in the movie. It started with the accidental touching of knees between the seats. That was when the male lead, the "leader of the vampires," entered the bedroom of the female lead ("first victim of vampirism"). The woman reacted "as though scalded." She was young and "exquisitely beautiful" ("a challenge to the vampire!"). She was also lethargic—in the film, in the flirt and in her own life. Like she had entered the movie theater by accident. It was not until she took off her light coat and threw her shawl over her gorgeous legs that I saw the hunger for domination in her eyes. I felt resolve. I also detected the weight of my origins.

Knees bumped each other several more times. She always reacted with mitigated surprise. Every touch increased my fear that I would lose contact with the picture on the screen. After the last two touches of the knees the woman even moved her leg "with a delay." Like she was sending signals that suddenly became clear signs of her intentions. The woman dropped her coat and shawl off her knees several times and each time she picked them up with an apology spoken in a breathy whisper.

She dropped her purse at the entrance to a building on the next street. Keys jingled.

The heel of her shoe fell off on the stairs. Suddenly she was a head shorter than me.

She lifted her skirt and took off her panties already on the first landing. (I don't know why I was reminded of my fourth wife.)

She dropped her keys at the door to her apartment. I smiled and firmly pressed her smoldering body. She did not let me through the wide open door, but stepped into her apartment first, moving backwards with disjointed, uneven steps, at times like a drunk, at times like a savage, at times like a sleepy child, at times like a wounded beast.

I was simply taken: first to the kitchen, then to the bathroom and then to the bedroom.

"Why did you breathe so unevenly during the film?" she asked. After the wild sex on the floor of her study, she smoked, passionately, the usual cigarette, and stared as usual at the ceiling.

I sat down, dressed, in the armchair and gazed at the luxuriously naked body of the beautiful woman, now transformed into an old woman intending to go into the kitchen and make some latte. Soft music by guitarist Bill Frisell came from the radio. Shadows on the wall: Julije Knifer's *Meanders*. All the books on the shelf: only by Handke. Silence. I felt great. Then a gentle wind started to blow. The breeze turned into a storm. The furniture, paintings, decorations, curtains and everything I could see in the room reminded me of the prewar (big) Yugoslavia.

And then cockroaches began to move in a corner of the room. The woman raised her long legs high and wide. And: plaster started falling from the ceiling. And: the woman's teeth started to grow. All the paintings on the walls fell to the floor by themselves. In the kitchen, the refrigerator door opened and closed. In the meantime, vegetables rolled out onto the floor. On the quilt cover under the woman's bottom spread a huge puddle of blood in the shape of the geographical map of a disintegrating country. Borders were not important. Not even the tearing of the cover (the sound was unpleasant, of course) was important. Importance lay in the feeling of fear: not of unpleasant dreams but of suspended origins.

✑ 28 AUGUST 1998

The story about the vampires starts in the west of a spacious country. Billowing clouds are visible on the distant horizon. The colors, of course, are strong and hot. The cameraman has paid special attention to the large grain in the picture of the shadows of objects illuminated by the setting sun.

With a sudden jolt of the picture and loud sounds (of what?) falling like pieces of a body, a jeep suddenly appears in the shot. It looks like part of the mountain on the horizon in the background, covered in evening, or morning, *sfumato*: moments in which every art historian with even the slightest experience concludes that all the figures on Leonardo da Vinci's frescoes are people of the night, inclined to debauchery. Horror story fans would be particularly delighted by that picture of a sleepwalking state. Not a single detail is meant to arouse fear. Someone who was moving about that time, going from one state to another, looking for new furniture, new clothes, a new face, new weight, could find something "nice and useful" in the abundant details of that truly hot picture. Not even the superintendent of a building on one of the most meaningless streets of the town, only visited because of the (always fresh) fishmonger's, could resist the sight of the enormous axe that the film's male lead tested on the trunk of a cactus, raised to his shoulder with a powerful cry, then turned resolutely to his friends and let out that resolute call, "To battle!"

Those were the commandos of a special unit to fight the vampires.

Let us also say that the sound of the call to head out on the mission reflected the exchange of short, resolute looks. They were so confident, piercing, important, formal, and also quiet, even a little sleepy, starry-eyed and amorous. And each one of the viewers—including the student of dentistry in the third row of the movie theater, and the florist in the twenty-eighth row, and the hairdresser in the seventeenth, and the bank clerk in the thirteenth, and the anesthesiologist in the eighth, and the jewelry saleswoman in the eleventh row of the movie theater—felt the need to draw closer to the person sitting next to them. I put my arm over the back of the seat (next to me) just when the leader of the commandos whistled loudly as a signal to get into the jeeps. Of course, the dust behind the hefty, heavy wheels of those cars as they took off recklessly, but also in a heraldic, almost formal manner, was heavy, thick, and fateful.

The vampires, however, were quite another thing. The physical appearance of these anti-beings deviated from every "standard." We cannot maintain that they are beautiful manifestations. By no means do they have an ideal shape. But each one has a "distinctive trait." ("Details again!") A detail suddenly stands out from the whole and unexpectedly appears as a special quality. "Dominant One!" It immediately returns to its "context" with (our) eyes. It is a slow "zooming out" to a "long shot." The view is calm and measured. It is guided, however, by the "distinctive trait" of the whole, accurately, rigorously and without deviation. The scene is therefore of a "powerful army" under the command of a leader with clear intensions. The movement is a constant advance, massing and conquering the space of the whole. Like viscous liquid, it spreads to every corner of the whole. Soon there is no empty space. The space of the view fills up, bends and almost twists under the weight of the preeminence of the One: the omnipotence of the "distinctive trait" of the vampire's manifestation. And this process is neither fast nor slow. The imperceptible but certainly tangible Advance establishes the despotic reign of details over the whole. And: the manifestation of the anti-being remains, as though forever, marked by a stigma that is unrecognizable but sensually present to a shudder. The distinctive trait of domination appears like a scar on an otherwise pretty and well-proportioned body. Like instant ugliness, compressed into the smallest thing emitting all its monstrosity and atrocity that suddenly fiendishly overcome the entire anti-being that is ready to empty itself of all such distinctiveness.

◎ 29 AUGUST 1998

For example, one female vampire was unusually slender, with an almost maidenly fragile build and small, firm, innocently exuberant breasts; she almost called out for protection; you almost felt like taking her in your arms. And then she suddenly showed her wall-eyes; this was not, however, an ordinary disturbance in the eye system; the anti-being had double vision; the pupils of her dark eyes alternated like day and night. The anti-being gradually, softly, hypnotized the victim; riveted him to the seat, bed or pillar; with her eyes. And then began the dance of the sorceress. And then the victim gave himself obediently to that extraordinary conquistador. There was no strength to resist the seductive power of the "aggressor." The power was manifest by several cheap tricks. Its effectiveness was proven by shamelessly playing out something that had never crossed anyone's mind. For example, the anti-being would say, "Come here and take me," or "Release me," or "Console me."

One of the vampires had an excessively large, protruding, round forehead, giving the impression of immense intelligence. This detail completely dominated the powerful corpus, a body that exuded only might. And the power of simulated intellect gushing from the bare, bulging shape of the vampire's forehead not only inhibited passion but acted almost hypnotically on the victim who immediately undressed, contracted, bent down and surrendered to the embrace, above all to the eyes of the fiend who did not do anything. He sat with crossed arms, following almost listlessly the dying victim and the change from day to night.

The nose of the third anti-being was exceptionally long. It was an extended arm of the olfactory organ, but also a device to catch the collocutor off guard. Smelling with such an organ also spread the infection to the outside.

The long, long legs of one of the female vampires were like sticky tape under a lamp, where beings got stuck until they died, transformed all by themselves into flies, mesmerized by the anti-being's gorgeous legs. They squirmed in the death rattle, overcome by the beauty of her skin, her sculptured muscles and the delicacy of the sorceress's long-dead body. And the victim was unaware when life ended, having surrendered exaltedly to the cheap trick of being shown the delights of nudity.

And when the main vampire appeared in the picture dressed strikingly in black, I wanted to join that group of anti-beings myself, even though I had been on the commando's side from the first shot in the movie: mostly because of my renegade origins. (My mother descended from a robber and bandit who attacked notables, most often at deserted crossroads. He fled to a neighboring country where he settled down and started a family. He transmitted the restlessness of his youth to his offspring. We are all powerfully built, just like these commandos. One, for example, has terrifyingly broad shoulders "like a three-door wardrobe." The hands of another are enormous, "like shovels." The legs of one of the female commandos, or relatives, are sturdy, strong and hard, "like beech logs." The breasts of another relative, or commando, are firm and pointed, "like knife blades.")

Now, the main vampire was in the form of a tall, slender man, his body swathed in a long black cloak. The narrow, sharp, regular shape of his nose simply protruded from the narrow isthmus between his eyes. They resemble two vast lakes with choppy waves in which the pupils, like two sailboats, tossed about wildly, do not wander but stare fixedly at the being before the anti-being and immediately turn him into a shipwreck. The other male and female vampires addressed that colossus as "Master" (lord). Unlike mortals, Master did not respond but simply appeared—walking, riding horseback, flying, advancing, encroaching and trampling. And he was truly handsome. With almost archaic manners. Lowered "fuck-me" shoulders. (Unlike us, descendants of a bandit, with shoulders mostly thrown out broadly to the side.) (Unlike us, "square-shaped!") Exquisite bony hands. (I'm talking about the main vampire, Master, and not us, the descendants of a bandit.) The most regularly cut lips. An elastic but oh so firm body. (Unlike us, the descendants of a robber, often with sagging lips, jug ears, stiff bodies.) (Unlike us, the descendants of a bandit, who imagined each other as Hollywood stars, heroes, and even vampires . . . Of course, I often saw Professor P. as a stand-in for the Hollywood actor Clint Eastwood from one of his later films. But that night, the "night of the vampires," I suddenly wanted Professor P. be in the role of the leader of a group of commandos out to "liquidate" the vampires. Because the professor was a "handsome man." Tall with a highlander's build, the face of a mild-mannered rebel, ready to burst out of all his cultivated manners and unleash the power of abomination. He was overpowering! A shot to "parry" Master.) So Master immediately adopted the style of a conquistador. He was accompanied by his closest and most loyal similars. (The words "likeminded thinker," or "members," would be too weak). And that little group of biological anti-reformers, those who truly changed the lifeblood of fate, acted as One. Not like a herd. Not united. Not as the chosen. They were truly a detachment of death. A unit of superhuman forces in a delirium controlled by no one. A team to destroy everything in existence. The reflection of the essence of evil. The very ends of death as a prolongation not of life but an imitation of life, pursuing the eternal, unnatural, unhidden urge to spread the infection and damnation arising from self-centeredness, an infection whose pith, moreover, is in that one physical detail ("distinctive trait"), a scar arising from the clash between the abyss inside you, your lack of origin and the chasm of modernity, from being self-centered and from the pressure of the outside, from the irrepressible desire for perfection and from being unaware of your weaknesses, from the clash between some sectarian clannishness and the irrepressible desire to spread that could never be opening but even more tightly closing, painful compressing, feverishly approaching implosion. Consequently, that anti-being was an instant of irrepressible longing for darkness, moistness, liquidity and somnolence.

Such a compact, indivisible group had a special way of communicating. Individual words were usually spoken: like vomiting what has been ejected, like putting a circle around a sign and what it denotes. These elocutions were immediately freed of any burden of information. They were multiply directed symbols. They were not to be received and decoded but to be taken inside oneself and closed up inside oneself. It was some sort of cage in which communicants languished forever. Consequently, without words, without eyes, without touch. Always advancing. Nowhere and everywhere.

✑ 30 AUGUST 1998

The commandos of the counter-vampire unit (in the movie) truly did communicate. And the communication was lively. The constant dispatching of information, interpretations, specific instructions, words, even if they were only "Get up," "Take this," "Don't," "What the fuck are you waiting for?" "Out," "Sit there," "What time is it?" "Get lost," "You didn't fill the tank," "Strip her naked," "Come on," "Stab him in the heart." (We too, descendants of a bandit, communicate clearly. We most often address each other with interrogative sentences accompanied by powerful gesticulations: "Didn't I tell you to take the pot off the stove?" my grandmother would say, hands on her hips. "Maybe you could give me a blow job?" a friend of mine would say, putting his hand on his genitals. "Did you swallow a drawer, empty bottle?" I would say and spit over the rug. "What's wrong with you?" came softly from the bedroom, accompanied by breaking glass. "He must have fallen into the cesspool again," seemed to come from the basement, accompanied by blows of a metal object on cement. "Are we going to stay here much longer?" said someone and spit in their hands.) (Professor P., "one of ours," who we saw as our leader, expressed himself clearly as well, but in short sentences, I thought. Of course, he gesticulated too, but he did it inconspicuously. "What now?" was one of his famous short sentences, always accompanied by turned-up palms. "He made a methodological mistake," he said once, also succinctly, in the hollow silence, his head cocked to the side, lips tightly closed, the tip of his nose trembling slightly. "Colleague Delić is right," he said succinctly, raising his left eyebrow, staring blankly into the distance. "Like John Wayne," "on that rise" above Monument Valley in the movie "The Searchers." And I looked at Professor P. again, sitting at the rostrum in the lecture hall at the university. And I saw him once again as Clint Eastwood staring into the face of a woman who was hiding a secret.) The commandos said all their Words passionately, hotly, and often roughly. But always personally. And you could instantly either reject what was said or use it skillfully. In any case you were practical. Mobile and able to act. And finally, to learn more about your surroundings.

Vampire words—"power," "night," "skin," "full moon," "might," "hole," "wolves," "hair in the wind," "coffin," "drops," "rats," "blood," "marble"—not addressed to anyone personally and even though vague, were uttered with a cry, straight from the throat, or even more often, in a whisper (so always abnormally), very breathy, so that collocutors could put their arms around what was said physically, bring it close to their body and with all their strength, with a new cry, with a groan, with a scream or with wild laughter and hissing giggles, thrust their nails into their body. That was the only possible interpersonal relationship between people communicating through utterances. And there was no substance for the vampires. The world, which they most often called "darkness" or "other-worldly" or "eternity" existed for them only in the corporeal where they existed by plainly showing their outsides, seizing other people's bodies, and killing and cutting up other people's insides.

The relationship between vampires and non-vampires takes place on the boundary between life and death. And that is an indefinite space. An emptiness between separated and untouchable worlds. And while the dead have always been uninterested in the living, preoccupied with pure, non-historical, thus non-vertical, generally non-dimensional memories, opening their world, other-worldly, a world of infinity (?) and totality (?), in all directions against life (which will be the subject of another story not to be related here), the living in their final (?) world defined by space and time (?), acted primarily in accordance with all the characteristics of their being, their ability to think, feel, observe (which will also be the subject of another story), giving special attention to fears of emptiness, the emptiness in that inter-boundary area, the inter-zone between, as we said, the worlds of life and death.

✑ 31 August 1998

It was a zone of darkness. From the viewpoint of life: nothing but the antechamber of death. Of course, colors cannot be distinguished there. Without shadow, taste, smell, and tangibility, objects appeared only as mockups. There was no coat rack, for example, or compartment to put your hat. Umbrellas with broken ribs, torn fabric and flayed handles lay on the dusty floor as the soundless wind whirled dried branches and withered leaves over them, catching them on crooked nails sticking halfway out of the rotting floor. With every gust of wind, the piles of things grew on these bare, dry bloodstained spikes. "Memory does not exist here," I wrote pointedly in my diary. I headed with uncertain steps across the dilapidated, squeaky floor. I did not feel the rats, cockroaches and pill bugs underfoot. "The senses are prohibited here," I wrote. When I entered the "prohibited zone," all perceptions, feelings, thoughts and memories were suspended, just like when one's head is cut off. So what are these notes based on? How do I know that everything was the way I presented it?

A "prohibited zone of consciousness does exist, however." (Available to everyone but not accessible by everyone . . . .) Closed, cocoon-like, impenetrable from the outside, bounded by the remaining, prevailing field of consciousness. It is not only *pars pro toto*. According to the feedback principle, it is *toto*. A dense, imponderably coherent colorless mass of body and soul. And it is resistant to every external influence. "The immunological system of the organism and the principle of withstanding environmental changes." "The liver and spleen of existence," I wrote in my notebook. Not available to a single anti-being. Simultaneously the embryo and center of resistance to everything external, including vampirism. Consequently, "the power of subversion."

Of course, in some living things ("in humans!") core consciousness is particularly strong. Of course, the homogeneity of the nucleus of consciousness is conditioned by the concentration of inherited factors. But ("I know that!"): the social context most certainly encourages subversion. "Experience is most certainly important," I wrote in the notebook (and squirmed with a shudder).

The commandos of the vampire liquidation unit are the toughest sort of beings. The physical strength of these "guys" and "dolls" is immediately visible. They are powerful. Strong, muscular, and robust. The women are always "hardbodies." The men do not all have shaved heads, but they always have "bodybuilder" physiques. They are more than autonomous individuals. They are indeed in a group. Nevertheless, they are always independent. And self-aware. Especially the special ones. A group of the chosen. Their selection is determined, or rather predetermined, by the degree of homogeneity and resistance of their core consciousness. Consequently, they are beings with a strong core. They are truly able to confront all the dangers that arise from crossing the "prohibited zone." Accustomed to being Undisturbed, they wander through the borderline space between life and death. And they are truly resistant to glances, voices, kisses, and especially to Vampire stories. Not even the sharpest vampire teeth pierce the rock-tough, not hard, so flexible and "erotically elastic" and thereby highly attractive skin of the men and women commandos of the vampire liquidation unit. The power of the male and female commandos' bodies, their build, the movement of their limbs, their sturdy gait, their resolute waving of the arms ("sharp from the elbow") of the male and female commandos is always guided and directed by the vibrations of the wondrous mass of core consciousness. Then, and always in "prickly situations," it appears ("only to those in the know!") as a *movens* of survival and superiority (or, at least, the not insignificant "will to power"). And then, suddenly "like lightning" or "like the blow of an axe" or "like a slap" or "like an unexpected grab at the crotch" it becomes clear to the viewer ("of that film") that they are before a picture of the incarnation of Freedom. Owing to this hidden core consciousness, the male and female commandos are free beings.

Vampires, as we know, feed on instant soul, primarily with peripheral layers of consciousness (since they are unable to penetrate to the core; because core consciousness is not accessible to them, because if it were, it would be a fatal tincture that would make even the immortal die unless they are ready to accept core consciousness; and vampires are not; since readiness to accept core consciousness requires the receiver to be thusly predisposed; because the receiver's qualities include love, solitude, gregariousness, dedication, reticence, modesty, loyalty, non-dissimulation; and vampires do not love anyone; because they are not loners; because they are not dedicated to anything; because they are not reticent; because they are not modest; because they are not loyal; because they dissimulate). Consequently, vampires feed on consciousness (its peripheral layers), they feed on the thoughts, feelings, perceptions and intuitions of the living; consequently, what they themselves do not have. Because they are manifested as a group. Because they always act as a group. Because they move in a group. Because One is always at the head of the group. "Master." Leader. Chief. General. Premier. President. And so on.

Recollections of Professor P as the leader of a group of students way back in 1968 are clear: perceptions are registered in the very core consciousness. They would be aroused, for example, by the fragrance of cheap eau de cologne the color of linden flowers. The branches were practically leaning against the windows of the corridor at the Faculty. Once I was standing in front of a urinal in the men's lavatory just as the enormous body of Professor Josimović came out of the stall. Professor Košutić spent all his time walking up and down the corridor with the female students, most often in front of the door to the seminar library. Professor Đurić would suddenly come out of his office and just as suddenly go into the office of Mrs. Bogdanović, and then suddenly come out of Professor Bogdanović's office and then suddenly go back to his own office, and so on. Why is it that the most festive moments I remember are the cleaning lady washing the floor (the rag she used had a strong smell), the eyes of student Dubravka V. (they were like a doe's), and the voice of student Vladimir B. (it was subdued)? Why is it that I do not remember Professor Gavrilović's body but only his voice, which I mix with the voice of student Zoran A? Why only teaching assistant Mužijević's walk ("like Robert Mitchum in *The River of No Return*")? Why only the pensive look of Ms. Gojković, the secretary ("like Greta Garbo just before the love scene with James Cagney")? (Suddenly there is the smell of the laundry room in building number four on Augustus Cesarca Street in Zemun. In the meantime, the name of the street has changed and so has the house number. No one is alive from the building where I used to live, except Jeremić, who lived on the third floor). It is noon. Professor P is standing in front of the door to the seminar library. He is wearing a long, loose, white or rather light beige coat. It is obvious at once that 80 percent of the students are female. The few males are withdrawn. Boško T. (from Bečej), for example, does not smoke. Mića R. (from Kraljevo, related to Snežana B.) avoids public transportation. Dragan (V., from Pula, later known for his book *Via Pula*) looks for sanctuary in cooking, eats alone, writes down and copies his own recipes. As soon as Jovan D. (from Borkovac) enrolled in the first year, his voice changed: he assumed the voice of Yugoslav

Radio-Television sportscaster Radivoj Marković mixed with the voice of his professor (P.). The professor was a brilliant speaker, though. For no reason at all he would take sentences out of context and repeat them importantly several times. In addition, the expression on his face never changed. And he whispered. He complained about his ailing vocal chords. Not even I know why I avoided passing him by in the street. And he was "my hero." Although he was not directly connected to Hollywood films of the 1950s, that professor spurred me to go to the movies and watch Westerns from the golden age. At the lectures on Plato, I saw the professor as Alan Ladd playing Shane in the film of the same name, in the scene where he is chopping wood: bent over, naked to the waist, he chops at the wood with an axe, looking lustfully at actress Jean Arthur playing the landlady, as his body glistens with sweat in the moonlight over the prairie. Thirty years later, when I was at Butch Cassidy Arch in one of the most picturesque regions of the Rocky Mountains of the "Wild West" (today only for tourists) and looked at the horizon, I saw the outline of my professor: he was riding slowly on horseback. The horse's hoof was bandaged with a cloth. His hand was hidden under the long sleeve of his coat and the barrel of a Winchester poked out from under the long coattail. Again there was that familiar movement of the eyebrow; again that unchanged expression on his face. And he seemed to be whispering. Like he was complaining about his ailing vocal chords. Not even I know why I avoided him in the street.

The Faculty building was an island in the river of daily life. Its banks were battered by the winds, undercut by the waves. They were jagged but nonetheless suitable ground where one could stay alive and even stay forever. That space was a bright world of intermission that needed little to become eternity, and not only for the new-comers.

So then, how do vampires come about? Where do they come from?

Once I remember standing on a crosswalk that led across a busy street. The woman next to me suddenly collapsed. She had twisted her ankle, she said. She had pulled a tendon, they said. I immediately went over to help her. Later, in my arms, she tried to bite my hand. She was out of control because of "the pain." I felt awkward. I felt unsafe above all. I felt nothing for that woman. We soon broke off our relationship. Perhaps also because of the venereal diseases that we gave each other. And the woman's face was too pale, which did not suit my taste at the time.

I was lacking anonymity. I was an average student.

There was the constant fear at work of getting too close to others. I did not feel close to anyone.

Even in elementary school, I was not part of the group. I always had one close friend, male or female. The first one I remember was R. L. (Raša Livada). All my friends later became Party members. And masons after that. I stayed to the side on impulse. If, on impulse, I was made a member of a political party at the proposal of one of those pale "friends" (not R. L.! but a guy named Z. B.), immediately, with the same impulse, at the proposal of another anti-friend (Z. R.), I was thrown out of the Party for not attending meetings, not paying membership dues and things like that. Why, I did not even know I had become a member of something. Just like I did not know what other people were joining. Now, after everything, I know that my initial absent-mindedness, not belonging, and even my stupidity, saved me from death.

A vampire bite is often only a look.

Often it is enough for someone to yell at you in public for you to feel your body going numb and that fatal loss of consciousness.

But the hardness of core consciousness weakens under the frequent embrace of pale women and under the severe, inquisitive gaze of collocutors.

Headaches, insomnia, listlessness, and in particular, feelings of rejection are the first indications of suffering from weakening of the core's hardness.

One night, in a sleepwalking state, I left the house and wandered aimlessly in the night. It was sultry. I took off my shirt. Threw it over my shoulder. Naked to the waist, sweaty body, lusting, I wandered through the streets, especially full of people that night.

The faces of the passers-by were exceptionally pale. The skin on their bodies was taut from great disquiet. The biceps of the rapidly walking men were popping. Chests heaved under the tight athletic undershirts. The women's bodies were disturbingly fragile and overpowering with their resolute strides. If those remarkable specters of the night walked in a group, they moved as though commanded by someone absent. He could be felt everywhere: in the air, in the walls of the houses, in the positions of parked cars, in the way the passersby were dressed, in the tree branches bending in the wind.

And the professor's voice was heard at great length in the room. And then it resounded through the corridor like an echo. It fluttered like a banner. It only stopped "waving" in the lavatory. But there was no way out of it.

☿ 1 SEPTEMBER 1998

I had a friend named Dejan—he came down with vampirism long ago. But the disease has been stagnating for some time. With superhuman resistance, he stopped the disease from advancing. Dejan does all he can to preserve his core consciousness: he reads day and night; walks every day; his steps are slow to exercise his powers of observation; he talks for a long time; sharpens his thoughts; uses special natural tinctures that stir his imagination to the point of derangement; he travels; changes his whereabouts; covers up his tracks; steadily withdraws from persecutors who insert an increasing dose of weakness into the eroded core of his consciousness.

That night ("Night of the Vampires"), I got together with friends. First, we had a drink in a bar on A Street. Several pale-faced women were standing behind the counter. A group of men with very striking features was on bar stools at a round table. The first had a crooked nose; the second had a visible scar on his cheek; the third one's beard was really bent out of shape; the eyes of the fourth had a colorless rim around the pupils. I gave them a bloody, seething look. That was the beginning of the showdown. A staring contest. At first I felt powerful. I resisted every attack. Like I was shifting to the offensive. Dejan, however, soon got sick. He felt weak and tired. With sharp pains around his liver. We moved at once to the next bar. It was a cramped place with a small bar and customers jostling in front of it. They were in lively discussion, trying to outdo each other in their desire to reach the bar; over it hung low wreaths of garlic bulbs, rungs with bloody, red, wind-dried sausages, knives, butcher's hooks, nails, stakes and meat cleavers. Dejan immediately ordered garlic bread. We drank lattes. Dejan quickly recovered. He even smoked a cigarette. A. and I felt "as strong as an ox." I felt the need "to stir up trouble." Dejan barely held me back from my manic intention to go back to the bar on A Street and have it out with the men at the high table. "What's wrong? Calm down," Dejan finally said sternly. He even tugged my collar. Suddenly his face turned red. "What's wrong with you?" I replied, thinking primarily of the strength that had returned to my friend's body, spurring me even more to have it out with the "trash!" in the bar next door. "Cool it! I know the guys, retired skinheads, they'll fuck our mother," said Dejan calmly. I admired my friend's level-headedness. Suddenly he appeared all-powerful. His voice was stratified. His cheeks were rosy. His nose was red. His ears were warm. Yes, yes, Dejan had revived. The words "wait," "damn it," and "easy" were like ukases and like the charming whisper of a seducer and like quotations. "Go to hell," I said lethargically, thinking of the time when we were all-powerful, when all those in our crowd (Žerminal, Sava, Mariola, Dijana and Dejan) were healthy, powerful, cheerful and dynamic "buddies."

We stayed in the smaller bar. Now it was even more crowded. Some were following a boxing match on television, commenting loudly. (Blood was gushing from the nose of one of the fighters in the ring.) Others were playing pool in silence. Some were playing cards. Others, of course, were keeping vigil at the pinball machines.

Dejan ordered another round of drinks. He lit another cigarette. He put his foot on the brass footrest under the bar. He stared lustfully at the waitress's bouncing breasts, rosy cheeks, hairy arms. Always in a good mood, Mariola (that was the waitress's name) had quite loud makeup that evening. Her lips were almost bleeding under the bright red lipstick. Her eyelids contested the light of the chandeliers, reflecting the gold and silver eye shadow and glistening, thickly applied makeup. Her long but blunt nails, each one painted a different color (purple, navy blue, coal black, light blue, green, blue, etc.) flashed in the sink like a fish in an aquarium.

And just when we ordered the next round of drinks and offered the waitress a cigarette, which she took with beautiful long fingers that were first wiped on the edge of her apron, under which a beautiful, hot little knife flashed, to which Dejan and I reacted by exchanging several sweaty looks, the front door suddenly opened. None other than Sava himself walked into the bar. He stopped for a moment. With the piercing eyes of a determined tracker, he tore the thick molasses off his field of vision in the smoke-filled room. Through one of the gaps torn by his wild gaze, he saw Dejan and me with our elbows on the bar, now surprised; he suddenly went up to the bar where, to the amazement of all present who were expecting the roar of a muscle-man and bully, he said, "Mariola," in the soft, almost vulnerable little voice of a mortal. It was the voice of a compassionate person, a living being of our times and a fighter for sensations, perceptions and feelings. A voice that brought tears to my eyes. A voice that I felt like a lump in my throat. A voice that was no longer that. And with that voice he ordered a new round of drinks. (This time for Mariola, too.) In the blink of an eye the crowd in the bar turned into a meeting. The newcomer was like a silent loud-speaker everyone stared at expecting the news of the night. But the newcomer's voice could not be heard. The speakers were seriously silent. Like they were not even breathing. The paleness of his forehead spread like a galloping epidemic over his shrinking face. Like the ends of life had drawn close to each other. And right away, with a look of horror, Mariola saw bite marks on the neck of her beloved man. The wound was fresh and open. Scratches zigzagged down his forehead as pale as ash. There was a large bruise on his neck.

✍ 2 September 1998

A vampire's touch is most often soft. Slowly fondling the soft parts of the body. The vampire's fingers slide without a sound over the victim's skin, leaving behind terrible devastation. The hair on the victim's body bristles and bends and stretches to the point of splitting. The skin starts to sweat, moistening the palms of the vampire's hands that, like a tick, or scorpion, or snake, slides down the nakedness of the victim who is now lustful too, waiting for the time and place of the fateful bite.

The prick is the goal of the attack, but it is also secretly coveted. (The victim is driven into a corner, but is also "overjoyed.")

The relationship turns straight into debauchery.

Suddenly everything serves to satisfy the torturer but also the tortured. (The heels in the shoe store are especially high.) (Food in the restaurant is spicy.) (Passers-by in the street turn to look at a convertible with the blaring base notes of synthetic music.) (The colors are light, but muted.) (Two naked women in the dressing room of a fitness center gaze at each other, stone-faced, for a long time in the steamy mirror.) (Twenty thousand fans at a sports stadium stare at one spot.) (Thousands of employees telephone at the same time, but not to each other.) (Silence.) (All that is heard is a buzzing wasp.) (It is autumn.) (The time when diseases spread.) (A man is lying on the sidewalk and quietly dying; leaving this life: moving to the "other side.")

Narcissism is one of the key traits of a vampire. There is no real mirror for a vampire. This is a well-known fact. A vampire looks at himself in an imaginary mirror, one that is actually in every mortal. Therefore, when a vampire looks at a mortal, he is always looking at himself.

Defending oneself from vampirism, one starts with paranoia, of course. Mental disorder, negative identification, mania, complexes, exaggeration, modification, psychotropic and schizotypal behavior are secondary manifestations of vampire phobia. The goal of the counter-vampire service commandos is to physically resemble the vampires.

Imitatio and disguise are mandatory subjects at the school that trains the counter-vampire service's specialists. The goal of the commandos is not to be recognized. The goal of the commandos is to infiltrate every vampire system. The goal of the commandos is to assume the "language" and "religion" of the vampires. The goal of the commandos is to destroy the vampires' "state," "government" and "people."

Imitatio and disguise are mandatory types of tactics that allow vampires to approach their victims. The goal of the vampires is not to be recognized. The goal of the vampires is to infiltrate every one of their victims' systems. The goal of the vampires is to assume their victims' language and religion. The goal of the vampires is to control their victims' state and government.

The paranoia of the living is always a byproduct of communicating with the nonliving. The goal of paranoia is to produce hostility. The goal of hostility is contrived love of our fellow man. The goal of such love toward our fellow man is indifference toward ourselves as possible victims of vampirism.

What happens in an imbalance between vampire and counter-vampire principles of living, dying, and death?

Someone banged a window shut on a two-story building. The glass fell out of the frame with a crash and scattered while still in the air. I stopped watching the process of the window breaking when the sheaf of glass started to fall and shifted my eyes to an elegantly dressed man just coming out of a bank. His face was as pale as ash.

I dreamed of the naked body of a woman from work. It was superhumanly large. Limbs like crane jibs. Pubic hair like a giant wire scrub to clean burned food off the bottom of giant pots and pans. Her eyes were of different colors, naturally. Her vagina was on her face, of course. Her face was as pale as a boiled rag, strangely alert. The strokes of her eyelids on her lower lashes were like snapping teeth. Her shoes had high heels, of course. She (my colleague) was bald. And had no breasts. Her nipples had moved to her hands.

A male colleague was sitting in the dressing room of a fitness center at the time. He was on the telephone. (Was he jerking off?)

I went out to a newsstand to buy cigarettes. I am not normal. I don't smoke, but I regularly buy cigarettes. Those, of course, are signs of paranoia and schizotypal behavior.

So, when Sava entered the small bar on A Street, Dejan, Mariola and I saw at once that he had had a bloody confrontation with the vampires.

"It started,"—he said in a calm voice, draining a second glass of vodka and slowly chewing a bite of garlic bread—"with short, piercing glances," that with each exchange turned harsher, stronger and harder along with (Sava's) words, "What the fuck are you looking at?" and (the vampire's) "Simmer down, slave," repeated and spoken with the formal voice of a radio show host.

Sava took off his jacket.

Mariola's lips slowly parted and out of her mouth, like a pacified whale, appeared her soft, moist, warm tongue.

"The rip on the front of his t-shirt gets bigger as he flexes his chest muscles. With a thud, his abdominals suddenly turn into a smooth, shiny slab and one of the vampires, staring as though at an imaginary mirror, catches sight of his row of broken teeth that snap like the canines of a veteran fighting dog."

Sava is bursting with power.

With a look sharper than all the knife blades in the nearby kitchen, its gust of forceful wind that threw open the front door and immediately broke it into component parts, now decomposed boards and laths, Sava detached a leg from the empty table next to him. With a flick of his tongue as he shouted "out," he whirled the leg at the bar where the bottles of whiskey, cognac, pear brandy and tequila toppled all by themselves in advance, as though out of immaterial, dead and now suddenly rejuvenated fear, into the abyss of the bartender's suddenly cramped quarters. Silence reigned for a moment. All that was heard was the gurgling of liquid that, like life, was pouring out of the broken bottlenecks. The place, transformed into a corner, became an acoustical hall where the words "tramp," "stink," and "toothless freak" echoed emptily.

◯ 4 September 1998

Dejan's "vampire" story was rambling. It was like porous tissue, a brick of soft wet clay that birds had walked on, leaving claw marks, like the letter of an open biography.

It started in the arms of a woman on the day her husband committed suicide. In despair, feelings of sadness intermingled with the desire for power. The woman was pretty and fragile. Early in the morning Dejan already felt slightly dizzy and feared estrangement.

Then winter set in. Unusual guests took turns staying in the basement of a friend's house. They came with dogs that growled and let out long, spiraling howls all the time, outside in front of the door.

Dejan was suffering from arthritis.

Problems with his spine started in early spring. That is when Lucia entered his life. Pale. White skin, long legs, soft, breathy voice.

Dejan lost weight. His brain was getting smaller. His eyes held a clearly focused fear of conspiracy.

He talked to himself, of course. He was out of sync with his desires. Objects piled up in a house that had no mistress. Lucia was gone all the time. That was the beginning of resistance.

Consequently, we ordered another round of drinks: Mariola kasha, Dejan a double whiskey, Sava barley brandy, and a double vodka for me.

The mist had not lifted outside. It rose up to the solidly closed sky. Since night already covered this part of the earth, only the sooty sky could be seen. The clouds were thick, dark and stratified. The lower, "first," immediately visible layer of sky was uneven, rough, full of bumps, cracks, wrinkles and defects. In some places between particularly large bulges, round holes stood out, deep, black and bottomless. They were so dark that they turned into sources of anti-light when looked at for a long time. Suddenly there was visibility. Like the other side of the day appearing in the night. And everything in the street was well-defined. Where there had been nothing, something suddenly appeared. A broken bolt of lightning flew through the clouds, made a beeline for the sidewalk, killed several random passers-by and with loud thunder and a brief flame, broke the cocoon of fear, bounced off the ground, and with the hollow sound of receding thunder, hissed toward the sky where it vanished in the blackness of a bottomless hole. In this light, our heroes (Dejan, Sava, Mariola and Žarko) saw the course of their next steps. It led across the threshold through the front door out into the street (where the wind was now bending the treetops, breaking branches, knocking them to the sidewalk, and whirling them across parked cars). Even though it was raining (pouring), it smelled like gunpowder. Even though everything was wet (and soaked), it smelled like the driest combustibility. The course of our heroes' steps cut into the sidewalk like a gorge, making its way through the thick, heavy walls of the hundred-year-old buildings. It tossed aside market stalls. Uprooted trees. Overturned parked cars. Drove sewer pipes out of the ground. Dug up train tracks. Twisted curbs. Approached the bar next door on A Street with all its force.

✑ 5 SEPTEMBER 1998

The clock on the steeple of the nearby church sounded on that unearthly night.

A cat started caterwauling in the darkness of a half-opened gate.

A dog started howling at the window of an apartment in a house.

More wind.

More rain.

More thunder and lightning.

It was clear at once that this was the showdown. Like a whirlpool where every thought of going back or retreating went under.

§2: WHEN WE GOT TO THE UNITED STATES

◯ OREM, UTAH, 13-14 SEPTEMBER 1998

When we got to the United States of America our field of vision immediately expanded. While the soil of Europe was constantly felt in the airplane (in the bitter tasting bread, the uncomfortable bend of the fork handle, the practiced, stiff walk of the cute stewardesses, and even in the hard landing of the plane), suddenly in the terminal building at San Francisco Airport, the carpet on the long, wide corridor seemed like a vast plain. Wide and soft under the walker's feet, it extended far into the distance. Feet sank through suddenly softened leather soles into a soft clover-covered underpinning. And the walker's face, respiratory organs and forehead were immediately struck by the warm air of a country in which the winds, sunrays and fans in spacious rooms acted in concert. (There remains, of course, the unpleasant memory of that showy movement of the customs officer when she refused the passenger's passport and said gruffly, "Yugoslavs have to fill out the 'white form' before they cross the border! . . . Next!") (There is the somewhat more pleasant memory of the young woman in an orange suit, pretty, really attractive and coquettish in her sternness when she replied, "Go left there, then right and then straight ahead!"). Of course, the obese people, primarily women, in front of the Delta Airlines window, erroneously chosen by the distraught traveler more out of excitement than lack of sleep, falsely altered the picture of a country just acquired by his first, childlike, uncertain steps. They were the only Indians in the check-in line, on their way to Alaska. They were like outsized pictures of themselves from the time that Columbus reached America. Like they had grown stronger in the meantime, expanded physically, puffed up, so to say. Unlike the South American Indians, for example, who were shrinking more and more every year,[13] allegedly because of increasing poverty and thereby lack of nutrition, these here seemed to epitomize all the power of the "industrially most developed country in the world." Like they were not living beings, but plastic figures that moved. Like they were wearing signs that said: "We are the biggest people in the world, because the country where we live is the richest in the world." (Scott said later that sixty percent of the American Indians suffered from diabetes because of the sudden "improvement" in their food, which did not suit the centuries-long adaptation of the organism to living in the sparest of conditions.) (This would never happen in the Balkans. Living conditions there are always the same, favorable. People never go hungry, not in time of war, not during economic sanctions, not during ecological catastrophes, not in years of drought, not during epidemics. The obesity of the Balkan man is always the result of suffering, which, of course, "has nothing to do with life.") In spite of discomfort at the thought of the coldness of far-off Alaska, the corpulence of the Indians stoked my feeling of security in the line. This was immediately actualized at the "right" window of the same airlines. A man, far, far thinner than the Indians, acted "perfectly," "in the here and now." His eyes flashed. He grinned. He drummed his fingers on my passport. (Did he have a pencil tucked behind his ear?) He was "normal" above all. (Unlike the first, unkind customs woman!) He was not contrite either. (Unlike the second, kind customs woman who let me into "the country" after I had finally filled out the questionnaire on the "white form" but in her "contriteness" made an "intentional?" mistake that later ended in a fine. More about that later!) So, I truly "felt good" at the San Francisco Airport.

It was much colder in the plane to Salt Lake City than in the plane to San Francisco. Not because of the small number of passengers. On the contrary, while still at the airport before takeoff, they seemed quite buddy-buddy. They were all dressed the same. Suddenly I remembered the beginning of Scott's and my previous joint book[14] and

---

[13] For more about this, see my book *Brazil*.
[14] Scott Abbott and Žarko Radaković, *Repetitions* (Brooklyn: punctum books, 2013).

Scott's description of a similar situation in the waiting room at the airport in New York.[15] The Mormons from the Church of Latter Day Saints there were dressed in a similar fashion too. Even though they were not related, they appeared to belong to the same tribe. They almost looked like each other. This familiarity, perhaps because of remembering Scott's text, was immediately transferred to the airplane cabin. Even though no one communicated with anyone else, between the passengers—either because of their similar clothes (all the women wore long skirts), or because of the positive voices of the stewardesses (they were all smiling or nodding their heads in the affirmative or looking quite clearly at the trays they were carrying)—there was a closed (or open) family atmosphere in which each individual felt safe. (The stewardesses were particularly warm. They were also untidy. Older women with slightly wrinkled clothes. Like they were in housecoats. But this increased the impression of motherly care for each individual.) (There is also the vivid memory of a mother with two little preschool girls. The woman had an unusually pretty face. The little girls were always smiling, concentrated on sheets of paper that they diligently covered with: circles, triangles, squares. Their mother spurred them to draw even more—underlining—in the game. And each time she smiled at me kindly over her children's heads. At one point she even stood up and her blouse was pulled out from under her belt and opened up on her chest, clearly showing swollen, juicy breasts, which gladdened me and prompted me to stand up, give a friendly "Hi," to the woman, "brush flanks" cozily with the stewardess and calmly take a blanket from the overhead bin, that I then cuddled into and, like the most normal Indian, sat there in the cold and stared out the window at what I could see outside.) (I looked at the little girls. They were like two tops, constantly spinning. And every time that the spinning would slow down, their mother would go up, now with the top button unbuttoned, smiling at me almost coquettishly, now more than normal, and start them spinning again.) (And that game lasted until the airplane landed.) And, of course, they looked out the window even before landing. The sun, of course, was setting. Its incandescent rays scorched the mountain tops that sizzled quietly down below. Bloodstained lakes, as though grilled on the spit, smelled up above like lamb, fried potatoes, baked apples, fresh cracklings and hot loaves of bread.

Silence.

---

[15] Abbott and Radaković, *Repetitions,* 1–2.

Now in a whisper, but audible, the local god makes himself heard. The plane had a soft landing. No one applauded the pilot. (Later it turned out that the pilot was a woman.)

The corridors in the airport terminal (in Salt Lake City) are illuminated by quite different light. It is stronger, more piercing and facilitating. (I went into the first restroom and washed my face with soft, fragrant water. A man brushing his teeth over the sink smiled discreetly over his toothbrush. I returned his greeting and, truly facilitated, touched the soil of the United States of America where I "immediately" spotted my friend Scott Abbott. Like a "local god" faithful to his believers—with me in the front row—he was standing to the side and quietly waiting for the one who suddenly looked at this story—now a travelogue?—as "set free.")

Scott, my friend, was wearing the same thing he had worn several months ago in Višegrad: blue jeans with a "funny" belt and a purple t-shirt. And the clench of my friend's hand was warm and wholehearted. (Did I feel in him the desire to change the contents of this story? Is that why the story turned into a travelogue?)

It was hot outside. The wind slowly descended over the town, advancing confidently down the wide avenue. The sidewalks were empty. The cars at the stoplight were like horses just before they are taken out of the stable. There was only one freight truck at the gas station. The food on the shelves in the supermarket was displayed in bright colors. Scott was quiet and slow, like the king of his territory, which would only be seen in its true light the next day after, of course, a weary, heavy and extremely complex sleep.

◈ 16 September 1998

Of course, the first trip outside my host's house was to the slopes of Mount Timpanogos. It rose like a neutral being ("neither male nor female"),[16] uninterested, lazy, but preponderant (sheer). At the same time it gave the impression of suspended history as shown by the unfinished stories on the surrounding massif ("History always has to be like that!" I thought and jotted it down), episodes ("Yes, episodes!"), and everyone has a right to them.

The path led up an incline overgrown with yellow grass scorched

---

[16] See Peter Handke, *Die Lehre der Sainte-Victoire* (*Lesson of St. Victoire*) (Frankfurt am Main: Suhrkamp Verlag, 1980), which I translated into Serbo-Croatian from the German in 1985, thus before the breakup of SFRY.

by the sun and wind, agitated and constantly whirling upwards toward the sky. And that field ("or skin") stretched like a carpet ("or blanket") across the bare flank of the sleeping animal ("or mountain"). It breathed heavily and perceptibly. The spasm of every breath set the population on a terrible, panicked flight. Swarms of grasshoppers exploded. Pollen burst from the plants. Birds took wing in flocks. Lizards, disoriented, crawled over broken (wounded) roots and dried (killed) plants. The animal (or mountain) where we were walking woke from a heavy sleep.

Of course, the streets in Orem (and later in Provo, and even later in "engaging" American Fork) were broad and empty. And only the foreigner noticed that the cars ("here") were considerably larger, more spacious and with quieter motors than "over there" (which the foreigner had left to come "over here"). And indeed the cars moved slowly on "such" an avenue. Like there was no one on them (the avenues) and in them (the vehicles). They were sufficient unto themselves. For example, vehicles parked next to the curb seemed to be resting before going to work. At a stoplight, for example, two whispering vehicles were gossiping about a third, the one coming from the opposite direction and "now" was stopped at the light . . . Not for a moment did the foreigner think of the drivers. They, if they even existed, were the embodiment of the car's internal organs: the carburetor, cylinders, universal joint, battery or spark plugs, for example.

Orem is just one of many towns on the plain between the mountain chains in the state of Utah and the lake of the same name. Owing to the diligence, enthusiasm and perseverance of the local (current) people, that brutal, dried, lifeless air of the desert was transformed into one of the "most fertile regions in the world." (The previous people, the "Indians," ate well, multiplied and exploded, consequently, they vanished, or, refusing welfare and underfed, thus scrawny, withdrew to reservations where they live as in the stone age, waiting for the return of their God and sleeping Nature to awake, thus "their five minutes.")[17] Along the fences around the spacious houses are rows of Fruit trees, branches bending under the weight of Produce. Between the posts are Bushes of multicolored and highly fragrant Roses. In the evening, a basket full of large, tasty Plums reaches the house. The spectacular Melons, Peaches, Apples and Pears on the counter in the kitchen simply vie with each. During din-

---

[17] See my book *Mount Timpanogos*.

ner on the spacious terrace at the back of the house, when we looked at the slopes of the Mountain, "bare, rocky, and steep,"[18] the contrast between the Desert ("high up there") and Fecundity ("down here in the lowlands") became so obvious that I saw myself doubled as well. I was like a foreigner and a local from time immemorial. I was both standing and sitting.[19] I was an old man and a child. I ate cooked corn with kernels like marbles and kicked a lemon-melon-like ball on the curly, grassy, bristling garden carpet. And the water streaming from the sprinklers was truly a sign of my vitality—exclamation point! I wanted to change clothes. Wear thongs instead of shoes. Of course, I chewed kernels of corn indulgently. My eyeteeth ground the kernels, the popcorn, the grains or stones, as the dog ("called Honey") played with an eaten but scruffy corncob. And my teeth became stronger with every bite. They filled their own cavities. Was I becoming younger with every breath? I ate, slept and saw everything. And acted.

Yes. I was in the United States of America.

That is how it was for the next few days as well.

The first signs of fatigue in my eyes went unnoticed. Although my face looked exhausted in the mirror, no one, not even I, noticed the traces of paleness. I did, indeed, blink more and more. My vision, however, was better than ever.

So, "the other side of the Mount Timpanagos ridge" is "quite different" (I jot down). No longer in the desert ("transformed," "by the diligence of the population" into "a fertile plain,") I walked on "truly black humus, thus rich soil." "The vegetation with its highly varied shades and the weight of its colors, the darker ones, of course, spread by the strong wind, occasionally hit the traveler in the head." "There is an abundance of water here," I say. "This is not a desert," I continue. We were in dense, succulent, green "Bosnian" forests. As a "foreigner" I must say that I trembled from, not even I know what kind of excitement. And I really did strip naked to the waist on a forest glade, sit on a pine log, and surrender to a swarm of flies that buzzed and softly caressed the skin of my utterly, utterly, trembling body. We fell silent and listened to the "local" sounds like a primeval text of "this" landscape.[20]

So, we took off (traveled) through the lands (territories) of the United (and yet individual and independent) States (republics) of

[18] Similar to *Die Lehre der Sainte-Victoire*.
[19] Scott was right. See Abbott and Radaković, *Repetitions*.
[20] Is this similar to that in the book *Die Lehre der Sainte-Victoire*?

America (just like the old Yugoslavia at one time). We traveled. And we experienced our surroundings first-hand.

⌒ PAGE, ARIZONA, 18 SEPTEMBER 1998

In the town of Kanab, not far from the Grand Canyon, in a restaurant at a gas station, all the ceiling fans are working. The wallboards are worm-eaten, creating the sumptuous relief of this "landscape." Looking at the pot of coffee on the breakfast table suddenly stirs hatred for the troop of writers who at one time undermined, smothered and destroyed their desire to describe their favorite landscape.[21]And then, moments of tranquility, poured from the cup, bottomless, of black coffee.

Only moments later, above the giant Lake Powell dam, came the memory of Peter Handke's enormous forehead . . . The landscape in this area on the border between Arizona and Utah is like the surface of the moon (seen the last time in Herzegovina before the collapse of Yugoslavia). Nevertheless, it is unusually lively. Sage bushes. Beautiful white flowers with an intoxicating fragrance. A truly strong desire to be silent and breathe evenly and softly. In the meantime the drivers' faces are clearly Indian. Just like the road, just then, is straight and rolling. And the traveling cars fly to the sky, bright and blue. Diaphanous and cloudless. And the rocks along the road are like scabs, pock-marks. They prickle the eyes of the passenger who suddenly feels chafing memories of certain parts of Lika. The thought of the ban on freely crossing borders is painful.

Right before the Grand Canyon is a green plateau. (Or just a flatland in front of a ravine.) Juniper trees and pinion.

⌒ GRAND CANYON

The Grand Canyon. Conversations stop. Thoughts stop. Forbidden, by conscious decision, to articulate words before the powerful sight. A picture of textures constructed by a multitude of details and countless tales in each particularity. And mist has brought the landscape to life, making it fateful, primordial and timeless, in which essential

---

[21] I will read about this later in my notes from 1998. Then I will (copying from my notebook) write a story about it. It will certainly not be a story about hatred.

movements (of the eye) are suddenly possible—back and forth. What freedom, spellbinding at the same time: Freedom from enslavement! If I have ever tried to get close to the "concept" (understated!) of "perceiving" (understated!) the "concept" (more than understated!) of "Exalted" (understated in all respects!), then that might be "here" and "now" "on Mt. Moran."

☉ GALLUP, NEW MEXICO, 19 SEPTEMBER 1998

Night in the little town of Gallup. It was founded during the construction of the first railroad from east to west. Our motel is on a busy access road, once part of well-known Route 66. During the Depression in the 1930s, it was the "highway of hope." (Scott said that instead of taking many people to "sunny California" and "salvation," Route 66 took them to "ruin.") (Many people "took this road" and moved "to slavery.") ("Many people disappeared forever.") (My friend's face is serious. Between sentences, spoken with his mouth barely moving, and between "this plain" "here," were long silent pauses.)

("Scott Abbott's face is silence embodied in an expression without mimicry. Nevertheless, "it is not pale," "it is not numb." "There are no bite marks on his neck.")

Today, "here in Gallup," Route 66 is a broad, busy avenue with rows of cheap hotels and restaurants marked by the usual signs on tall poles that can be seen from a great distance.

We stop at one of these roadside motels. Its name is also on a signpost on the road, *Lariat Lodge*. (That was last night, after a long ride through the deserts of Arizona and New Mexico.) That hotel with the usual row of suites in a three-sided square, had an opening for cars from the highway (Route 66). There is a parking space in front of the entrance to every suite. Several cars were already there when we arrived, mostly old American cars, rattletraps. One van, two jeeps and a car with a trailer full of enormous, round, fat, truly convincingly large watermelons.

The rooms in the suite were cramped. In one, the bed literally ended in the walls. In the other somewhat larger one, there was a television, a little five-hook coat rack on the wall, a chair next to the bed, a mirror on the door (oh, yes, and a telephone on a small dresser).

They were two "cabins" like wooden boxes placed on a wooden base placed on a narrow belt between the highways (Route 66 and the highway going north) with railroad tracks going along it. The noise of traffic, particularly the trains, invaded the silence of sleep.

What did I dream about that night on Route 66! About nothing and everything. About a herd of cows, for example, quietly running over a stream in a ravine. A naked Indian was standing in the water combing her thick black hair. She had a silver bracelet on her right wrist set with green and turquoise stones. She rolls in the soft bed when the train sounds its horn. The humming engine of a late-night guest at the *Lariat Lodge* is also heard. The Indian's eyes are turquoise-green. And the flames pouring from her vulva are turquoise, too. She stood quietly in front of the dresser with the telephone. I started to sing.

Gallup showed its full splendor in the morning. Empty avenues colored by the bright sun. Stores selling beautiful Indian goods, still closed. Empty gas stations shining in the magical dawn of the day. Only one restaurant was open, its customers (crystal-clean faces, of course), all Indians, happily "normal," concentrated on their breakfast.

We sat right down at a table by the window. Outside, in front of the place, cars were talking softly like horses tethered to a fence, in a small group—a Ford jeep, a Chevy pickup and a Nissan sedan— parked in front of our window as though waiting for their masters, the drivers. The owners, in cowboy hats, Wrangler jeans, and brown cowboy boots, sat calmly at the counter like horses in a stable and ate slowly, like hawks circling above the desert.

I immediately ordered two fried eggs "sunny-side up," two pancakes, and two sausages. (In the menu this was denoted as *Two Plus Two Plus Two.*) I smiled at the waitress. She was loose, plump, a happy expression on her face, Indian. She comes right up to our table and pours coffee (limpid, brownish liquid, thus not "with milk") into cups (white, ceramic). I immediately pour a large gulp into my wide-open mouth (like an eagle's). "Thank you," I say. Bob Dylan's music comes from the radio softly, as though far away. The crossbeams on the ceiling of the place are bent out of shape. Even though it is morning, the sun is shining like it's going down.

Later, in the restroom, a look in the mirror: in the picture is the one who is looking, and standing next to him is a man with an enormous hat. He combs his hair with a wetted comb. He smoothes his sideburns with wet palms. Of course, a strong jet of water is pouring from the faucet.

So, we travel (move around) the United (and, again, individual)

States of America (just like those of the old Yugoslav republics). We travel. And experience our surroundings first-hand.

The road to Chaco Canyon goes through a vast barren area covered with clumps of grass as far as the eye can see. Not a single vehicle on the horizon. Just a few ravens in semicircular flight. Just a few snakes, rattlesnakes, winding in spirals. Just telegraph poles. A few rocks, washed by powerful downpours, cleaned by strong winds. Van Morrison is singing with a "regally" confident voice (from a cassette player, of course). And suddenly, the fear of losing my friend. And at the same time the desire to die slowly in the silence of the desert ("Ah.")

✎ SANTA FE, NEW MEXICO, 20 SEPTEMBER 1998

Then loss of self-control. Physically absent. And nothing. Nothing. But thanks to the gentle, smooth walls in the ruins of an ancient Indian settlement in Chaco Canyon, a magnificent Nothing.

I spent some time searching the ground intently for the remains of broken ceramics. The soil is sprinkled with tiny stones. They sparkle in the strong sun and their sharp reflections prick the eyes. That is the most magnificent picture of Indian (or late) summer. The horizon is vaster than anywhere else! Of course, the pressed flowers in my notebook, where I persistently tried to describe my preposterous corporeality, are large, bright and vibrantly colored.

Evening in the city of Santa Fe is fresh. A cool wind is blowing. People, filling the streets, seem frightened.

"Finally in a city," I think as I catch sight of a group of policemen next to the railing on a bridge under a knoll. They stand there almost nonchalantly. Laughing uproariously. Was one of them telling jokes?

Later, in a restaurant (of course, the oldest one in town, built way back when tracks were being laid for the railroad that never got there), I feel, probably because of the inexplicable bond between all the customers, like I'm in a German beer hall. For example, a woman of about thirty, "classy" looking, gracious gestures, pronounced Indian features, is sending brief smoldering signals, as though drinking beer, not coffee. At another table a man, also alone, with sunglasses raised above his eyebrows, seems to be drinking beer and not three different drinks in three different glasses. (Why? What happened to him? Afterward they took him out half-conscious.)

Almost never have I felt such aversion to the urban environment. I almost started crying for Bajina Bašta, a place that I keep in a tiny part of my memory as a green oasis in my personal wilderness. Why the feeling of such alienation right there at that convivial moment, in a restaurant in Santa Fe?

Later: Walking through the city streets is just more wandering aimlessly. Even the police have left the little bridge under the knoll. ("No more help.") (Did I physically feel Peter's desire in all his travels through Serbia to "urgently," "as soon as possible," "flee," "from the city," "to nature"?) (Was this the "beginning" of that "expected" "disease"?)

Then: a dream, of course, intense and interrupted.

The feeling of imprisonment continues in the morning, after the dream. Irritability right away. Coughing and spitting in the bathroom not only brings no relief but causes alarm with one look down the drain in the sink. The top of a tube of toothpaste appears there menacingly. ("Who threw it down the drain? And why?")

Walking through town. ("Finally on the move!")

There is no one on the bridge above the dry ("empty") bed of the Santa Fe River. Not a single car in the parking lot. Not a single pedestrian in the street. ("Am I allowed to count myself as being present?")

In the "Coyote" coffee shop. The usual coffee ("weak"; and no limit to how much you drink). First sitting in a gallery with unpleasant artificial coolness produced by an air conditioner. Later, in the lower area in the unpleasantly pleasant atmosphere of more pleasantly unpleasant air temperature but an intensified unpleasant feeling of imitating everything that does not exist. On the walls are pictures ("American imitations") of a European painter (Van Gogh). (Reminiscent of the "European" imitations of the paintings of American painter Edward Hopper on the walls of a restaurant in the center of Cologne.) "Roman mosaics" on the floor. Chairs decorated in the French prerevolutionary style. Even the "purely American details" appear Italian, Danish, Finnish or German. Nothing of that authentic force of nature seen in previous days. Not a shred of challenging or aggrandizing oneself in that magnificent atmosphere. (Did I sleep poorly?) Just absurdly, or irrelevantly, and repulsively, catching myself imitating and unproductively repeating the desire to wake up something else ("European" in this case?). (Am I sick?) Not an ounce of "historicity" (brought to the point of absurdity in Europe), so needed here (it seemed to me). (Have I gone mad?) (Suddenly every "American," even Scott, or above all Scott, seems like a Reject who persistently, or by any means, wants to be in the "center," the long nonexistent center, mostly nonexistent, or primarily—it suddenly seems to me—the destructive action resulting from the pure survival instinct, "cultivated" then in some sort of hard and cold pride. As though the psyche of each individual here, and of my friend too, appeared to me in some conscious reduction.)

(Did *core consciousness* self-destruct or had it consciously re-treated into the shadows: "for now"?)

The Georgia O'Keeffe Museum sharpened the line that separates the interior from the exterior.

First, I tried at length to get close to this famous artist's paintings. (I went from painting to painting slowly, heavily, bated breath, no blood pressure.) But the canvases rebuffed me the whole time owing to (what I imagined to be?) the (artist's) overemphasized desire for "introspection," which (it seemed to me) repressed, almost destroyed the primary principle of communicating with this "environment" ("it destroyed observation"). If observation was defined, then they denot-ed it by "deviations" represented by the incomprehensible need, or unconscious desire, to physically inscribe themselves (and their in-satiable hunger for the routine) in a landscape that was completely lost, gone forever. The question "Why?" arose at once. Behind it all seemed to be a bare, incorrectly used and thereby weakened force (*coming from the desire to compete*?) ("With whom, exactly?").

Of course, the impression of the museum building was all the more striking. The floor was earth-gray. The visitors' sandals and feet appear clear, plastic and "ambitious": just like every detail of the mountain, prairie and desert, illuminated by the strong, late-summer or early-autumn sun. All at once, I physically loved the building I was in.

What I loved above all was the color of the Georgia O'Keeffe Mu-seum floor. In the cracks of the dirty-gray earth-colored cement I caught sight of the broken line marking the middle of the road (lane) as a generator from a previous life filled ("in spite of all the com-petitiveness") with love and warmth? And the crack between the floor and the thick plastic wall (on which the paintings, only with my deep suffering, sobbed in their helplessness) was so beautiful that I wanted to keep looking, silently (and quietly whimpering) "forever."

I must say that I particularly liked the dark room where films were shown. Georgia O'Keeffe appeared truly beautiful and produc-tive on the film screen. I am thinking primarily of her name. It swell-led with its beauty. It spread like paramecium.

After leaving Santa Fe, did the plot of this story (travelogue?) become reflectively deeper and broader, emotionally duller and longer and perceptively more scattered and shorter? It finally turned into a travelogue! (That was yesterday.) (That was yesterday in the late afternoon hours.)

During the ride to Dulce, Scott and I had a short conversation in which we "looked back" on the "tension" during the day spent in Santa Fe. It had been painful in the blind, aimless wandering through (the otherwise pretty) town. The awkwardness hindered me from remembering a single scene from my favorite movie, *Desperado* by Robert Rodriguez, most of it filmed in that city. The whole time I saw Scott as falling out of our common context. Like he was obstructing the memory of that movie by imposing his own (more important to him) role in a movie of the same name that he had thought up and produced on the spot. Like I had a secondary role in Scott's movie. The whole time I felt a dullness that spread until it pressed against my senses. I experienced almost nothing, because there were no observations to induce feelings for the surroundings and an opinion about the surroundings. There was nothing but a dull queasiness that went on and on and only cleared up later during the visit to the pioneer museum and the city of Santa Fe. I finally felt something tangible there: real sorrow filled me. When I saw the museum displays of men's and women's shoes worn during the time of the pioneers and conquering the west and south of today's United States of America, tears welled up in my eyes. It was not ordinary staging. I trembled over my very self and the fate of all emigrants, outcasts, loners. I was truly frightened of Scott's new "movie" in which his main role (I imagined) would push all of us into the wings (a reservation), preparing for our final disappearance. (Yes, that was my "great imagination"! Of course, the whole time I observed, felt, and thought, and thus experienced only the scenes and sequences of all possible Hollywood movies from the past. Even today, I think I need therapy to purge my consciousnes—decontamination of core consciousness—of all the Hollywood movies seen back then in the Yugoslav Film Archives in Belgrade. Not, for example, because I imagined that on a visit to Cologne, Dinko Tucaković, in the meantime the main editor of the Film Archives' program, had a face that was too pale; not because I imagined that the small group of people who went to the Belgrade Film Archives museum, to which I belonged with my whole being, lived only at night and that each one left their daytime lair only in the evening, wearing dark glasses; not because I imagined that many of those employed in the Film Archives had died in the meantime of paleness, blood loss, sunken eyes and the transformation of feeling to the nails and teeth. I wanted that therapy primarily in the desperate attempt to prevent the destruction of *core consciousness,* which I suddenly saw as "wretched" and in a "secondary role" in Hollywood movies: like the bus driver of a band of vampires in a night action, in the Coen Brothers' film *Barton Fink*; or like the attendant at the entrance to the lavatory in a restaurant on the edge of town, a place where vampires hang out in the movie *From Dusk Till Dawn* by Robert Rodriguez.

In another museum with an exhibit of items from the apartment of Lucy R. Lippard, I found myself. Because that is where I clearly remembered the formation period of my personality and *core consciousness,* which is so important to me today. I stood for a long time before artwork from the 1970s, gifts from different artists of the apartment owner's time, imagining my apartment as the central place where my personality was formed. The series of drawings by Hanne Darboven was seen in parallel with the rug in my room on Avgusta Cesarca Street in Zemun, and I suddenly saw a drawing by Dubuffet as the incarnation of Raša Livada whistling below the window to my room. There again, I saw Scott as a soft line on a drawing by Pablo Picasso, the one on the hip of a nude young woman.[22] That is also where I realized that the *core* of my anti-vampire *consciousness* was formed under the auspices of the sexual revolution of the 1960s and 1970s, but not in swimming down the river of sexual freedom those absurdly free years (as "accurately" noted by my former, third, wife), but in resisting all cupidity. While my peers were "screwing" in apartments, parks, on canals, in basements and garrets, wasn't I looking for hours out the window at nothing, that is at my *consciousness,* seeking the elementary substance of my identity, consciously blunting my libido, conscious, and increasingly so, of the fact that my anti-vampire creativity could only emerge outside of the corporeal? That is why, at the time, I had the habit of going out at night into the open and confronting the werewolves. That is why I preferred listening to the Stones at the time. Because I perceived them right away as being "ethnically uncommitted." Thus, not at all as a group. The frequent "intonation" and "bullshitting" today that the Stones and Mick Jagger

---

[22] And I saw Dinko Tucaković as a figure on Giotto's fresco.

are some kind of ethnic enlighteners is a misconception. No! The Rolling Stones are *Everyone Together*, but not a People, rather *Both Them and Us*, so Nothing, so an instant of rhythm and music, and that, seemingly, irrelevance, irrelevance of being against. Unlike Bob Dylan, who appeared to me paler, thinner, more religiously indoctrinated and vampire-like as the years passed. Consequently, today I don't like myself from the phase of liking Dylan. I don't even want to remember myself from Tri Kaplara Street, when I sat on a dumpster and played the guitar and acted like Bob Dylan in a wailing voice, and down in the audience, seen from above on the dumpster, only a random passer-by applauded, a guy named Ratko Adamovič. (Of course, I'm exaggerating!)

I remember the colonnade on the main square in Santa Fe and the row of Indians selling souvenirs and homemade goods. "Who to?" I wondered. They were pale, bitten all over, dirty, with scratches and large scars.

Later (enjoyably?) sitting in a little park on the main square with mouthfuls of tasty Jamaican food that tumbled rhythmically in the stomach from one organ to another. They rolled toward the body's exit, transformed into their antipode. It was a rare moment of world musicality in which I imagined everything—people, insects, domesticated animals, objects and even the surrounding mountains—as reggae beats.

Every kilometer away from Santa Fe and closer to Farmington brought relief. (Scott was less and less pale. His eyeteeth got smaller. His nails shorter. His ears redder and redder. He hiccupped, softly and amiably.)

Night fell somewhat heavily in Farmington, above all physically. (Someone kept turning a car motor on and off right below the bedroom window.)

✑ 22 September 1998

The time spent in famous Monument Valley most certainly sharpened my feeling for the sublime. Back when I read Kant, I imagined the sublime as standing above a yawning chasm, staring dumbfounded at the gulf for a long, long time, while here I saw myself at the bottom of it. Looking at that "nowhere-else-in-the-world," plastic, all-encompassing, wide-open Space, was always twofold: I was looking at myself at the bottom of the valley and at someone up above. So I saw the whole space as my realm and myself in the space as insignificantly small. My first time here several winters ago, I concentrated on the snow, while this second visit clarified a number of details. Wandering among the magnificent natural monuments in the valley, I practiced my feeling for size in the enormous space. And two perspectives intertwined again. One was pulled to the very core of nature, truly powerful here. The other perspective was determined by the camera angles in films about Monument Valley. On famous John Wayne Peak, I was immediately reminded of the actor's boots in the foreground of the panorama of Monument Valley in the movie of the same name. (Of course, I also remembered the joke about John Wayne in front of a urinal in a public restroom in Belgrade.)[23] I immediately included John Ford in the experience, the director of that film, as a great mythmaker. Like Cezanne, he took a truly, in itself magnificent work of nature, a landscape, and made it into a mythical story of world and historical importance. Thanks to those striking scenes in several of his Westerns. Everyone who loves movies and visits Monument Valley feels the need to find the same angle to look into the distance, or the need to walk just like John Wayne in John Ford's films (slowly, with a gait, dragging his boots on the ground).

Later, on the road to Teasdale, I read excerpts from Scott's and my book *Repetitions*[24] in the voice of the great Hollywood actor, although without a cigarette between my lips and without my coat collar turned up. The road was like part of the moving scenery in a film that had yet to be filmed. And the reader's voice was like the first course of the dinner at Scott's friends Nancy and Sam's house in Teasdale.

◌ 23 SEPTEMBER 1998

Yesterday was spent hiking together (Nancy, Anne, Sam, Scott, and me) in Spring Canyon in Capitol Reef National Park. The hike lasted

---

[23] Dejan told me the joke: "Why does John Wayne stay away from urinals in public restrooms in the center of Belgrade? Because the man in front of the urinal on his right side always tells the man in front of the urinal on his left side, 'There's John Wayne!' The man on the left turns and John Wayne always leaves the restroom with wet pants."

[24] I was reading in preparation for the presentation at the Kennedy Center in Provo. I was supposed to read an excerpt about going to Gazimestan in Kosovo in 1989, described on pages 96 *ff* in Abbott and Radaković, *Repetitions*.

around six hours and was like an endless story about rocks, mountain massifs, cliffs, stones, sand, and highly diversified flowers (mostly desert and canyon roses).

✍ OREM, UTAH, 24 SEPTEMBER 1998

The presentation, after the presentation and right before the presentation in the Kennedy Center: I remembered yesterday's hike to Cassidy Arch in Capitol Reef National Park.

Sunny weather; rays pass through the scattered clouds; sultry.

I am wearing new black oxfords, new dark-blue pants and an orange-green t-shirt.

✍ 25 SEPTEMBER 1998

In the meantime, events are piling up with all their weight and at great speed. Experiences become fossilized spots that suddenly should be treated with the patience of an archeologist.

What all happened, for example, in Spring River Canyon? The answer hides in the picture of a rock covered with layers of sand already hardened under the pressure of the glance and memory.

In the meantime, I read an excerpt from my text *Under the Stone Bridge* from Scott's and my book *Repetitions*. I read that text, taken from the whole, and called "Kosovo" (in the "excellent" translation into English by Ivana Đorđević), before an audience gathered in the Kennedy Center. Never once did I raise my eyes from the paper on which the letters appeared like a column of ants following the course of a maniac. Of course, the reading for me was primarily music, harmonic or disharmonic. The rhythm was determined by the meanings of individual words, clearly distinguishable in even intervals. As though spurred by the ticking of a metronome, the meanings emerged from the darkness of the text, turned on like the lamp of a lighthouse, illuminating the space around them, showing the outlines of rows of chairs in the auditorium, like waves on the ocean, in which the public, like shadows of Eastern theater, showed the lower part of their faces. The text was also a heavy mass of water in which we floated in an unknown direction. All that was heard was the speaker's breathing. And at one point, I felt like I was on a swing (I said that later).

It was hotter in Salt Lake City than in nearby Provo. The avenues are much broader and seem more powerful. Had they been blood arteries, for example, the liquid ("of life") in them would have flowed quietly, calmly, and in moderation.

Elaine (Scott's friend) appeared in one of the quietest streets that afternoon in town. She trod on the clean, smooth and compact space with the foot of an elastic, slender ballerina. That woman, who is a journalist by profession (which was only supposed to upset me) (in her free time the drummer in a female pop band), was "so charming," "so attractive," and "so nice," I told Scott later.

The atmosphere in "The Pie" pizzeria had something conspiratorial about it. People sat in twos or fours at square or round tables that were black or had tablecloths. One, two, or three enormous portions of pizza were on each table. (Why had I previously imagined that in some restaurants in towns in the USA—in New York? In Santa Fe?—people mostly sit alone or in twos, and if they are alone they stare blankly and greedily toss pieces of food into their mouths like into a machine to process food into calories, recognizing already by the bites the future shape and density of the feces?)—(I imagined it like that because I was not normal.)—(Why at the time did I think that at large dinner parties in restaurants in some cities of northern Europe—in Sweden? In Denmark?—people are mostly silent? That words are side dishes in the plate, on the fork, or in the mouth? That they "eat" like one common mouth? That teeth, also in common, are perfectly filled, maintained, and polished, and sharp, like nails, hammering, loudly clacking at bites that are the same in all the mouths? That conversation, that added "salad," is inarticulate, produced by moving the jaw, like a ruminating cow, left-right-up-down? And that these, actually, these maxillary balletic movements of the "eaters" are celebrated in many operas by European composers?)—(I saw it all like that because I was not normal.)—(Why did I imagine at the time that the restaurants in countries of former and present socialist countries are all the same? That food there was part of brotherhood, equality, unity? That words in conversations at lunch crumble through spaces between teeth? That the tongue, like a shovel, turns over food like hay in a barn? That a chewed bite is already the gulp of a heavy little ball sliding down the esophagus to the stomach like the common reservoir of the state where the members of the government count the mouthfuls? That during the meal, some ministers go around the restaurant tables and gently, but authoritatively, after all, and promising "even better" food, stroke the hair of their fellow citizens, the "eaters"? The "head of the health department," as the waiter, announced at one point that it is "provided by law" to drink liquids, most often beer, regardless of the type of food.)—(I imagined it all like that because I was not normal.)— . . . Here, now, over real plates at a real table in a real pizzeria in Salt Lake City (thus, in the United States of America): real glasses and pitchers of beer. Although the patrons are "talking" all the time, the basic sound of voices comes from the television that seems in the darkened room like a special guest has arrived and wants to have some fun and wants to check out the manners and behavior of those who are there (because the rules in this regard have also been established in advance).

Elaine had a restrained smile, somehow from her forehead, and more from her lips than from her stomach or chest, unlike me. Tongue-tied, I wanted to tell the joke about the peasant who wanted to sell his cow. On the way to the market he dropped by a tavern where potential buyers were sitting. As the seller and buyers got drunk, the cow grazed outside and several hours later lay down to ruminate. It moved its jaw up-down-right-left. After a while the peasant came out of the tavern, firmly resolved to continue the trip to the market, even though the buyers had stayed behind to have a few more drinks, intending to go to the market the next day or the day after. When the peasant pulled the bridle to get the cow moving, it swore at him and spit in his face. A quarrel ensued ending in a fight and all those in the tavern took part. Someone called the police. The peasant, of course, was defeated . . . I simply could not stop myself from preparing to tell the joke. I probably seemed intimidated. I might even have fallen silent. But I laughed boomingly several times, from my stomach and chest. And I think that everyone at the table looked at me worriedly . . . . Elaine managed to bring her curiosity in line with the investigative soul that emanated from her firm breasts. Although she was slight, she seemed extremely ambitious. And loving. It was only when she asked me at one point whether I had ever "ruined someone's life" in my "journalistic career" that I remembered scenes from horror movies. Of course, I fell silent then. Later, I laughed again. This time, I wasn't thinking of a joke. This time, everyone accepted my laugh.

Alex Caldiero[25] was having a show in the gallery across from the pizzeria. The performance was held in conjunction with a wider pro-

---

[25] See, for example, Richard Kostelanetz, *Text-Sound Texts* (New York: William Morrow, 1980).

gram marking exhibits by two local artists. First an astrophysicist spoke, a university professor and associate at the High Energy Astrophysics Institute in Salt Lake City, "on energy and mass." ("Why?"—I wondered the whole time.) He stood at a small rostrum in front of a microphone (just like me several hours earlier in the Kennedy Center at Brigham Young University in Provo), holding a little lamp that shined red rays on a screen that projected an outline (foil) of the lecture ("on what?"). The lecturer was in his middle (the best) years, wearing ironed pants, an ironed shirt, with a tie, but without a jacket. He looked like a preacher in a church. Later during the socializing in the gallery, he seemed like he had "wandered in." (Like one of the "committed" gallery goers had brought him along by chance.) What did he actually talk about? The content could be read on the faces of the audience. They too were sitting in seats, in rows like lines on note paper. They too were looking at the speaker from the bottom of themselves. One was sitting with crossed legs and nodding his head "in a relaxed manner." A second was staring at the rostrum like at an icon above an altar. A third was turning around looking for someone to talk to, primarily a likeminded-thinker. A fourth was a woman who crossed her legs every time the speaker stressed a word. Of course, they all clapped thunderously at the end of the lecture. Of course, after the lecture many went up to the speaker who, in his ironed pants and ironed shirt, had an ironed smile on his face.

Alex performed "from the rear." Like an Egyptian sphinx, he stood for a while without moving. He looked straight ahead. His eyes pierced each spectator individually. He glided over the rows of seats and stopped at each one, raised his eyes, and then suddenly, like a pin, with a flourish nailed the eyes of the spectator sitting there immobile, but staring straight ahead, periodically emitting inaudible shrieks of horror that, then, fell right into a basin full of viscous liquid that was part of the installation of one of the artists who, of course, were sitting in the room and anxiously awaiting the "beginning."

"The beginning of what?" I wrote discreetly in my notebook (from which I am now rewriting those same words). Elaine noted that at once. "As a journalist, did you every ruin someone's life?" she asked. I shrugged my shoulders, raised my eyebrow, winked and, with a smile, looked meaningfully at Alex.

What Alex Caldierio said during his show was something I had thought about twenty-five years ago, sitting in a half-empty restaurant in the center of Novi Sad. At the time, a man with a shaved head was sitting across from me at the next table, talking to himself. What he was saying could not be heard. The man only opened (and closed) his mouth. Nevertheless, I understood him quite well: "word for word."

Alex Caldiero spoke with rigid eyes. His mouth supported his strong forehead. He kept balance with his breath. He floated in the air. He stood on his tongue. He drew the audience's attention with his ears. He addressed the paintings on the wall with his stomach and in those "dramatic moments" it (the wall) did not obstruct the field of vision. Alex Caldiero moved through the exhibit area full of spectators like a centaur through bacchantes and bacchants. Sitting with their legs crossed, they firmly squeezed their tightly bound genitals in which the flesh puffed up, swelled, expanded and fell apart. And the words that Alex Caldiero spoke that evening were the connective tissue of presence, at the same time fecundating cells of absence that would later, in repeated presence grow into a "great event" that would distinguish itself from history by its shape: it would not be fixed, it would be described with broken lines, often noted just with periods, all in open surfaces from which colors would spill into each other, and between them would certainly remain empty surfaces, not, however, like gaping holes, but like a very delicate painting, easy on the eye.

Morning. Sharp, cold air. Through the openings of the venetian blinds over the window onto the street: contours of the Cascades, a mountain range extending from Orem toward Provo. Round black clouds are on the mountain peaks: a sign of bad weather. Nevertheless, the music of silence, broken by the even background noise of passing cars.

At exactly nine o'clock, the bell rings at the front door of the house at 300 North Street. I get out of bed with heavy movements paralyzed by sleep. Fortunately, the floor underfoot is a reliable support. I go to the door with energetic steps. (I imagine the energetic movements of a pen writing a letter to my friend: *Lieber Peter, eine fast unwirkliche Reise kommt leider bald zum Ende. Die Erlebnisse sind komplett. Es fehlt nur noch der Geruch des Fussballspiels heute mittag . . . . Liebe Grüsse von Deinem Ž., der sich sehr freut auf unsere nächste gemeinsame Reise nach Jugoslawien.*)[26] At the door in the Penelope pose stood Alex Caldiero.

The ridge of Mount Timpanogos, seen from the base, clearly separated the background of the picture from the part that we might call the face of the mountain. Either because of the clouds pouring from the top of the mountain or because of the strongly illuminated sky above the mountain's head, the line of the mountain ridge did not disturb the view or restrict the two-dimensionality of the picture. Suddenly the picture gained additional expanse that was manifested by the plasticity of form. The line of the mountain ridge formed a face with a full, lively expression. The mountain slopes descended from the top in broken crags, not like lines drawn on a sketch, so not like steaks but like the plastic sides of a sculpture. The clumps of trees were not the shadows of the drawing but protrusions in space, forms of gentle bristling. The large boulders, rubble, rough sides, thighs of the mountain scratched the limbs of the eyes with such feeling that they either moved away painfully or else, from some indistinct physical passion, rushed to the heart of painful pleasure.

The conversation with Alex Caldiero was unusually friendly and filled with mutual respect. We each felt the other to be an important person, struck by the emanation of enormous mutual trust, but also like humble beings of a planet divided into chambers, spheres, zones and, above all, sectors. We were in an interstice: the foyer of the house of our common friend Scott Abbott, a particularly dark room today. A ray of sunlight pierced the blinds and with a gentle caress warmed my foot that had simply fallen off my body sprawled in a rocking chair. Alex was sitting in an armchair across from me. We looked each other in the eyes. We were talking.

"I'm an optimist," said Alex. He was sitting without moving, in the position of a sphinx, denoting the desire to prolong everything: the mood, time, position in space, the species.

"Europe is in a bind," I said, my eyes piercing the border of the corona around Alex's head that now truly turned a dark brown color.

Did the keys on the piano behind my rocking chair move by themselves? Did my heart tremble (from love, happiness, satisfaction, the liberating fear of emptiness)?

---

[26] Dear Peter, an almost surreal trip will, alas, soon be over. The experiences are complete. All that is missing is the smell of the football game this afternoon. Greetings from your Ž, who is really looking forward to our next trip to Yugoslavia.

If there were restraints in America (and there were!), then I perceived them primarily in religious rites. At church services, I almost saw them in the thrall of the church. Perhaps it was the kitschy cloyingness of individual believers that alienated me the most. I was also astonished by the desire for public confession. This was something I only got to know after surviving terrible catastrophes, such as the death of a loved one. On the day of the funeral (or rather after the funeral) you catch yourself in some sort of pleasant self-pity, shown by the desire to recount your memories of the departed, a story in which you feel like the bad guy. That is how I saw the ascetics at the service in a church on the outskirts of Salt Lake City. One, for example, talked about himself as a former soldier in Vietnam who, by the grace of God, had escaped certain death in the hell of the battlefield. Another started crying "out of happiness because God had given him a pretty wife," and he was, "well," "the ugliest man in the world." A third was "overjoyed" because he was still living "with Mama" and because, "well," he could express the hope that his father, who left before he was born, was also "fine."

On the way back to Cologne, everything seemed highly implausible. The passengers who got on in Paris gave the impression of a dispersed bunch of random arrivals from somewhere on the outskirts of cosmic events. I suddenly realized that I was not returning anywhere. I realized that where I was returning did not belong to me. I was simply being taken from one end of the planet to the other. I almost did not care where it would land, this plane that had taken us on the long, sad trip across the ocean.

Of course, this was not the only reason for my abnormality. It was certainly not the only reason for my completely abnormal views, my more than abnormal observations, feelings, thoughts, experiences. They were strung together like something inevitable, like a chain reaction, one producing another. They even surprised me.

The passenger in the seat next to me on the airplane from San Francisco to Paris, a man in his fifties in tight pants bursting with the flesh of an aging ex-gigolo! Of course, he answered the stewardess's customary question, "What would you like to drink?" by ordering "a beer." As though long ensconced in futility, he spilled it the very first time he brought the glass to his cracked and twisted lips. Of course, he ordered another beer.

That is how all the passengers in the plane looked to me. Decrepit, tired, old. A child in its mother's lap did not sleep but breathed with a rattle in a nightmare between the dream of a (future) monster and reality deformed by the trip. A young woman leaning back in a worn-out seat appeared like a superannuated "nag," physically used in all kinds of ways. The triangular crease on her pants around her vagina was like ruins after a powerful earthquake accompanied by a heavy downpour. The woman's skin was bruised, with open wounds and half-dried scabs, over which the tongues of prematurely aging men had hung. Their voices echoed the over-ripe secretion of puss and bloody spit that poured slimily down the body shuddering with pre-death fever that shook an observer from the side, like a maniac behind a bush watching a couple on a park bench, with the fever of most lustful excitement. When one of these men, not the perverse, but the truly, naturally, unnaturally-naturally bent old man vomited over the woman's stomach, I screamed with a voice cracked by horror. The echo was so loud that its blow opened the overhead bin, spilling out suitcases, coats, handbags and sacks of goods bought in duty-free shops. Of course, a bottle of Wild Turkey whiskey hit me on the head, the one I had bought for a relative in my homeland, which I would only reach after a long "odyssey," consequently in several months. Of course, I was knocked out at once and the bang of closing the overhead bin (done with the attentive hand of a stewardess) immediately (or somewhat later) turned this into a long dream. I cannot say it was unpleasant. It was periodically too bright, causing strong pain in the depths of the negative view. I dreamed of the stewardess sitting in my lap, dissolute, bare breasts and legs wide apart. Her skin was smooth, taut, cold, and covered in oil. She had a ripe, red, smooth, and cold apple in her teeth. The woman's hair was straw, of course. She smelled of hay. Naturally she had lively almond eyes. They twinkled like pieces of glass in the rain. I felt good. I breathed evenly. I did not cough. Periodically I sneezed, expelling the remains of pepper after the meal on the plane. With motherly care, the woman wiped my nose with the bottom of her t-shirt. It went on like that until we landed. (Those were moments in which I found my abnormality pleasant.)

It was cold in Paris. But it did not start raining until Cologne.

Nothing spectacular at the airport. Disciplined travelers, like cattle guided by trained dogs, took their luggage to the exit. There, in the shadow of sad thoughts, was a friend. I thought at once that he was sick. Of course, as we embraced in greeting (three times on the cheek), I saw fresh signs of bites on his neck. (Another unpleasant experience of abnormality!)

On the way, in the nervous ride through the city, the threatening sign of a flickering lamp warning that the radiator was not working. My friend's apartment. Silence. The sleepy eyes of my friend's wife. Pale face and sad eyes that, when I announced that I would soon go "to Yugoslavia," shone with a wet, metal gleam, accompanied by the barely audible snapping of eyeteeth. Finally, soft rain fell outside.

❧ 5 OCTOBER 1998

Two days "after that"—in the desperate battle to stop the process of forgetting, in the feverish battle to preserve my memory, and almost superhuman efforts to keep my increasingly sluggish and cold memories awake—I left the room "for some fresh air" "out into the street."

("Stinking") rain was falling. The thought of the "pleasant" return to the room was immediately "rejected" by the "simultaneous cold" that, I could see quite well, had "snuck in" through the slightly open window onto the street.

I went deeper into the molasses of the day: at first glance, the picture did appear "kitschy," but thanks to the shadows of the forms in it, "smelled" like letters in the famous essay on old age.

It also appeared physically at the entrance to the supermarket, in episodes from great genre paintings: a man without a single front tooth; leaning on a woman without any hair; bloody mucous pours out of his snout; the man is missing three fingers on one hand; the woman talks in a whisper nonstop; she has no vocal chords.

Three days later: again at my (tired) friend's with his pale wife (sleepy-eyed). Sitting in front of the television for a long time. Silence. Exchanging silent looks in which large tears evoke memories of melancholic music from the radio in the corner of an empty restaurant.

Later, in the street, several pairs of worn-out shoes. Vagrants. The dirty skin of a woman's décolleté on a bus without a windshield. Curtains, carried by the strong wind, fly through the opening in front of the driver and bats get tangled in them at once.

Silence. Only footsteps echoing on the sidewalk. Only dry leaves on the empty street, then on the wet sidewalk, then on the shoes of the slow walker.

In front of a crooked lamppost: No one.

There actually were no official changes "at work." The furniture was the same in the rooms. People at the desks were like flowerpots on windows. No one raises their eyes from their desktops. No one changes place. Place is only formally defined. You do not exist mentally. Physical existence is the only reason for being employed. Employment is weightless, consequently incorporeal, sitting on what only the cleaning ladies still call "chairs."

Indeed: one female colleague was sitting there, hanging in the air so to speak, sucking into herself, like a vacuum cleaner does dust, the letters of a processed text that puff up the weightless body to the envisaged weight. One man was even sitting like a grasshopper, waiting for the "gong to sound." Another man had identified with the cactus plants on the window ledge and his body was completely covered with barbs. I was sitting standing up, wrapped in a blanket under which my penis swung slowly, loudly, and accurately. I watched a female coworker as she leaned her bare back against a space in which I suddenly saw all the inhabitants of the earth without an economic system. A third coworker was sleeping. The man next to him yawned.

§3: THE DAY I LEFT FOR BELGRADE

↻ DÜSSELDORF, OCTOBER 14, 1998

The day I left for Belgrade: rain dampens the picture of the city (Düsseldorf). Heavy freight trucks: wheel marks in the puddles; the sky is burning, weary, sick, tissue.

At the airport (in Düsseldorf), passengers in the vehicle approaching the airplane are helpless. Numb faces. Tired. Still marked by the night.

↻ ZÜRICH

The picture is then slightly (or essentially) changed. Weak sunrays burn the eyes through the arched windows in the hall of Zürich airport. Only a few penetrating rays pierce the pale, sleep-exhausted, and thin skin on the neck of the woman, head resting on the shoulder of an unshaven middle-aged man with bloody eyes. Of course, no one in that icy space reacts to the thin voice from the loudspeakers that gratuitously, with the sound of a tuning fork in approaching silence, seems to announce the grieving after a crime against a dear one, felt in long, dark, sweaty sleep . . . Then a sluggish look at the screen and the word "Belgrade," denoting the destination of the next flight, like the faded trace of a mother tongue constantly forgetting itself.

✎ "Zürich-Belgrade"

The faces of the passengers in the plane are shriveled. The eyes of the passengers in the plane are moist. The clothing of the passengers in the plane is black. The voices of the passengers in the plane are lifeless.

✎ Belgrade

Belgrade. Ponderous and alone. The baroque of the city, and of the whole country as well, is so pronounced that eyes fix on every rough spot on the ground. Gutters are crooked and twisted. The face of a woman in the bus is square. The taxi tires are cogged. I immediately noticed the uneven spots on Handke's book *The Innerworld of the Outerworld of the Innerworld* (translated into the Serbian by Zlatko Krasni). (On the next-to-last page of the book, the titles *Child Story, Sorrow Beyond Dreams, Lesson of St. Victoire* simply fell out of their place in the original titles.) The city is pretty. People are good-looking. The president of a local political party whom we meet in a bar is handsome as well. The theater director we meet at the entrance to the police building is handsome, too. We are first drawn into "everyday life" on the central city square of Terazije. Then we are "transported" to the floating river restaurant "Bahus." There we are "graciously" "lowered" to the very bottom of an "independent" dark story that will only take place several months later. L.L. and D.B., B.K., and S.J. are with us. The river widens toward the sky on that spot. It stretches its skin. Tightens its flesh. The river's blood circulates with all its strength. It pounds from the center of itself in the name of God who, in the shape of an enormous heart, breathes deeply and laboriously. Waves carry off a swollen board. Waves carry off the distended carcass of a horse. Waves carry off a boat with no one in it. Poplar leaves applaud soundlessly. Never have I seen so little knowledge about one's surroundings. Never have I seen so little interest in the evil that will come crashing down on the innocent suburban shadows at any moment. Self-confidence is so absurd that everything that moves with determination in one's immediate surroundings slips right out of the hand. With every subsequent movement, everything breaks up. The place where we were located was a pile of junk, where you sat like a king. It was truly a country without neighbors. People existed there without a state. (And not, as they maintained "imprisoned in the cage of the state.") Freedom. An empty field where we were negative tourists.

The stay in Banja Luka? Real presence? We were employed most of the time? We worked off every bit of the hospitality of the people of Banja Luka? We were, finally, asked to work. And those unforgettable nights when I felt like an empty log cabin with the wind blowing through it.

The same feeling continued in my sleep in the night on Fruška Gora's Iriški Venac. During dinner, I tried to stop my thoughts and reduce them to feelings. They were too dense. My body felt like the log of a tree with rough bark.

I awoke in the morning empty. I stood above the hill in front of the hotel ("Vojvodina") for a while and stared as though through a narrow opening at the Srem lowland. Like saying to myself, "Is it possible, that you are really here?! Am I dreaming?" Last night's visit to the monasteries of Hopovo, Grgeteg and Krušedol turned out to be only bruises after a salvo of slaps in a fight with myself. Now I was calm. Tired. Conversations in which I transmitted Handke's sentences to others exhausted me completely. Like hearing in a song on the radio about the end of translation, an issue that my friend Scott pressed all the time.

Of course, I remember the bright face of a woman named Teodora: pretty face, elegant, proud build and a little acerbic, readiness for measured, long, truly meaningful conversations about everything.

What really happened on that seventh (?) trip with Handke? What?

It started with frequent excursions with the media close by and eavesdropping.

Conversations about nothing and everything most often developed slowly, nonchalantly, without any specific intentions and showing no fear for the times in which we lived.

One might even say that this time the trip took place through telephone calls. The direction we took, the stations, means of transportation, guides and even the accessory equipment were already frequent topics in those short or long phone conversations. The discussions were not heated. But not lukewarm either. Conversations about everything. Wistful, attentive, warm and passionate. With every conversation the trip that we were planning became more real, clearer, brighter and "more plastic." And not only was there no more reason to postpone the trip: any thought of any change was excluded.

✑ 25 October 1998

I arrived in Belgrade two days after Handke. It was the first time that Peter had preceded me in my own town. That fact surprised me with the additional consideration of "changing places," whereby I would immediately feel like "a stranger in my own house."

The changed places were already portended by how one traveled to Yugoslavia at the time: while I must say I was afraid of the announced "bombing of Belgrade," Peter was cool, at least on the phone. While I thought of postponing the trip, periodically in the grip of panic, Peter stayed true to his intention to go to the capital of Yugoslavia and, as he said, see "with the naked eye" "what was going on" and "personally" catch the "smell of the country." While Peter had landed on time back on Monday (October 14), flying with "Air France," I was forced to stay in Cologne because the German air carrier "Lufthansa" had cancelled its flights to Belgrade (fearing the announced bombing).

✑ 26 October 1998

The next day, Tuesday, I tried Peter's "Air France."

Peter had already been in Belgrade for some time. I called him by phone around noon. I was in the DW building.[27] The telephone was

---

[27] *Deutsche Welle*. See my book *Pogled* (Belgrade: Stubovi kulture, 2002).

in an empty room on the twelfth floor. Peter was in his room at Hotel
"Moskva."

Dead silence. Then noise echoing like explosions. The voices
seem all the more subdued.

"You really can't come today?"

"No, even 'Air France' is going to cancel their flights to Belgrade!"

It is cold in the restaurant as I write this. The place is just about
empty. That is why I notice that all the stools along the bar are different. Why can't I remember the face of the journalist from Banja
Luka who mentioned going to the office of *Književna Reč* (*Literary
Word*) (in the "old Yugoslavia").

Silence. Methodical movements of the woman's hand at the next
table. If the spoon bringing foam from her coffee cup to her mouth
were to slip out of her little hand, the clang of the metal cutlery would
echo so loudly that the ceiling fan, alarmed for a moment, would stop
its otherwise methodical but—I have no idea why—sad rotation. And
the waiter would only cough. The man at the table by the window
would sneeze. I would wipe my nose loudly, of course, not in place of
the man. And it was only after a woman with very long legs entered
the place, causing the bartender to choke—we have no idea why either—that I remembered the face of the journalist from Banja Luka.
It was the unmistakable picture of a man in his forties.[28] The tired,
suffering face, unshaven, with wrinkles (like escape routes in the war)
deeply chiseled in his forehead, and pale, almost bloodless complex-
ion, aroused me from my sleep. Did my bright eyes pass over the
prominent cheekbones of that half-dead face? Did my stern eyes search through the charred remains of his nose? I wanted to stop such
thoughts, so that is what I am doing. I have no idea why there is such
a strong desire to write in the present tense. There is also a strong
desire to go to the movies. Suddenly it seems to me that the book I'm
writing here that I want to finish right now is not a story about re-
collection. The unfinished state of this text is primarily shown in that
Knifer-like constantly starting and only periodically finishing what
has been started. This gives rise to the need to write in the present
tense, which suspends any storytelling. Because this is an observation
story and an "observation story" must report on the present. Of
course, this kind of "storytelling" seems like talking emptily and like
talking to yourself. Because who listens to a storyteller of the present?

---

[28] Several years later, as I was rewriting this text (for the seventh time), I
found out that the man had committed suicide.

Who wants to be in the audience of the absent? Because listening to a storyteller of the present is the same as removing yourself from the present. Closing your eyes. Extinguishing the fiery images. And wholeheartedly abandoning yourself to listening.

✍ 28 October 1998

So, right after I get to Belgrade I meet Peter in the restaurant of Hotel "Moskva." We are sitting at a table "in the point" of the room, like on the bow of a ship anchored in a harbor, which is what this square looks like with its two streets that meet right in front of the hotel's front façade.

"Hi," I say.

"Hello," replies Peter, getting up politely. That movement is so familiar to me, so pleasant and tangible, that the embrace, patting my friend on the back and his friendly slap on my forehead, turn into the signs of a story that suddenly needs to be recalled. It was summoned by those light, soft, short glances. Silence, of course, sweeps away the roar of daytime traffic in the street.

✍ 2 November 1998

That afternoon after I got to Belgrade is memorable for my meeting with L., and less so for meeting M.J.[29] Let me explain, L. is that artist whose art did not seriously interest me before, perhaps because of the "rebellious image" of "1968-ers" who in my (not apolitical!) "anti-moralizing" "purism" were abrasive from the very beginning of my awareness of the "truth" about art. Didn't fellow student Z.R. openly say at a meeting of general literature students in Takovska Street that I should be "ideologically processed" for my "unsuitable apathy," "amoral aloofness," and "complete political absence"? In the mass of exalted rebels in the student protest demonstrations of 1968, didn't I truly seem like just a loser? After the decisive, declarative meeting of student rebels in the Hall of Heroes at the Faculty of Philology, when Z.R. himself screamed into the microphone and called everyone there to go out into the street, I, who just happened to have wandered there, accidentally ended up in the front lines of the mass of students, inflamed not only by Z.R.'s speech. Many of the students were truly

---

[29] He will be discussed in my book *Handke.*

dissatisfied. Nevertheless, the whole time I seemed to have a premonition of my later despair. And I said so to my parents right then: articulating my vision of the "ruination of everything," speaking in the agony of a nervous breakdown that only seemed to be feigned. That was when I left my parents' home, forever. So, on the way out of the Faculty of Philology building, the police beat me up. Not only did I not feel the truncheon blows, but I felt bad the whole time (owing to the accidental nature of my being there, because I felt guilty at having taken someone's "heroic role"). The same feeling filled me on the ceremonial balcony on the front of the Faculty of Philosophy, which the students took over that day. Down below on the sidewalk in front of the entrance, film director Želimir Žilnik, a young documentary filmmaker at the time, filmed me on the balcony (for his later banned film *Rani radovi* (Early Works) later celebrated throughout the world). And I was not brave enough to leave the balcony right away ("run off") or shout at the cameraman ("stop filming"). On the contrary, in my dull-wittedness I "posed," establishing a distance from my present time. My eyes were "fastened" on the director's face; he pointed at me to the cameraman as he gave orders triumphantly and a little despotically. During the night in the courtyard of the barricaded faculty building, when Minderović ("Minda") played Beatles tunes on the piano, I was lying on the ground, head resting on the stomach of a half-naked girl (not Drinka!) looking at the starry sky, imagining myself in prison. Even Dilajla, a good buddy, who had lit a joint, seemed to me like the hero of a drama that would not end happily. I felt the sharp taste of deceit: in the marijuana smoke and in the beats of Minderović's music, and in nudity of the woman with whom I later moved to the armchair of the University rector. Unlike some students, I felt unnatural the whole time. I did not physically feel the words in the speeches of professors P.O.[30] and D.M.,[31] not even in the fateful speech by Josip Broz. It was like none of it attracted me, even though I was present the whole time, and even active. (I moved from one place to another. I talked. I clapped.) Later, several years later in "Kolarac" restaurant on Knez Mihailovoja Street, I saw L.—he was at the top of his artistic career. He was in jeans and white tennis shoes. "Like Tito in a formal white suit," I thought. Like the "wrong hero in the wrong place at the wrong time" in a drama that was not all that good, I wrote. In words and sentences

---

[30] Today the president of a Serbian political party.
[31] Today president of the Yugoslav Assembly.

that, allegedly, carried the truth itself, there was something of the illusionist. Perhaps that is why I don't remember anything that was said. Only images remain: sweaty brow; moustache falling into a spoonful of fish soup; dirty hair; a voice like that of an announcer reporting on a coup d'état. I wondered the whole time about the motives behind the hero's actions. In a number of public appearances—later primarily as an ideologist—L. was not lively enough, thus unconvincing. Or else he: seemed level-headed, quite diplomatic. (I am speaking here of someone I have never met.) (This is, therefore, an opinion without a tangible foundation. So it is not even an opinion. It is more like a feeling.)

Everything the artist said that afternoon in Belgrade and later in Zemun neither confirmed my previous thoughts nor brought any new ones. Of course, I took pains not to show my feelings. I am sure that those present did not deduce them either.

On the other hand, I was curious about the outcome of the meeting with the artist. I certainly was hoping for all that. Was it also because of my hurt pride, bitterness and spite caused by the words in a letter from a female friend, M.Č., who "scolded" me for having "wrongly" "taken" Handke on "those" trips through Serbia? "You should not have gone 'through villages.'" "You are creating a myth about Handke." "You are mixing with the wrong people." Suddenly I saw friendship like the picture of a pile of wood on a clearing in a forest, with despondent people standing in a row in front of it, as a forester gives them instructions: "You take this log," "You take that log over there," and "You take that log," "Go on, take them, and go home," and "Don't anyone touch those logs over there," "Dismissed!"

◔ 5 NOVEMBER 1998

So there was a meeting: October 16, 1998, at high noon. (No! It was somewhat after 2 p.m.) It was next to the fountain in front of Hotel "Moskva." (No! It was next to the hamburger stand.) The day was sunny. (No! It was raining.) ("Look, storytelling in the past tense again!") The air was filled with the smell of that familiar Belgrade "sfumato" autumn. The particles of that picture were not only "large grain" but also the quite shaded, pale colors of the background where the bright shades of summer had truly disappeared. This is why nothing present took effect "at first glance." Even the artist's car (a Honda sedan), parked ("illegally") at the top of the Balkanska Street descent, seemed to take effect "at second glance." The picture, of course, was "quiet." The strong smell of rancid oil came from a kitchen window. The outline of scattered split logs and lumps of coal could be seen (only "at second glance") through a half-open basement window knee-high to Peter. "Down there," from Zeleni Venac green market, came the smell of rotten fruit in slow, heavy and long waves, plaguing the positions, gestures, limbs and hair of those passing by in the street. Seen "from Mars" (so a "long shot"), people looked "like ants." It was only "clearly seen" "at second glance" that the eyes of these fellow citizens were "ringed" with dark circles. ("Like pools in the middle of concentric circles of ripples on swamp water, set in motion by a jumping frog.") The black circles under the artist's eyes were also evident "at second glance." The dark circles under Peter's eyes were also evident "at second glance." "At second glance," my dark circles were also evident. And we all stood there and looked at the "Albania Palace" building, once the tallest and most magnificent buildings in the Balkans (so they claim in the country), today only the symbol of a "superseded empire" (claim some foreign media). It is still a symbol of "growing up without maturing" (many say in some foreign media, but also in the coffee houses in the country). A symbol of "educating children with books having no substance" (they say). "A symbol of punishing offenders before they commit an offence." (Do I, here and in general, reject symbols as denotations in talking about experiences and expressing feelings?) And at one time the Albania building (stressing "at one time") was the perfect picture of success. In the streets around the building: Tito's pioneers with red kerchiefs around their necks. Mothers wearing stockings "with seams" were not "streetwalkers" but were "virgins" one and all, giving birth to us by "immaculate conception." There are no dog droppings on the sidewalk. Sport aircraft fly over piles of coal deliveries (for winter heating) and split wood thrown around it (also for winter heating) ("on the sidewalk"). In Belgrade, the Albania building was the very embodiment of a small cosmos in which everything had "its place" (say many even today in the country). And only madness will shatter the frame of that picture." (Or that picture frame will shatter on the very crags of reason that were too hard and too harsh for all those there?) Only a troubled mind will break the coordinates of that system, the vectors falling out one by one. (Or the coordinates of that system will be broken pre-cisely by someone's vigilance, pure, cold and complete, drawn out to the point of being evil, warped and debauched?) And (they said in the country) that was a "time of the avant-garde" in which every word in a sentence and every brick in a house was immediately clear to everyone at first glance. "There was no trace of the later 'postmodern' blurring of the picture," I write (today) (neither in the country nor abroad). "Clear view through the window to the street where pedestrians, flocks of sheep, camels, cats, ants, wolves, workers, lions, pigs, horse-drawn carriages, cars, and policemen truly pass by, all together, not bothered by each other, and smiling when they meet."

Of course, I am not normal.—"Today, consequently, everything is different. The claustrophobics, as we know, have the upper hand. They all wear sunglasses. Villages no longer exist. (So, the present tense again!) The towns are pens for cattle that were slaughtered, eaten, digested and ejected in the form of feces long ago. Figures in human form take public transportation, taxis and private cars from nowhere to nowhere. Consequently, no one goes on foot. Even if there are pedestrians, they are drivers. They jingle keys in one hand. A mobile phone is shining in the other hand. The sun does not shine but presses on the heart. I am suffocating. In front of the grilled meat stand I can't find my wallet. I don't have any cigarettes. Under my arm is a bundle of a dozen 'daily newspapers.' The weather is 'cold and clear' making everyone shiver and grin unnaturally."—Of course, I am not normal.

✎ 6 November 1998

And this meeting will, consequently, be remembered. We will remember these moments later. The meal, scruples, uncertain steps toward the restroom, gazing at the other bank of the river, the story of a woman with moist eyes. What primarily sticks in my mind is the expression on the waiter's face as he recognizes the customers, but remains calm the whole time, "ostensibly" "uninterested" . . . And it all started with an absurd handshake. As one pressed the other's hand as hard as he could, the other was concentrating on what he was looking at. His hand seemed to float in the air.

✎ Stuttgart, 21 November 1998

Much, much later I visited a city that in my earlier adult life had been an important foundation of the grubby awareness of what was then and continues to be the unfinished edifice of my Balkano-Slavic persona.

It was a time of possible storytelling based on the ability to control thoughts and experiences. The narrative system was quite clear, tangible, and sound. Above all, it was indestructible. And enabled the slow, zigzag or roundabout movement around a center that immediately ceased to exist or else immediately became something else, or immediately changed, etc.

At the time, I was hungry for something new.

At the time, I wanted more.

At the time, I sought the Other.

Going to museums, for example, was ("at the time") a "holiday," an "event," an "amorous encounter." Standing (or sitting), for example, before a master's painting brought trembling owing to the very closeness of the uneven areas in the layers of paint.

Today, in the same museum, in front of the same painting by the same master, uninterested so to say, my eyes go out the window into the grayness of the wintry late autumn landscape of the street "with a bus passing a car" and "with" several "random passers-by."

There is not a bit of the controlled flow of narration. The story, if it still exists, develops in fits and starts, with sudden interruptions, breaks, jumps, degenerations and tearing of the fiber of an increaseingly drawn-out story. It is reminiscent of dough, saliva, and spit.

The storyteller's interest in the secondary is captivating. First, he observes the exhibit goers. In front of a canvas of the Mother of God, for example, a group of people resembles spectators watching a sport aircraft review.

In the meantime, a touching letter arrives from a friend. He makes special note of wanting to get together . . . . Later, on the phone, shudders of loneliness. Along with fear of illness.

Then H.S. called.

Unpleasant surprise at work yesterday.

Rain. Thinking of going out into the street: drowning.

Suddenly a passer-by like an "adolescent" or like the picture of childhood turned ugly. He seems so silly, inauthentic, wrong, but convincing, that only after he leaves, consequently in his absence, do I feel myself.

On the telephone, I have to shout. Annoyed by the picture of someone who never ever looks "flirtingly" at anyone. Everything in the picture seems so purposeful that you really see the primordial picture of the future. "Does that guy ever sleep?"

Reading the protocols of polemics, I feel helpless. The first thought is "attack the artist again." At the same time, the image of smothering the soul with definitions and one-beat interpretations. I see misreading as being both twisted and an autistic reaction. But they, it seems to me, really seem like "professionals" and linguistic "lawmakers" .... And then those polemics appear to me like an issue that touches those who are truly affected by something, but also those who benefit from the subject of the polemics .... "Old folks of ancient history."

And why was it that when I looked at something I felt the increasing need to listen. As though expecting the sound or voice of the story. And I strained my ear every time. And the picture in my field of vision blurred.

When they spoke about "tolerance," I wondered whether all of us, the speakers, audience, guests, "were in church" ....

That problem of expressing myself, particularly after some letters that arrived at the time, suddenly boiled down to the need to reform my correspondence and translations ... What first came to mind was the idea of stopping all communication, so that the missive became sufficient in itself .... Right afterwards I thought I should screen the senders, so the missive would take on what I considered its necessary aura. I imagined the recipient of the missive in a happy position, sitting on a bench in a park. He is reading the missive like his favorite novel. Of course, his face is beaming with joy .... Then I thought I should intensify the correspondence. I thought I should reduce the vocabulary of the epistles to the smallest number of words so that, when used, they were also an injection, a serum and antibiotic in the battle against a disease that was spreading perniciously.

Several brief conversations with A. . . . .

A brief conversation with S. along with a lot of roaring laughter
. . . .

A missive from P.

A long conversation with R. First in dark tones and rough. Later soft but not sunny as well.

A letter sent to Z. denoted the beginning of the "reforms."

Oh, yes! And a brief conversation with H.S. . . . .

END

BRIDGE

Žarko Radaković & Scott Abbott

§

BRIDGE

In the summer of 1998, Peter Handke, Scott Abbott and I traveled together through Yugoslavia and Bosnia and Herzegovina. Several months before this trip, I thought that along the way Scott and I could continue the joint travelogue that we started in our book *Repetitions*. That book resulted from reading Handke's book *Repetitions*—and Scott and I traveling together through the "geography of the novel," intending to "verify" just how much the narration in Handke's book corresponded to the "reality" of the described "locations." Now that Scott had become Handke's translator too, having translated and published Handke's *A Journey to the Rivers*, I felt it would be worthwhile to go to the geography of that book—we, Handke's translators, traveling together with our author. And we would write another double manuscript. Again, we would be One looking through two different optics. That way—we thought—what was Seen and Experienced would be enriched. And I again—as I had with *Repetitions*—made the proposal. We got ready for the trip. And we set off on the journey. Scott, as always, was efficient. He noted down every detail "on the ground." I, as often when traveling with Peter Handke, wrote down as little as possible and let myself surrender to experiences that I would later repeat. But this time Repetition became lost in Experience. As soon as our trip ended, new events followed each other at breakneck speed. So much that was new. The country continued to break up: a takeover was portended in what remained of the state; NATO intervention loomed on the horizon and soon came; I traveled to the U.S.; I moved; my closest friends fell ill; I withdrew inside myself and fell silent; I left my job. All the new things I experienced during that period before and after the trip with Handke and Scott simply buried the experiences that were to be the basis of our writing a book together. My manuscript developed into another story. The connection with Scott's text took on new dimensions. I suddenly took Scott's manuscript as a crucial context in which the book *Vampires* arose. Instead of keeping a distance with regard to my partner's text, regarding it as parallel to what I was writing and another way of looking at our joint reality, I kept going back to my friend's manuscript. I suddenly experienced the reading of Scott's text as a solid part of myself. The danger arose: instead of a writer, I would remain a reader. Consequently, I had to remove myself from that reading material. I had to write. But repeating what my traveling companion had already written seemed impossible to me. Owing to the proximity of my friend's text, owing to the intensity of the new experiences. Consequently, I had to write something new. I started writing the novel *Vampires*. Today I experience Scott's writing as an extremely important environment for my novel. Because if there was anything I wanted in *Vampires*, it was a description of the time and space in which we lived in 1998 before the NATO intervention in Yugoslavia, which made us all suffer so much, which changed us essentially. I thought, if Scott has already recorded everything so convincingly, shouldn't it be up to me to do some storytelling? In my case, there was no longer any question about a travelogue. All I could do was take what already existed as a travelogue, Scott's manuscript, and insert it into my book. That is what I have done.

Ž.R.

The year Žarko and I traveled up the Drina River with Peter Handke—between the wars—was a nearly fatal span for my dear friend. The events of the same year may have saved my life.

I remember standing next to Žarko in front of an audience at Brigham Young University (was it his first visit or his second?). I had invited him to speak about his work with Peter Handke. For two hours he had engaged my students, delighted them, questioned them —all in German (which is the language he and I share—we're both foreigners when we're together). Now he was to address an audience that didn't understand German. I was to be the interpreter. I was to say "I" and mean "Žarko."

It was 1992 (the first visit, then). Žarko's lecture was so personal, so elegiac (tragic) that I stood transfixed even as I repeated in English the words my friend spoke in German:

> Approximately fifteen years ago, I left my country. Back then, in 1978, it called itself the Socialist Federal Republic of Yugoslavia. In late autumn as I left the Belgrade train station to travel to what was then the Federal Republic of Germany, I didn't have the least suspicion that in fifteen years, that is, now, my country would no longer exist . . . .

He/I continued:

> Can I, in the midst of these tragic events, appear as an "omniscient narrator"? Can I, as an isolated writer, produce stories? Can I, as a writer in this situation, react publicly, draw conclusions, show emotions, move about freely, take part in discussions? Can I write about this brutal present at all?

Years later, Žarko answered those questions with his novel *Vampires*. The answer, of course, is no. He can't appear as an "omniscient narrator." He can't produce stories. He can't draw conclusions. The answer, of course, is also yes. He can, in fact, write about this brutal present. Or better said: He can write this brutal present. That writing—that tortured, broken, but not un-dead writing—questions narration. It undermines stories. It deflates conclusions.

The tremendous costs such writing exacted on my dear friend weighed heavy on me as I tried to write my own text in the context of a country split so brutally that it now required a Serbian dictionary *and* a Croatian dictionary. How could I possibly put what I experienced with Žarko, in Žarko's homeland, into sentences?

What I did know was that my own life was in danger—my emotional life, my future life, my spiritual life (No, not my spiritual life. I no longer wanted a spiritual life). If I couldn't somehow write my way out of the drying cement of my life . . . .

S.A.

A REASONABLE DICTIONARY

SCOTT ABBOTT

My work is of a different sort. To record the evil facts, that's good. But something else is needed for a peace, something not less important than the facts.

Peter Handke, *A Journey to the Rivers: Justice for Serbia*

Let this story begin, perhaps, in 1998 in Belgrade among the well-kept ruins of the Kalemegdan fortress that overlooks the confluence of the Sava and Danube rivers. A barrel-chested man walks along a path with his two little girls. They lag behind. He shouts at them. They catch up. They turn aside to play among wildflowers. He threatens them. The girls join him momentarily, then disappear among the tall flowers. He roars a command. They return. The youngest girl begins to cry. The older girl takes her hand. The big man steps off the path and rips a bunch of wildflowers from the high grass. He hands them to the crying girl. She stops crying. He shouts again. They walk away, all three of them, holding mismatched hands.

Or let the story begin just after the turn of the century with the younger brother of my friend Christian Gellinek's grandfather. Otto Gellinek was an Austrian officer, Christian says, a ladies man—he died of syphilis—and a fencing instructor who liked to show off by walking on his hands. In 1907, disguised as a painter, Gellinek traveled in Bosnia-Herzegovina to sketch fortifications and make notes for a possible war. In 1908, despite Gellinek's report arguing against a formal annexation, the Austrians invaded the country. Catholic Croats welcomed the invaders, but Muslims and Orthodox Serbs opposed them bitterly. The battle lasted three months and cost the Austrian Army 5,198 casualties. More importantly, it aroused virulent anti-Austrian sentiment among Serbs, manifest most pointedly in the person of the 19-year-old nationalist who assassinated Archduke Franz Ferdinand in Sarajevo to set off the First World War.

Translating Peter Handke's *A Journey to the Rivers: Justice for*

Serbia from German into English, I called my old friend and long-time collaborator Žarko Radaković to ask about the phrase: "Do we need a new Gavrilo Princip?"

What kind of principle is this? I asked. Is it a term from business management?

Gavrilo Princip? Žarko laughed. He was the young assassin.

It's not easy to begin a new story about the old land of the southern Slavs (Yugo = south). After all, what do I know? A foreigner in the country for a few days. A self-styled translator with no command of this language. A potential verbal assassin.

> . . . in Shefko's translation the old man's words seemed suspicious, smelled of politics and seditious intent . . . Shefko, who was obviously putting the worst possible construction on the old man's exalted phrases and who loved to stick his nose into everything and carry tales even when there was nothing in them, and was ever ready to give or to confirm an evil report.
>
> Ivo Andrić, *The Bridge Over the Drina*

Caveat lector.

◯ PROVO, UTAH, 20 MAY 1998

Tomorrow, when I leave Utah for Yugoslavia, for Serbia, for the Republika Srbska along the Drina River, I'll carry with me the bruise-enhanced memory of this afternoon's mountain-bike ride up a section of the Great Western Trail on the southern flank of Mount Timpanogos. The ride began with a good omen, the first lazuli buntings of the year, those orange-and-white-chested, slash-winged, blue-headed and -backed beauties that nest here in the spring.

My friend Sam and I climbed the familiar twisting trail over an outcropping of quartzite and then pedaled along a ridge of blue limestone. Sam, a botanist, spoke the names of the wildflowers: evening primrose, hound's tongue, sweet vetch, and death camas—see the three petals characteristic of the lily family? Higher on the mountain, he pointed out the delicate white petals of woodland star, mountain forget-me-nots, and upland larkspur. The larkspur, Sam explained, like death camas, contains a potent poison, a fine, selective sheepicide.

The trail rose more steeply now, switch-backing upward, stealing our breath, and testing our will. An unexpected trickle of water down the trail and then, around the next curve, the massive toe of a months-old avalanche, a 10-meter-high wall of densely compacted snow, dislocated trees, and boulders.

Standing atop the snow mass, looking down on our bikes, I shuddered. Was it the sudden chill, I wondered, or awe at the snow's blind and ponderous presence, or was it how the avalanche reminded me of my marriage?

What does that mean? Sam asked. You have seven beautiful children. You've been married for a quarter of a century.

You're right, I answered. My marriage has been no avalanche. I love my children. I respect my wife. Still, it's telling that that image sprang to mind, don't you think?

Sure it's telling, Sam responded, but what it's telling is another story.

We gazed up at the evident history of the avalanche: that line in space—from the distinct break under the mountain-top cornice to the constricting limestone gate halfway down to the botanical and geological destruction at the toe—that in retrospect became a line in time.

In the untouched grove of maples to one side, Sam showed me the small purplish-pink flower of a spring beauty. It is also called Indian potato, he said, because of its tasty bulb. And here's a violet, Nuttal's violet. Look at the backs of the yellow petals.

I lifted a delicate petal. Underneath, hidden from passing glance, the petals displayed bright crimson fuzz, splendor reserved for attentive pollinating insects.

I would like, I thought, to see Yugoslavia this closely. No, not that national abstraction "Yugoslavia." I don't want the blindness that comes from generalizing. I would like to see some specific thing in that specific place this closely.

On the way down, admiring a swale carpeted by blue forget-me-nots, I lost track of the trail and went over my handlebars, somersaulting down the steep slope. I lay there and wondered why my hip hurt so sharply when I had fallen into deep leaves. A scrub-oak stump had done the damage, it turned out, raising a knot I would still feel three weeks later on the plane ride home.

✑ DÜSSELDORF AIRPORT, 22 MAY 1998

Žarko, his eighteen-year-old daughter Milica, and I wait in an isolated and locked room to board the JAT (Yugoslavian Air Transport) plane for Belgrade. With medals flashing on bright uniforms, colorful scarves streaming in their wake, the plane's crew strides in. One of them strikes me as especially haughty—as in high, erect. She has loose dark hair, a sharp nose, and beautiful legs; but it is her self-consciousness, her extreme defiant uprightness as she sweeps along that draws my attention. It is too bad, I think, there are so few of us to witness this triumphant crew.

Triumphant?

Defiant.

We are in Germany. The Germany that bombed Belgrade in April of 1941. The Germany that interred and murdered 200,000 Serbs, Roma, and Jews in the Croatian concentration camp at Jesenovac. The Germany that in 1992 so precipitously recognized the independence of its WWII puppet state Croatia. The Germany that was quick to impose sanctions on Serbia during the ensuing and perhaps consequent war, sanctions that included an air embargo grounding JAT planes.

"Dobar dan," the flight attendant says when we enter the plane. Žarko beams.

In the plane, as always, Žarko and I speak German. We met in Germany, at the University of Tübingen. German is our only common language. Were it not for the German language, for translation from English and Serbo-Croatian, this American and that Yugoslav would not be friends.

◇ BELGRADE, 22 MAY 1998

Žarko's mother, Ljubica, is 72 years old and not at all well. She refuses, however, to go to a doctor. At my age, she explains through her interpreter son, it's better to steer clear of potential disaster.

Her hands turn and weigh and rub a cigarette lighter. She smokes "Partners," a brand she says comes from Macedonia. With a cigarette holder between long fingers she reminds me of Greta Garbo.

She snuggles up to Žarko, smoothes his hair, and asks what barbarian cut it.

She complains that she has but a single grandchild. Žarko tells her I have seven children. She nods her head approvingly. My son, she tells me, pointing her cigarette at Žarko, is lazy. Just one.

I picture Joe and Maren and Tom and Nate and Ben and Sam and Tim. What a brood! How would they deal with the breakup of a 25-year marriage?

The TV flickers interminably. For one half-hour stretch, we watch an episode from an American series in which beautiful, piano-playing young people with bare midriffs and taut biceps try to figure out a murder.

A news report shows students demonstrating at the university against newly announced education reforms. The news is read by unblemished mannequins who, had they spoken English instead of Serbian, might have read their lines on American TV.

Late in the afternoon Yugoslav TV features a rebroadcast of the third playoff game between the Jazz and the Lakers.

Here in Belgrade—in a third-floor apartment above a dentist's office, on a TV that produces only occasional hints of color, in front of a table bearing cups of Turkish coffee, glasses of water, and shot glasses of Rakija (an amber Šljivovica or plum brandy produced by Ljubica's 75-year-old brother who runs the family farm near Novi Sad)—here in Belgrade the Utah Jazz beat the Los Angeles Lakers to take a 3-0 lead in the series.

I tell Žarko and his mother about TV interviews with Vladi Divać and Toni Kukoć. To questions about the war and how Divać, a Serb, and Kukoć, a Croatian, now view one another, Divać replied that he still respected Kukoć and wanted to continue a friendship that had begun when they played together on the Yugoslavian national team. Kukoć said the war had changed everything and that he hated Divać like he hated all Serbs.

You must learn some Serbian, Ljubica says: "Srbi su dobri ljudi." She says it again: "Srbi su dobri ljudi."

I repeat the phrase. She corrects my pronunciation. *Srbi su dobri ljudi.* "What does it mean?" I ask.

"Serbs are good people!" She laughs, pleased with herself.

"That goes without saying," I respond. "Teach me something else."

"Muštikla," she says. "Muštikla."

"What's that?" I ask.

She points to her cigarette holder: "Muštikla."

It's not on the vocabulary frequency lists, I'll bet. But I learn it. For her. And add, later: filteri.

In downtown Belgrade, the windows of a large bookstore are hung with book-fair posters featuring the luscious headless body of a naked woman holding an open book. The text reads: LEPA, MUDRA, AĆUTI (Beautiful, Wise, and Silent), and then asks: "Where Can You Find It?"

It?

Headless advertisements for a book fair?

Misogyny. Where Can't You Find It?

What images do I have in my American male brain that have colored my marriage over the years, that have inhibited intimate companionship?

Žarko translates the title of a book by Professor Dr. Jovan Marić: *Kakvi Smo Mi Srbi? Prilozi za Karakterologiju Srba* (In What Way Are We Serbs? Contributions to a Characterology of the Serbs). I imagine a characterology of the Americans, of the Jews, of the Germans. Slippery terrain.

A characterology of Scott Abbott? Not if it involves Professor Dr. Jovan Marić's procrustean abstractions. But translating myself into new words, mobile and supple words, words flavored with Yugoslav accents, that's one of the reasons I'm here.

Along the crowded pedestrian zone stand racks of glossy magazines: *Guns, Handgunner, Gun World, Rifleman, Guns and Ammo.* Yugoslavia is a country of killers, I think. My nostrils flare and I imagine a bloody headline in the *Salt Lake Observer.* This is a story I can sell.

Easy, easy.

There are other magazines on the racks, a more complete picture of the reading habits of English-speaking Belgrade Serbs: *Bimmer, Sportscar, Yachting, Sailing, Playboy, Cosmopolitan, Lingerie, Wet & Wild, Brides, Sports Illustrated, Forbes.*

Were I to highlight the gun magazines for the *Observer*, I'd present a characterological Serb obsession with guns. But where do the English-language gun magazines come from? And remember that of the 88,649 gun deaths reported by the world's 36 richest countries in 1994, 45% occurred in the United States.

✿ ZEMUN, 23 MAY 1998

Yesterday, when Žarko told his mother we were going to spend today in Zemun, she begged him to reconsider. Neo-fascist Vojislav Šešelj, head of the Serbian Radical Party, now Slobodan Milošević's assistant, came to political prominence as mayor of Zemun and she thinks an American might run into trouble there among his radically nationalist constituency.

"Zemun is our hometown," Žarko says.

"Precisely," she answers.

"But Zemun has a long history of openness to difference," Žarko argues. "There is a synagogue in the park, a Jewish section in the cemetery."

"That was before Šešelj," his mother says sadly. She marries a cigarette to her muštikla.

With a hundred fellow passengers, Žarko and I ride a creaking, tire-bulging bus across the Save River to Zemun.

"This," Žarko says, pointing at an outdoor café fronting on the Danube, "is where I used to come with a friend after school to drink sodas and smoke cigarettes. One day my father walked by. We ditched the cigarettes. He came in and asked if he could join us. He sat down and ordered coffee. He offered to buy us something. He took out some cigarettes and started to light one. 'Do you want a cigarette?' he asked, holding out the pack. We didn't dare accept. Finally he went back to work. As far as I know, he never told my mother."

Not far from the café, a century-old barge rides at permanent and waterlogged anchor. A sign on the long plank gangway declares that "Bicycles and Dogs are Absolutely Forbidden!"

We find a table in the sun, welcome on this cool afternoon. At the next table, two men play chess. A white-jacketed waiter stops regularly to see how the game is going. Most of the guests on the barge are drinking Jelen Pivo, "Stag Beer," brewed in Yugoslavia since 1756. The shoulders of the stubby brown bottles are rubbed white with use and reuse.

A motorboat docks alongside the barge. The man who climbs the ladder and joins us at our table wears canvas boating shoes, jeans, a sweatshirt, and a canvas vest. His long hair has been raked over a balding crown. His name is Pera, and he and Žarko have known each other since grade school.

In varying combinations of Serbian, English, and German, we talk until the sun sets and cold air begins to rise from the Danube.

Žarko introduces me as the co-author of *Ponavljanje/Repetitions*. Pera says he hasn't heard of it. I tell him that's a scandal, that everyone else has read it, that it was selling like crazy yesterday in the Plato bookstore near the university. "I'm ashamed," he says, "but at eight o'clock tomorrow morning I'll be at the bookstore to buy a copy."

Pera asks if there is a film industry in Utah. I mention Trent Harris's "Plan Ten From Outer Space," with Karen Black as the alien feminist.

"Karen Black!" Pera says. "I know Karen Black. She was here in Belgrade twenty years ago making a low-budget movie I did some photography for. I fucked Karen Black. More than once. She's not as interesting personally, let me tell you, as she is on screen."

"What have you been doing recently?" Žarko asks.

"Two years ago," Pera answers, "short of money, I agreed to make a campaign film for Mira Marković's political party. She's Slobodan Milošević's wife," he explains for my sake. "It was kitsch, pure kitsch, and very effective. I had a whole sequence with neon lights that shot the word PROGRESS across the screen: PROGRESS . . . PROGRESS . . . PROGRESS. It was a brilliant piece of propaganda. Since then, I've called myself Pera Riefenstahl. I learned everything from Leni. She was a genius at making the people so small and the great leader so large. I don't worry about having done the job. I needed the money and the country is absolute chaos anyway. It doesn't matter what you do or don't do, it doesn't change anything. Absolute chaos, and so I just made the film and now I can keep my boat running."

I have drunk a lot of pivo. Carefully I walk the length of the barge to the restroom where I piss into a hole opening onto the grey Danube.

The sun sets. Between us and the shore, frenzied frogs raise an orgasmic din.

Osloboditi reč znači probuditi je iz sna, učiniti da ona znači sve ono što je sanjala da znači. . . . Za reč nema večeg užasa od razumnog rečnika.

To release a word means to wake it up and make it mean everything it dreamed of meaning. . . . There is no greater horror for the word than a reasonable dictionary.

Branka Arsić, *Rečnik /Dictionary*

I am fond of my little dictionary, given to me by a friend the first time I traveled to Yugoslavia. Although it was published in Belgrade in 1973, the dog-eared book looks like it might have been printed in the nineteenth century. I like the subtle contrast between the blue of the one-quarter cloth spine and the black paper sides. The pages are Smythe-sewn with red-orange stuck-on endbands that add a fine touch of color to the book.

Rečnik, the book calls itself. Dictionary: English-Serbocroatian, Serbocroatian-English. On the spine, and only on the spine, the word "standardni." A standard. A standard for Serbs and Croats married to one another for over forty years in Tito's multi-ethnic Yugoslavia.

The book has 620 pages. Nearly half the green pages in the center (pages 281–314) are a dictionary of synonyms: Rečnik Sinonima. ("True—right, sound, sterling, upright; real, actual, positive; certain, exact, accurate, precise; faithful, constant, loyal, staunch, strict, catholic, orthodox." Synonyms in whose mind?) On the same green paper, pages 315–368 explain English grammar.

The rest of the book translates words from one language into another.

This equals that.

Walter Benjamin argued that translation, at its best, both uses and undercuts the identities posited by a dictionary:

> Translation is so far removed from being the sterile equation of two dead languages that of all literary forms it is the one charged with the special mission of watching over the maturing process of the original language and the birth pangs of its own.[32]

✑ TRG REPUBLIKE, BELGRADE, 24 MAY 1998

It is a good-sized square, this Yugoslav Place de la Republic, a broad space that has retained its human dimensions. Bounded by a museum, a theater, and department stores, the square sits astride the city's backbone ridge.

A fine place to sit in the late morning sun, to take notes, to watch passers-by.

A teenaged boy sits down on the concrete planter behind Žarko. He lights a cigarette and looks at the notebook Žarko is writing in. "Are you a poet?" he asks.

---

[32] Walter Benjamin, "The Task of the Translator," in *Illuminations: Essays and Reflections*, trans. Harry Zohn (New York: Schocken Books, 1969), 73 [69–82].

"I'm a writer," Žarko says.

"I've never seen a writer taking notes," the boy says. "I'm skipping school. I'm a good student. My parents are teachers, but they aren't getting paid. I feel like I ought to help them. They want me to go to Switzerland. I see no purpose to life. Maybe I'll kill myself." Žarko and the boy talk for some time. They stand and say "do vijenja." Žarko and I walk to the market to buy flowers for his mother.

In her four-room apartment, Ljubica Radaković feeds us chicken soup, then new potatoes and carrots and chicken with gravy. While we eat, she smokes. "You remind me of Greta Garbo," I tell her. Žarko translates. She shakes her head and says: "Greta Garbo with diabetes."

A parliamentary debate on the education-reform law flickers silently on the TV while we eat. If the reform passes, Žarko explains, university deans will be appointed by the minister of education, faculty appointments will require ministerial approval, and all faculty members will have to sign new contracts affirming their support for the new policies.

That's how they do it where I work, I tell him, at the Mormons' Brigham Young University. Not a healthy system, unless your main concern is preserving an established way of thinking.

Ljubica, who has begun to practice her native orthodoxy again, is surprised to learn that I work for a church university.

It's an odd fit, I explain. I grew up Mormon. I served as a Mormon missionary. I have a Mormon marriage. I raised my children to be Mormons. I teach at a fundamentalist Mormon university. But over the years I've lost my faith. I disagree with the conservative politics of the Mormons. Now what should I do? Leave my job? Leave my marriage? Abandon my people?

"No, no," Ljubica says. "Be careful. Move slowly."

"Do vijenja," I say as we leave. Ljubica beams and waves her momentarily empty muštikla.

Back in the square, Žarko finishes reading the *Danas* newspaper, an independent paper financed in part by the Hungarian-American who made his fortune buying and selling currencies, George Soros.

These are journalists talking with journalists, Žarko complains, journalists reporting on each other, writing for each other. Why can't they be practical? Why can't they deal with reality? What kind of opposition paper is this?

"There is supposed to be a demonstration tonight," Žarko reports. Here in the square. Against school reform and for freedom of the media. Djindjić is going to speak.

"Who is Djindjić?" I ask.

"He was elected mayor of Belgrade," Žarko explains. "You remember the elections Milošević tried to steal? Djindjić had been a student of the philosopher Jürgen Habermas in Frankfurt. He's an intelligent man. But he never figured out how to deal with reality. So Milošević, who isn't all that bright academically but who has his fingers on the pulse of things, could step in after the fact, divide the opposition, and take over again."

Not far from the square, we enter a bookstore owned by a poet Žarko knows. I'm not sure what I expected, but it wasn't the following (all in translation—even the authors' names!—or in the original Serbian): Raymond Carver's *Cathedral*, a new edition of Shakespeare's *Collected Works*, Ričard Rorti's *Consequences of Pragmatism*, Julian Barnes's *Flaubert's Parrot*, F. Niče's *Thus Spake Zarathustra*, a 1997 translation of Novalis's *Heinrich von Ofterdingen*, Žarko's *Emigration* and *Knifer*, and even our book: *Repetitions*. It's the first time I've seen it in a bookstore. I buy copies of *Emigration* and *Repetitions*.

You already have those books, Žarko points out.

Yes, but I like the feel of buying our books in a bookstore.

Let me introduce you to Gojko Djogo, Žarko says as a small man approaches, dressed in a dark sweater, white shirt, precisely knotted tie, pressed brown slacks, and shiny black wingtip shoes. Žarko introduces him as the store's owner and a poet of some renown.

We shake hands and sit on three chairs in a cramped space behind a counter piled with books. The two Serbs speak for some time in Serbian, catching up, I suppose. I look around the small store, then back at the poet, who wears a red-and-white watch with the Serbian national cross on its face. In the angles of the cross are the four Cyrillic S's that stand for something like "Serbia Safe Only When United."

Djogo became famous in 1982, Žarko explains, when he published a book of poetry called *Vunena Vremena*, translatable as something like "The Anxious Time." The book featured a bear that some people took to be Tito. The poet was sentenced to two years in prison, time that was shortened to four months after he developed severe stomach problems. He subsequently received a prize in Hamburg at the 1985 Pen Congress, where he sat between Günter Grass and Susan Sontag. "I was there," Žarko says, "and he was a big hit."

Gojko Djogo is pleased to hear the story, and when I ask about his sense for the political future, he is anxious to speak. "We have turned a corner in world opinion," he says. "Brigitte Bardot recently spoke out in favor of Serbs, and of course Peter Handke is our champion."

"But you know Bianca Jagger wrote a piece against the Serbs," I tell him. And there the conversation ends.

Rain falls across the afternoon and onto the nighttime crowd that has gathered in the square, a thousand people perhaps, standing under umbrellas and yellow street lamps.

Students hand out color posters that feature a microphone lit brightly against a threatening black cloud, gripped by a hand with its middle finger extended. At the top are printed a question and a command:

KOLIKO RADIO STANICA ČUJETE?

MISLITE O TOME.

I understand the photo perfectly, but to translate the words, I bend over my rečnik/dictionary: How much/how long the radio stopping place audible? Does it mean: How long will the radio station be audible? And then: Think about it.

Not likely.

At the bottom are the words: Radio Index. And then a brave and/or foolhardy "claimer": Fotografija, Art Concept and Design: KA-MENKO PAJIĆ.

Twenty people, most of them men, stand on a stage built up against an equestrian statue between the museum and the theater, lit by inconsistent spotlights. Students wave the opposition party's green and yellow flags and one red, blue, and white Serbian flag.

The steady rain soaks a huge sound system.

Speakers, one after the other, take the microphone and work the crowd. The words are incomprehensible to me, but I understand the rhetorical devices: the repetitions, the pauses, the crescendos, the climaxes.

The crowd is dripping wet. Hundreds of umbrellas block the view.

Žarko translates as much as he can. Every speaker, it seems, is denouncing as devils Milošević and Šešelj, who himself once called Milošević a devil.

Shrill whistles from the crowd.

Milošević is a fox, one speaker shouts, a fox scheming with Richard Holbrooke to sell out Kosovo.

"Isn't this the liberal opposition?" I ask Žarko.

He nods.

Couples are embracing throughout the crowd.

"Have you noticed that there is an erotic buzz in any demonstration?" Žarko asks.

A speaker compares Milošević with Hitler.

On the periphery, young men tell loud jokes. People buy cigarettes and magazines at a kiosk. Ambulances stand by. A Red Cross worker in reflective clothing walks through the crowd with a radio.

Finally, Djindjić takes the microphone. He led the street demonstrations just a year ago, hundreds of thousands of citizens marching and blowing whistles and demanding that the results of the democratic elections be honored. They achieved their goal. Djindjić and friends took office. But here they are again, out of power, outside in the rain, speaking to a scant thousand demonstrators, participants in a revolution that is running out of steam.

Still, Djindjić is a consummate orator. We'll go to the people, he says. We don't need the media. We'll simply walk with the people . . . We will not stop until the Milošević government is toppled . . . We will not allow him to cripple the education system . . . And we will never allow him to give away the birthplace of Serbia. Kosovo is sacred ground!

"This is nuts," Žarko says.

"What is nuts?" I ask.

"One way to explain Milošević's drastic educational reform," he says, "is as an attempt to maintain Serbian control of Kosovo by keeping the Albanians there out of the universities. So when Djindjić demands that Milošević keep Kosovo Serbian, he works against his own demand for academic freedom."

Complicated.

"We'll continue the demonstration tomorrow morning at 10 o'clock," Djindjić says. "See you there."

And that's it. The demonstration is adjourned.

After a minute, the sound system blares some sort of heroic, overwrought film music. I think of Woody Allen's line: "Listening to Wagner makes me want to invade Poland." How do you move the masses without playing to the mass instincts that are part of the problem?

Before the lights dim, Djindjić gives an interview to a man in a red rain jacket holding a tape recorder and then another to a TV journalist (so who doesn't need the media?), and it's over. We walk back toward my hotel. Around the corner stand eight vans full of policemen. One of them shouts insults at us as we pass. I don't need a translator.

Radio Index posters adorn every wall, every column, every door. Someone has been busy. And brave.

In the hotel, a couple of men shake the rain out of their hair and off their coats and explain to the desk clerks: "We went out to overthrow the government, and it rained." They laugh uproariously.

Žarko says good night and walks on to his mother's place.

I sit in my room and remember Djindjić's broad, handsome smile in the spotlight. His practiced wave. His rhythmic sentences. His forceful repetitions.

I think of the sentences I translated in Peter Handke's *A Journey to the Rivers: Justice for Serbia*, of a very different rhetoric—Handke's dialectical stammering, his pragmatic detours, his incessant questions.

How does a country move from "crowds and power" to a self-conscious and skeptical democracy? Education? Books that teach another kind of thinking? But then, in a crisis, as people look for answers, for comfort, right-wing rhetoric and left-wing clichés blossom. The leader promises purity, points to unambiguous solutions, incites to absolutes, and starts wars.

I've read the theory. Tonight I saw theory in action.

Don't get me wrong. I admire Djindjić. Leaders aren't perfect. But I can wish for a different kind of people. And I'm not thinking of Yugoslavs.

○ BELGRADE, 25 MAY 1998

Walking through the city this morning, I got lost. An hour later, I finally recognized the building where the parliament was voting on education reform. Demonstrators packed the sidewalks, hundreds of people shouting and blowing whistles and pushing past white-coated policemen who were trying to keep them off the street.

Žarko appeared out of nowhere. He smiled nervously.

A flood of angry people swept into the street. The police stepped back. The crowd stormed past. A line of blue-coated policemen stepped in front of them. The crowd moved on, more slowly, filtering through holes in the line. A white-haired couple screamed at the policemen, blew their whistles, gestured wildly. Green-and-yellow flags waved.

Ten short-haired men, big men, in black leather jackets and jeans stepped between the police and the crowd. When the next person moved forward, a black-coated man pushed him back. An advancing woman got the same treatment. Skirmishes ensued. Quick exchanges of blows. Flashfights. Thugs against citizens. No match. The crowd fell back while cameras rolled, five or six TV cameras, a dozen or so still cameras, held high to record the fighting. Footage, in seconds, for the evening news.

The thugs stood in a line. The crowd chanted the ultimate insult: "Ustasha! Ustasha!" A young thug cupped his ear and asked: "What? A little louder?"

The crowd sat down on the street. Whistles. Shouts.

Blue-jacketed police reinforcements filed in from around the corner and formed two lines perpendicular to the line of thugs that stretched across the street. At some signal, the policemen hustled the thugs off the street and themselves formed a shoulder-to-shoulder dam.

Cries of rage from the seated crowd. Looks of concern on their faces.

Was there concern on the faces of the young policemen?

The line advanced on the crowd. The crowd began to chant. A tiny woman at the front blew her whistle and shouted and pointed at the policemen.

The police moved another step closer.

The crowd chanted: "Go to Kosovo! Kill Albanians! Go to Kosovo! Kill Albanians!"

The police advanced.

"Red mob!" The crowd shouted.

A policeman drew back his boot and swung it at a seated person. Then again. Other policemen kicked at crossed legs and bent knees.

The crowd jumped up and turned and drew back and began to run. The police moved rapidly with them, kicking and swinging nightsticks.

We trotted along the sidewalk, not quite sure what was going to happen, curious, nervous.

There was a shout behind us. What were the policemen doing? People panicked, running, pushing their way up the street, ducking into doors.

Žarko and I followed a crowd into a door, down a hall, and into a courtyard. A dead end.

We ran back up the hall and out the door. In fits and starts we retreated from the parliament building, running when the crowd surged behind us, walking when the pressure eased.

Minutes later we stood in a bookstore holding a new Serbo-Croatian translation of Thoreau's *Walden and Civil Disobedience*, sweating, wondering what had just happened.

Fifteen minutes later, still clammy with sweat, having fled officers of one sort, we went looking for officials of another stamp. This was a scene I had translated from Peter's book:

> Departure finally from the over-heated capital city . . . outfitted with a laconic permit from the Serbian Republic that we had obtained in . . . central Belgrade . . . . At two quite empty desks . . . two women in summer attire, elegant in that characteristic Yugoslavian manner.[33]

🖎 ŠABAC, 26 MAY 1998

I sit alone at a table in front of the Šabac bus station. Žarko has gone to report the loss of my notebook, dropped, I suppose, on the floor of the crowded bus as we got out.

At the Belgrade bus station, men had climbed onto the bus to sell drinks and nuts and pulp fiction. From the bus's rear-view mirror hung a silly German "WUNDERBAUM—KOKUSNUSS" air freshener. Underway, I woke from a nap to see a geographically accurate but politically naïve freeway sign listing the number of kilometers to Zagreb and to Llubljana.

Žarko returns. "I filled out a form," he says, "but they weren't hopeful. I lost a notebook two years ago," he tells me, filling the silence. "When I tried to reproduce it from memory, I still had all the general events, but the details had sifted away."

Here, he adds: "For you."

My friend of 15 years hands me a schoolgirl's notebook: lined paper between cardboard covers decorated with photos of two sexy young women lying on their stomachs writing in notebooks decorated with photos of two sexy young women writing in notebooks.

---

[33] Peter Handke, *Sommerlicher Nachtrag zu einer winterlichen Reise* (Frankfurt am Main: Suhrkamp Verlag, 1996) 12.

I'll start over. The Düsseldorf airport. Žarko's mother. The demonstration. Zemun.

Let's go for a walk, Žarko suggests. Peter and Zlatko won't be here for an hour or two.

Šabac is an unremarkable town located on flat and fertile land, its low buildings spread out in orderly blocks. Žarko and I photograph one another in front of a shoe store called Borovo ("The Pines," my little dictionary says) whose three stone stories exhibit a hint of vertical aspiration.

Peter Handke and Zlatko Bocokić arrive in Zlatko's little red Peugeot. We shake hands. Peter and Zlatko tell of a brush with Croatian officials at the border. We pile into the car and head southwest.

Where the flatland meets the first hills rising up from the south we intersect the much-storied Drina River. Not far to the north the Drina flows into the Sava, which flows into the Danube between Zemun and Belgrade. Turning south, we follow a twisting, climbing river road, driving into the gathering darkness.

"Let's stop here," Peter suggests, and Zlatko pulls into a tiny parking lot. We unfold ourselves from the Pugeot and enter a one-room café. We sit around a chrome-rimmed table.

Peter asks the proprietor to sauté some mushrooms he pulls out of his pocket. We watch the darkness thicken. We exchange inanities. We drink a bottle of white wine—*bello vino*, as opposed to *czrno vino*, Žarko explains. We sit at the chrome-rimmed table and listen to the Drina flowing past just below us.

Time passes. We get up from the table and leave the café. Shortly before eleven we arrive at Olga's apartment in Bajina Bašta. Olga was Žarko's high-school sweetheart and is Milica's mother. Again, we sit. Olga serves plum brandy. Žarko shows me the James Dean poster in Milica's room.

It's after midnight when we walk to the cavernous hall of the hotel. I'm game only for a single round of bello vino. Then I turn in.

✍ BAJINA BAŠTA, HOTEL DRINA, 27 MAY 1998

The telephone rang this morning at 6. "Da?" I mumbled. A woman's voice said something that reminded me of "ustashe." Croatian quislings, enemies of Serbs! I panicked. She hung up. Through blurry eyes, I searched my dictionary and finally found "ustati"—to rise, to get up, to stand up.

Who ordered this wake-up call?

Last night, well after midnight, I glanced up and saw my image in the mirror. No connection, I thought, to the person I think of while writing in the first person. What I saw was a cadaver-white man with a bad haircut and reading glasses. A man with folds under his chin and a flabby chest. A man heavy with a marriage long since settled into the clichés of quiet desperation. A man settling into clichés about clichés.

Dead tired, I had left Peter, Zlatko, Žarko, and Olga in the hotel's hall where a grand total of nine people sat at two of 100 well appointed tables listening to a seven-piece band armed with all the latest technology—left them only to stare at my cadaver self in the mirror and then to fall into a troubled sleep in a room so clean and white that I dreamed of hospitals.

Thomas Deichmann, editor of *Novo*, joins us for breakfast. He is returning to his home in Frankfurt from a media conference in Greece, or if his sunburned face is any indication, from a fruitful tour of Greek beaches. For the rest of this trip, we'll be a quintet.

I'm pleased to meet you, says a bald man whose thin lips and large nose remind me of a Breugel peasant. "I've spent the morning cutting grass," he explains, pointing at his work clothes and beard stubble. "My name is Slobodan Rogić."

"Žarko has told me about you," I say. "It's a pleasure."

"I've read your book," he tells me.

"So you're the one," I reply.

He insists that the town's librarian has also read the book. Two readers in a town of 10,000!

Slobodan hands Peter a recycled Johnny Walker bottle and kisses him on both cheeks. "Serbian whiskey," he says, "šljivovica, plum brandy."

"I've been watching your Utah Jazz, "Slobodan says, turning back to me. "After their games against the Lakers, I think they'll beat Chicago. Bajina Bašta has its own sports hero," he continues. "Bora Milutinović—the former coach of the U.S. national soccer team and current coach of the Nigerian national team—is from Bajina Bašta. And Steve Tesich, the U.S. screenwriter, is from here as well. Do you know Tesich?" he asks.

"Didn't he write the screenplay for "Breaking Away"?"

"That's him. He's from Bajina Bašta."

Before we leave, Žarko tells him about my lost notebook.

"A catastrophe!" Slobodan says.

Hearing the words from my reader, it seems a worse loss than ever.

Over the slow course of a quiet afternoon, we sit under an apple tree in the village of Peručac, just up the Drina from Bajina Bašta. It's the garden of Olga's mother, the proud partisan Peter describes in *A Journey to the Rivers*: "The grandmother, the former partisan, who a half-year earlier had worn a peasant scarf and winter slippers inside the little house and who was now blithely bareheaded, her hair bronze-colored, very erect, with shoulders set at a commanding angle, like a chief, on her feet the finest leather shoes." Set off by her black-velvet blouse, Dušanka Nikolić's hennaed hair gleams red in the sun. Gold teeth, one on each side, light up her mouth.

Žarko and Milica, who has arrived from Belgrade, inspect her grandmother's garden. They stop to watch a cat slink through high grass. They walk across a steep pasture. Chickens scurry out of their way. Olga sits with her mother and the rest of us at a garden table heavy with food. A couple of neighbors come by and the women talk about the refugees crowding Peručac, Serbs driven from their towns and villages on the Bosnian side of the Drina.

They're a lazy bunch. They refuse to get jobs . . . . While we work, they stand around town, all dressed up . . . .

Across the river, the steep hills are thick with trees. Looted and burned houses, roofless, dot clearings. Muslim dwellings. Former dwellings.

. . . or get their hair done . . . . They get food and other things from humanitarian organizations then sell them to us in the market.

A helicopter rises from behind the hills, hovers. I think of the fuel it is burning. Another helicopter arrives, swings around, hovers. Maneuvering precisely, the hunters zigzag their way up the river, toward the dam.

Hunters?

Back in Bajina Bašta. In the fading twilight, the five of us make our uncertain way to Slobodan Rogić's house. "I know right where we are," Zlatko keeps telling us. "Don't worry. I know right where we are." And, it turns out, he eventually finds the house.

It's just an average Serbian house, Slobodan says proudly of the large two-story house surrounded by an orchard and garden.

"Scott," Slobodan says, "I want you to meet a friend of mine." I shake hands with a slightly built man wearing a thin mustache. He bows and hands me a shiny white bus-company sack: Spremić Rade, Belegija Prevoz.

Inside is my lost notebook.

I hug Slobodan. I hug the man who handed me the bag. I repeat my thanks, *hvala*, again and again. I hug the bag. I smile like an idiot. I wish I knew more than ten words of Serbo-Croatian.

Slobodan explains that he called this man, a bus owner, who called the man who owns the bus company whose bus took us to Šabac, who located the book and shipped it by bus to Bajina Bašta.

Small-town ties. Small-town hospitality. A gift beyond my comprehension.

Slobodan introduces us to a stately man in his sixties, the author, Slobodan says, of a book about monasteries on Mt. Athos in Greece. He has brought a copy of the book for Peter.

Slobodan's wife lays out a beautiful platter of smoked trout, a platter of fried trout, a bowl of potatoes, a plate of bread, and a bottle of Macedonian white wine. Despite requests for her to stay, she retires for the night, leaving eight men around the table.

We attack the trout. I admire the fine bald heads of all three of the men from Bajina Bašta. Zlatko too is a member of this tribe.

A life-sized painting of a provocatively arranged nude woman hangs in the living room. On the adjoining wall hangs an equally large work of art, a highly stylized orthodox icon of a gold-leafed Jesus Christ.

For nearly an hour our conversation is light, a meandering exchange slowed and flavored by Žarko's and Zlatko's translations. We spend fifteen minutes, for example, trying to correctly translate an obscene and labyrinthine Serbian curse that moves from the law of gravity to one's own mother.

Finally someone brings up the war.

Although I'm not religious, says the stately author, although I don't believe in God, nor, however, am I an atheist, but having said that, I think God has given the Serbs more than they can bear.

Slobodan expounds on the impossibility of the Serbs ever expiating their perceived guilt in world consciousness: It's like the rabbit, he says, that tries to prove it's not a donkey by fucking until its balls wear out, at which point it can no longer prove it is no donkey.

"We need better leaders," the bus owner ventures. "Like who?" Žarko asks. "Like Václav Havel, the bus owner suggests." "No!" interjects the stately author. "Havel is gay." "Which means nothing," Slobodan says.

Slobodan leans toward me and asks if I know what "skot" means in Serbo-Croatian. "No," I say. "It means the runt of the litter, beast, or vermin."

"What does Slobodan mean?" I ask him.

"Free, independent, free man. It's a name given to many Serb babies during World War II, a defiant response to the Nazis."

"Lucky you," I answer. "My American parents simply didn't pay attention. But your name isn't faring so well these days either."

"Serbs are weary of American moralizing," Slobodan opines. "America has its own history. Putting Indians on reservations was a kind of ethnic cleansing, after all."

"America as a moral authority is a bad joke," Peter says. "A country with a death penalty that insists on its moral superiority! Please."

The expert on monasteries introduces a long and winding speech by means of a legitimating biography: "I am not religious, but neither do I deny God. I was in Buchenwald for eight months. My father was a Partisan who died in the war. My brother was a Partisan who died in the war. I was a Partisan in the war."

The evening wears on. There are stories about refugees, about Muslims in a prison camp, about a camp guard who had been Slobodan's pupil, about shelling from across the river, about Muslim aggression, about Serbian stupidity.

"Why," Peter asks, "did the Serbs lob artillery shells into Sarajevo, creating the damning images that turned world opinion against them?"

Peter has a tiny yellow Langenscheid's dictionary he pulls out of a jacket pocket now and then. It claims to be "Kroatisch-Deutsch/Deutsch-Kroatisch." With a pen he has added "Serbisch-" to the mix.

✑ Bajina Bašta, 28 May 1998

We've had a hearty breakfast in Dušanka's garden and are packing for a two-day hike on the Tara Mountain.

Peter carries the sturdy canvas pack used by one of the characters in his film *Absence*. He wears an old pair of high-topped leather shoes I imagine to be the same shoes featured in his story "The Shoeshiner of Split":

> In the following weeks, however, he wore the shoes in the snow of Macedonia, in the leafy dust of the mountains of Peloponnesos, in the yellow and gray sand of the Libyan and Arabic desert. And even months later, one day in Japan, it was enough to rub the leather with a cloth and the original shine from the promenade in Split reappeared, undamaged.[34]

Žarko has a good nylon daypack and a pair of generic white athletic shoes. Zlatko, Thomas, and I carry our things in high-fashion vinyl shopping bags—black-and-white, lemon-yellow, and pink bags supplied at the last minute by Olga. Zlatko and Thomas wear city shoes, black-leather low-topped shoes that are the antitheses of my heavy leather hiking boots.

What to note about the 35-kilometer hike? The wildflowers. The changing views of the Drina from ever-higher vantage points along the switchbacking road. The blind-worms copulating blindly on the roadside. The sunlit meadow where we lie in the grass to rest our weary feet and legs. The rare Serbian spruce Peter points out. The ski-resort inn where we re-hydrate. The serpentine logging roads. Peter's ongoing search for mushrooms, which he stuffs into a compartment of Žarko's pack. The desultory conversations. Our growing weariness. Žarko's incipient and then pronounced limp. The moment late in the day when Peter picks up the pace and Thomas and I fight to match his strides while the other two fall back. The huge Tara Mountain conference and sports center swarming with sweat-suited volunteer firefighters gathered for a training session. The little roadside restaurant where the owner has been waiting for us.

While we eat a hearty dinner that includes the mushrooms Peter has picked, the restaurant owner tells us about the years he spent playing an accordion in Germany. After his back gave out, he says, he tried racing cars and finally came back to the Tara Mountain.

Sometime before midnight the racing restaurateur proves his

---

[34] In Peter Handke, *Once Again for Thucydides*, tr. Tess Lewis (New York: New Directions, 1998), 18.

prowess by speeding us up a winding road, leaving his slow head-lights hanging in the trees at every tight corner, accelerating and braking, screeching and honking, torqueing and turning to pull up abruptly at an A-frame cabin where we spend the night.

✏ KREMNA, 29 MAY 1998

Sleepy Kremna, maybe fifteen kilometers east of the Tara Mountain. After the morning's march we sit relaxed in front of a bus-stop restaurant. Olga and Slobodan arrived early with Zlatko's car and have a story to tell.

While waiting for us to arrive, Olga went to help a baby bird that had fallen from its nest. She bent to pick it up and was attacked by the mother bird. She points to a nasty scratch on her cheek.

We eat and drink and talk and order another bottle of wine. An occasional bus provides the only structure to our aimlessness.

Down the street stands a beefy blue truck, a muscular winch bolted to its front. Unmatched knobby tires give the truck clearance enough for a tree stump. Three burly uniformed men stand next to the truck. Forest rangers, probably, but they feel threatening to me, a foreigner, within 25 kilometers of a recent war zone.

Passengers return to a bus parked in front of the restaurant. The last passenger climbs on and the bus rolls down the street. From the side door of the restaurant leading to the restrooms flies a middle-aged woman. She chases the bus down the street, arms flailing. The bus turns a corner. She follows, gesturing silently like an actor in an old movie.

Beside their truck, the uniformed men break into grins. They look at us. We are grinning too.

✏ VIŠEGRAD, REPUBLIKA SRPSKA

"Was denkt in dir?" Peter asks.

"What?" I ask, unable to hear him over the noise of Milka and her band.

"What is thinking in you?"

"Sorrow," I answer.

For two months in 1992, there was intense fighting here. Marauding Muslims. Marauding Serbs.

And now the town is devoid of Muslims.

Since we crossed the border into the Republika Srpska, I have been imagining Muslims and Serbs lying in bed those 60 nights. Worrying, as they lay there, about possible futures. About a sudden end to possible futures.

Tonight, we sit at a long linen-covered table in the dining room of a large resort hotel tucked back into the forested hills above the town. Guests of the Mayor of Višegrad.

Aleksandar Savić is an outgoing young man, a good mayor, I think. He's dressed in a striped shirt, a bright tie, dark brown slacks, and a double-breasted black blazer crossed vertically and horizontally by white stripes. Occasionally he raises his right arm, cocks his hand, holds it momentarily behind his head, strokes his slick dark hair. The gesture of a beautiful woman.

"Of the 20,000 inhabitants of Višegrad," he says, 2,500 are refugees. 97 percent of them say they want to remain in Višegrad. 1 percent want to go home. 1 percent want to go to Serbia. And 1 percent want to leave Yugoslavia altogether."

Yes, there is high unemployment. The town's factories have shut down.

There are, of course, no tourists. The hotel is a cavernous home to men convalescing from the war.

The mayor's driver, a large and gentle man, is from Goražde, now a Muslim enclave. He left there in 1992, he says, and hasn't been back, although it's only 30 kilometers up the Drina. He admits to having left a girlfriend there. Peter asks if he wouldn't like us to contact her for him when we drive through. "No," he says, "No thank you. It is impossible."

A young man limps painfully into the dining room, accompanied by two women, one his girlfriend perhaps, or sister, the other old enough to be his mother. They take a table. They talk. They drink a bottle of wine. They sit silently. The young man twirls his box of cigarettes between the table and his finger.

Milka, backed by an accordion, a keyboard, and drums (was there a drummer?), is a sultry lounge singer with a Serbian repertoire, traditional sad love songs sung in a middle-eastern quaver. Her black-stockinged legs under a very brief skirt draw Žarko's and my attention until Peter points out that our mouths are open and couldn't we be more discreet? When she approaches our table and sings into Peter's ear while stroking his neck we exact revenge by remarking on his adolescent smile. We all redeem ourselves by tipping her handsomely. And remark on how her long legs and double-sized head make her tiny body into an afterthought.

"She has lost 50 kilos in the past six weeks," the mayor says.

The mayor describes the first local casualty in the war: a 24-year-old, fighting with a small group, hit by a "dumdum" that took off his shoulder. His father and a priest buried him there in the forest with some branches and leaves over his face. A monument now marks the grave. A holy place.

"I was recently in Bulgaria," the Mayor says, "to accept a literary prize for the Bosnian Serb leader and poet Radovan Karadžić. Karadžić couldn't leave the Republika Srpska because he is currently under indictment for war crimes, so he asked me to represent him. In my acceptance speech, I referred to him as President Karadžić. Later, I was summoned before a Norwegian judge and asked about the reference, illegal now that Karadžić is banned from holding office. I had thought about it, and had an answer ready: 'The Americans,' I told the judge, 'refer to Richard Nixon as President Nixon, even after he is no longer president. That's what I was doing.' "

"And how did the judge react?"

"He let me go."

Someone asks about Višegrad during the war.

"The town," the mayor explains, "was two-thirds Muslim before the war. In 1992, the Muslims chased the Serbs out of the city. The Serbs retook the city through the grace of the Muslim Murad Šabanović who captured the hydroelectric dam above the city and threatened to blow it up. The Muslim population fled the threat of flooding. The Yugoslav army arrived and dislodged the crazy terrorist. And the Serbs moved back in."

While the Mayor talks, a small man with a dark beard pushes past a concerned waiter to crutch his way toward our table. He breaks into the conversation and with a sweaty palm shakes each of our hands. He pulls two photographs out of a coat pocket.

The waiter signals to Milka. She skips toward our table, cordless microphone in hand, armed with a vigorous Serbian song.

The small man holds out two worn photos. The first is a glossy celebrity shot of Radovan Karadžić. The second is a snapshot the small man identifies as his brother, killed in the war: "My brother, killed in the war. My brother."

Milka belts out the song "Oh Višegrad!" The waiter takes a hesitant step toward our table. The convalescing soldier puts away his photos and retreats slowly on his crutches. Milka hits three quick high notes, kicks up a shapely heel, and dances away.

Well after midnight, we disperse to the rooms the Mayor has reserved for us in this hall of echoes.

✍ VIŠEGRAD, 30 MAY 1998

The only other guests at breakfast this morning were well-dressed French speakers. Thomas spoke with them and found it was the entourage of French General Jean Cot, for a time the controversial commander of UN forces in Bosnia. He was collecting material for a book on the war. "His translator," Thomas says, "was the second wife of Danilo Kiš, one of Yugoslavia's best contemporary writers."

Back in Višegrad, Žarko and I walk around town. Tomato and pepper seedlings are on sale in an outdoor market, the dark earth around their roots wrapped in damp paper. A wedding procession sweeps past, flowers clamped under windshield wipers. Horns blare. Serbian flags flutter from radio antennae.

I remember my modest wedding, remember the hope for the future we shared. What was the defining moment in the end of that hope? There were twenty-five years of defining moments, any of which might have tended in another direction.

Affixed high on the wall of a house, maybe 12 feet up, is a brass historical marker: "Hochwasser vom 10. Nov 1896." This I can translate: High-water mark on November 10, 1896. The German-language sign marks a powerful flood, and a hundred years later it stands as a reminder of the Austrian occupation.

Last night, I read a passage from Ivo Andrić's Nobel-Prize winning novel *The Bridge Over the Drina* in which a Muslim town leader refuses a Turkish request to fight against the approaching Austrians. The exasperated Turk has his fellow Muslim nailed by the ear to the Višegrad bridge. From his awkward and painful position, he can read an Austrian proclamation posted on the bridge:

People of Bosnia and Herzegovina!

The Army of the Emperor of Austria and King of Hungary has crossed the frontier of your country. It does not come as an enemy to take the land by force. It comes as a friend to put an end to the disorders which for years past have disturbed not only Bosnia and Herzegovina but also the frontier districts of Austria-Hungary.

The Turks leave. The Austrians arrive. An Austrian Red Cross orderly pulls the nail out of the Muslim's ear. The Muslim, as wounded in spirit as in body, walks through town:

> Beside him walked some soldiers. Amongst them he saw that fat, good-natured, mocking face of the man with a red cross on his arm who had taken out the nail. Still smiling, the soldier pointed to his bandage and asked him something in an incomprehensible language. Alihodja thought that he was offering to help him and at once stiffened and said sullenly:
>
> 'I can myself . . . I need no one's help.'
>
> And with a livelier and more determined step he made his way home.[35]

Žarko guides me down six steps into a half-dark room fronting directly on a busy street. "You need to try a *burek*," he says. We order, and a woman cooks and serves us eggs and cheese in dough that is flaky and greasy at the same time. "It's not very good," Žarko says. "A typical *burek*."

At the hotel, we are met by the Mayor, none the worse, it seems, for the late night. He has some things he'd like us to see.

We drive to a construction site on a hill overlooking the Drina River. Three stories high, typical orange-brick construction. A line of women and men unload a truck, passing orange tiles from hand to hand in a long chain. On the high roof, men are interlocking the tiles in undulating rows. A small evergreen tree, a ragged red, blue, and white Serbian flag, and an improvised rack from which hang three bottles of brandy and three new plastic-wrapped shirts adorn the rooftop. I'm not sure what the shirts represent, but from the boisterous singing, it's clear what the brandy is for.

"These are refugees from Sarajevo," the Mayor says. "They have formed an organization and with a government grant of land, tools, and materials are building 158 apartments here." He introduces us to the president of the refugee group, a thin man, maybe 70 years old, bright-eyed and erect, who speaks an eager English as he shows us around.

"Mr. Handke," he says, "you are a writer. And I too am a writer. I

---

[35] Andrić, *The Bridge Over the Drina*, 121–123.

write children's books. We are colleagues. You are big and I am small. But we are colleagues."

Peter introduces Žarko and me as his Serbian and American translators. The president has eyes only for Peter.

We meet the young architect. She and her husband, she says, have moved into an abandoned Muslim house. Through third parties they are trying to exchange their house in Sarajevo for the one in Više-grad.

TV cameras arrive and Peter joins the chain to pass a few roof tiles for Serbian television. Then it's time for lunch.

Most of the workers sit on the floor of a large shaded room. The rest of us are seated at a long table in the glaring sun. We share cold cuts and tomatoes and plum brandy.

"This is the Austrian writer Peter Handke," the President announces. "He has come to visit our building. We will now hear words of wisdom from this great man. Mr. Handke, would you please honor us with words to remember on this proud occasion?"

Peter stands and raises his cup of brandy. He looks at the President. He looks back into the shaded room where the workers are seated. He turns back to the President. He speaks words to remember: "Jebi ga."

Fuck it.

The surprised workers raise a boisterous cheer. Peter grins and raises his cup again.

The afternoon slips by like the Drina River, whose green waters we overlook from a vine-covered restaurant terrace—Žarko, Zlatko, Thomas, Peter, the Mayor, the Višegrad city planner, and the Mayor's driver.

The table is loaded with baskets of bread, soft Kajmak cheese, tomato-and-onion salad (*Srpska salat*), platters of meat with spicy little civapcici, pork chops, veal, chunks of lamb on spits. Bottles of white and red wine. Shot glasses of rakija. Mineral water in bottles bearing the portrait of Karadjordje—the Serbian hero named Black George by the Turks.

Light rain spots the river.

Two white OSCE vehicles stand in front of the restaurant. Six representatives of the Organization for Security and Cooperation in Europe are having lunch at the other large table on the terrace. Their common and loud language is English. The two women speak with French and Spanish accents. One of the men has a Hungarian, another a German accent. And the remaining two men, one sporting a ridiculously small red bow tie, speak with high-pitched buzz saw American accents. There's something about these two Americans, an overbearing, know-it-all smugness, a brazen self-righteousness, an unreflective sense of entitlement, that makes me want to strangle them. To apply for a different passport. To learn a different language. Peter's face suggests something well beyond strangling.

Finally, the English speaking functionaries leave their table and enter the small hotel adjacent to the terrace restaurant. The Mayor's driver gestures to the Mayor and leaves the terrace. The city planner describes rebuilding efforts since the war.

Zlatko scans the menu and recommends that I order tufahia for dessert. When he says the Turkish word, it sounds suspiciously like "to fuck you" in English. Zlatko assures me it's not a joke. He describes tufahia as a baked apple with whipped cream. Tufahia, I tell the waiter, itching to add por favore or bitte or s'il vous plait, anything that would make it more than an order. But I'm an idiot in this language. He makes a note and leaves.

We don't call this dish by its Muslim name anymore, the city planner tells Zlatko and me, admonishing us with his index finger. We call it "Srpska jabuka," a Serbian apple.

On the bank of the Drina a magpie swoops down from one tree and up into another. Native Americans called magpies black-and-white longtails. Or "the bird that eats shit." European-Americans called them magpies.

The Mayor's driver returns with the news that three Serb soldiers have just been killed in Kosovo. A drive-by shooting. The Kosovar Albanians are trying to provoke a war, the Mayor says. The city planner adds that Albanians have been waging a demographic war on the Serbs in Kosovo: They have eight or nine children, he says.

I go into the hotel to use the restroom and to escape the city planner. The OSCE people are sitting around a table in a room off the hall, a laptop computer open in front of each of them. Flipcharts and flowcharts and posters graph the RE-REGISTRATION PROCESS— VIŠEGRAD CITY ELECTION.

Outside, I report on what I have seen.

We'll go in one by one to use the toilet, Žarko tells the Mayor. We'll leave bribes (*baksheesh*) to help with your re-election.

A long-legged man strolls by, his hips and legs preceding his upper body *á la* Charlie Chaplin. He carries a thick-handled hoe. Cotton drifts through the warm air. Not from the cottonwood trees I know at home (*Populus fremonti*, called *alamo* in Spanish), but from closely related poplars.

Most of what I have witnessed on this trip is somehow related to things I know at home. Still, two nights from now, when I hear the first nightingale song in my 49 years, I won't need anyone to explain what I'm hearing.

⟫ Goražde

Up the Drina River, past the hydroelectric dam and the reservoir, Zlatko pilots his Peugot through a dozen tunnels. A railroad track with its own network of tunnels snakes along the opposite side of the river. In ten minutes we reach Muslim-held territory. There are, contrary to my expectation, no borders to cross. "Since the Dayton Accord," explains Thomas, "this is one country."

Border or no border, the tension in our little car rises as the familiar ruins begin to appear, Serb houses this time. We have been welcome in the Republika Srpska—two Serbs, the author of *Justice for Serbia*, two translators of that text, and the journalist who demonstrated that the ITN photos of the concentration camp at Trnopolje were a fiction. The welcome wouldn't be as warm here.

"Here" is a town stretched along both banks of the river. Fierce fighting with machine guns and artillery has marked, has scarred the once prosperous face of Goražde. Between the highway and the river rises the brilliant white tower and five domes of a new mosque. Goražde was taken by the Serbs and retaken by the Muslims. It is connected now by a thin corridor to the Muslim-held area around Sarajevo.

In less than five minutes, we have passed through the town. We'll come back this way tomorrow.

⟫ Foča, 31 May 1998

I've been reading about these towns along the Drina in Misha Glenny's *The Fall of Yugoslavia*:

The Serbs stormed the urban centres of eastern and then southern Bosnia . . . . Bratunac, Srebrenica, Višegrad and Foča all followed suit quickly although in Višegrad the army's path was stopped by the extraordinary Murad Šabanović, a desperate Moslem fighter, who took control of the hydro-electric dam on the Drina above Višegrad and threatened to blow the installation sky high, a move which would have had incalculable consequences for the entire region. Dramatic negotiations over the airwaves of Radio Sarajevo included Šabanović telling the chief of the JNA in Bosnia, General Milutin Kukanjac, to go fuck himself . . . .

Soon after Foča was taken by the Serbs, Andrej Gustinčić of Reuters succeeded in entering the town after a hair-raising journey through the barricades:

Gangs of gun-toting Serbs rule Foča, turning the once quiet Bosnian town into a nightmare landscape of shattered streets and burning houses . . . . The Moslems, who made up half of the town's population of 10,000 people, have fled or are in jail. Many of their houses have been destroyed or are in flames . . . . The Serbs say that despite the damage, only seven or eight of their own men and about twenty Moslems were killed in the fighting which began on 8 April. They say the Moslems began it. A feverish distrust of all that is not Serbian and a conviction that they have narrowly escaped genocide at the hand of Islamic fundamentalist has gripped Foča's Serbs.[36]

We spent the night in the Hotel Zelengora, a high-rise tourist hotel built by the Tito government, populated at the moment largely by refugees. Many of them are children.

A dark lobby, dark stairs, and halls. There is permanent but not wholesale leaking into my toilet, and water drips but doesn't flow from three sources in the sink and shower pipes. The mirror still has several places near the center that reflect an image. The room's thin green unpadded nylon carpet sports a perfectly melted iron imprint near the window. The two chairs once had upholstered arms. Light fixtures have disappeared, leaving holes in the walls.

I'm glad to have a room.

Last night, Zlatko and I waited in front of the hotel for the others to appear for dinner. On the steps of the hotel stood a pack of boys

---

[36] Misha Glenny, *The Fall of Yugoslavia* (New York: Penguin, 1996), 169.

ranging from ten or eleven to maybe thirteen years old. Their attention was fixed on the girls and young women walking past. "Hey sister," one of them called to an especially beautiful woman, "how about an hour for me?" His friends laughed at his bravado. She chortled at the absurdity.

Foča is an ugly town in a beautiful setting. What was it that inspired socialist architects to construct so many identically shoddy boxes? Twenty-six kilometers upstream, the Tara and Komarnica rivers flow out of the mountains of Montenegro to join and become the Drina River that flows swiftly between Foča's steep hills.

In the morning sun, we sit in front of a café for breakfast. Around us sit several dozen citizens of the town drinking Sunday-morning coffee. One table is occupied by four German soldiers. An SFOR jeep flying a French flag drives past. Two women in US uniforms stroll by. A couple of SFOR armored personnel carriers roll up the road.

After breakfast, I climb steps to find the bricks of what was once a mosque, still topped by a copper-covered dome but with holes gaping where the large doors had hung. The ruin is choked with refuse and blackened by smoke.

I flee down a cobblestone street, past shops with clever wooden shelves that fold out from the outer walls for displays, past an open-air market doing a brisk business this morning. The sun is bright. I find a concrete bench. I sit.

A girl on rollerblades pushes her way to a bakery window and leaves with a loaf of freshly baked bread.

A small lizard hunts along the edge of a sunny concrete slab.

Two men walk past in nylon soccer shorts and jerseys and striped soccer boots.

Young parents follow a little boy pedaling a tiny tricycle and wearing an abbreviated baseball cap. His older brother clutches a soccer ball between fat arms.

Dressed in heels and a red dress, a woman carries roses wrapped in crinkly plastic.

A young mother pushes a stroller up the hill on one side of the square, leaning into the task, her bare calves beautifully muscled.

Fifteen men, silver-haired all, most in white shirts and suit coats, stand and converse in the shade of linden trees. They shake cigarettes out of packs labeled Lucky Strike, Lord, Marlboro, Partner.

Dressed in black, a young woman with brilliantly hennaed hair turns heads all around.

A young soldier wearing blue-grey fatigues ambles past with three friends who wear no particular uniform.

A grey-haired man, suit coat slung over his shoulders, steps off the street and greets the men under the lindens.

Carrying a newspaper and a denim jacket, a bearded young man saunters up the street alone.

Behind him a woman with a tray of several dozen eggs.

Across the square stands the café Palma. Bright red canopy and red plastic chairs.

Two boys licking ice-cream bars.

A man in a sweat suit passes, leading a taut-skinned tan dog with cropped ears and a blunt nose. Its weight balances mostly over its front legs. Between the small back legs are packed a potent pair of shiny balls.

A soldier in green-brown fatigues strolls by with a pregnant woman in a red blouse, both of them eating ice cream.

Two soldiers in blue-grey uniforms, carrying radios and pistols. Their patches say MILICIJA.

A white-washed wall across the street is pocked with bullet holes.

A big blond woman strides up the hill with three bottles of cooking oil and a cabbage.

Across the way is a taxi stand. A driver works on the front door of his vehicle. He slams it. Opens it. Works the latch with a screwdriver. Slams the door. Opens it. Adjusts something. Slams it. Opens the door.

We spend most of the afternoon in Brod, just outside Foča.

Cross the bridge, says the woman in high rubber boots. There will be a sawmill on the left and on the right, a kiosk. They live right next to the kiosk.

"They" are the girlfriend of Novislav Djajic and her mother.

Novislav Djajic is a 34-year-old man from this area who fought briefly in 1992 with Bosnian Serb forces. He and several others were escorting fifteen Muslim prisoners to Foča when two militia soldiers drove up, furious because three Serbs had just been killed by a mine. They opened fire on the prisoners. According to testimony by the single prisoner to survive, Mr. Djajic did nothing to stop the shooting.

In 1993, Djajic moved to Munich, where he had relatives. In 1996 he was arrested in Munich and was subsequently tried and convicted as an "accomplice to murder." He is currently serving a five-year sentence.

We are here because of Mr. Djajic's correspondence with Peter, most notably a letter written on the back of a copy of the police order to arrest him. After stating that Djajic has been notified, the order reads: "Nehmen Sie den Ausländer fest"—Arrest the foreigner.

Arrest the foreigner?

Justice from a bureaucracy that can produce such a sentence?

Misha Glenny (*The Fall of Yugoslavia*) and others have speculated that there would have been no war had Germany not rushed to recognize Slovenia and Croatia as independent states.

At breakfast we asked the waiter if he knew Mr. Djajic.

"Of course," he said. "I know him. He is a gentle man, a little strange. If you went up to him in the pub and hit him in the head he would just get up and leave."

In the kiosk, a tiny building with a window whose sill is the counter, sit two men in their late teens or early twenties and a woman of about the same age. Zlatko explains who we are looking for and they point to the apartment building across a dirt driveway. Zlatko buys them a round of brandy. One of the men shows Zlatko a revolver from behind the window and laughs: "Here, this can be your calling card."

A woman in her early twenties greets us cautiously. Zlatko explains to her and then to her mother that Peter has a letter from Novislav Djajic. Peter shows them the letter and they invite us in. We sit in a combination kitchen and living room. An oven, sink, and cupboards line one wall across from a couch and chair and coffee table.

The apartment is hot from bread just out of the oven. Thomas sits with a long silver coffee grinder between his legs and grinds coffee Peter has brought as a gift. He begins to sweat. I take my turn with the grinder. The mother boils Turkish coffee in a small metal container.

Do they still call it Turkish coffee?

The mother serves coffee in tiny cups. The daughter hands us small glasses of pear brandy.

Peter asks about Novislav Djajic. The women answer alternately.

He was an unwilling participant in the war. He was right here in this apartment just an hour before the incident on the bridge. His gun was there on the couch. He didn't want to go. They came and made him go with them. He never wanted to hurt anyone.

"What was it like when the NATO bombers came?" Peter asks.

They tried to bomb the bridge. But they missed. The bombs were too close so we ran up onto the mountain. We grabbed a blanket and ran. For seven days and nights we crouched in the forest while the jets were bombing. It was October and it rained the whole week. The bombs were made out of uranium. People here are dying of cancer. Two women just down the road.

"Do you hate the Germans?"

"No."

"What do you think of Muslims?"

"They were good neighbors."

The mother brings out a Polaroid snapshot of a lanky young man sprawled back on the couch we are sitting on, a shy smile on his face.

People called him a traitor here because he didn't want to keep fighting the war and left to go to Germany.

Peter teases the young woman about what will happen when her boyfriend returns. She turns her head and covers her smiling mouth with a hand, her teeth victims of the wartime breakdown in health services.

And then we are outside, saying good-byes. The mother kisses Peter three times and hands him a bottle of her pear brandy and a loaf of warm bread.

In the late afternoon we sit on the terrace of a restaurant overlooking the Drina River, a hundred meters downstream from a modern bridge. What was once a modern bridge. It now juts out from the highway, plunges at an abrupt angle down to the river, and then crosses in a tangle of concrete and steel.

Heavy rain unsettles the surface of the river. A woman under an umbrella follows a little herd of sheep grazing on the steep slope between the highway and the river. A younger woman appears, swaps a rain cape for the umbrella, and departs.

A man walks along the highway, turns at the bridge and climbs athletically down the hanging structure, then picks his way across the wreckage and scrambles up the steep bank to enter the town of Foča.

Besides the five of us, the only other guests at the restaurant are four men at the next table. They are working on a second bottle of wine. Zlatko leans back and strikes up a conversation. He points at Thomas and I hear him say *nemački*, German. He points at me and says *Amerikanski*.

A bald-headed man points at me, then at the ruined bridge. In the torrent of angry words that follow I recognize only *civilizacija* and *demokratija*.

A black-bearded man leaves the other table and joins us. Several Dinar coins drop from his lap onto the floor. I pick them up and hand them to him. He throws them back onto the floor.

"Serbs," he says in Žarko's translation, "leave fallen money for the poor."

"Read the revelations of John," he tells us. "You can know the end from the beginning."

"Did you go to church this morning?" Peter asks him.

"No," he answers, "I am a medical doctor. I was on duty until five a.m. I don't need a church to practice my religion."

"It would do you good," Peter says, "to spend an hour every week being bored in a formal church service."

"I am the mayor of my town," he replies. "I don't have time to be bored. Who are you? What are you doing here?"

Zlatko answers by explaining first that Thomas is the Thomas Deichmann who proved that the ITN footage of the purported Serbian "death camp" at Trnopolje was a deliberate fiction of the camera, that the cameraman, not the emaciated refugees, had been standing inside the barbed-wire enclosure.

The doctor stands up, pulls Thomas to his feet, and kisses him three times. "Thank you," he says, "thank you from all Serbs." He asks Zlatko to take a photo of the two of them together.

Peter is next, and this once, even the author of *Justice for Serbia* takes second billing. "Thank you as well, Mr. Handke," the man says. "You are an Austrian writer. I know that. But remember this: History will forget the Austrians. The Serbs will live in history forever."

"Do you speak English, German, or French?" Peter asks him, looking for a way to converse that doesn't require Zlatko's translation. "No. I speak Serbian," the man asserts. "I speak only Serbian. We will speak only Serbian and soon the entire world will speak Serbian."

I'm introduced as the American and as Peter's translator. Like Thomas, I am pulled to my feet. But not for kisses.

"You are not an American," he says. "What are you?"

"An American," I say.

"No, where did your people come from? From Germany? "

"England."

"There we have it," he says. "You are English. There are no Americans."

He grips my shoulder in a strong hand and points to the bridge. "Who bombed this bridge? Look at that bridge, and tell me who bombed it!"

"We did," I say, slapping my chest. We did. The Americans did. We bombed that bridge. For democracy and civilization!

Driving out of town, clattering over a partially blocked smaller bridge, I gaze out the window and curse the language that speaks me.

✏ GORAŽDE, 31 MAY 1998

Late afternoon. Where the bridge over the Drina meets the main highway, we sit in front of a cafe and drink "chai," which Zlatko pronounces with a careful and delicate Muslim lilt.

"No reason to attract attention," he says.

Across the street is an apartment complex. With laundry hanging to dry in every window and on every balcony, the building looks like a ratty overstuffed couch. A white truck stands in front of the building: UNHCR—United Nations High Commander for Refugees. Stacks of firewood rise high in the courtyard.

Three children run past the café. Two of the boys wear tennis shoes. The third runs with a practiced shuffle in the adult shoes he wears, their backs flattened like slippers. He looks up and smiles at us before following his friends down the riverbank.

A woman with a wheelbarrow full of kindling shoves pieces of wood into a basement window.

The main street of Goražde is called Marshal Tito Street.

"Good for them," Žarko says. It's a crime that most Serbian towns have renamed their streets. You can't just wipe out 40 years of your history.

✏ VIŠEGRAD

We'll spend the night in the Hotel Višegrad on the bank of the Drina River. From the second-floor landing, I can see a long roof covered by bright orange plastic. UNHCR is stenciled on it every few meters.

Up the hill from the hotel, among houses and gardens, stands a small white Serbian Orthodox church, its copper-clad onion dome reminiscent of Austrian architecture. (It *is* Austrian architecture.) Next to it is a "Serbian Soldiers' Cemetery." Polished black stones stand in rows. A half-circle of varnished beehives, numbered 1-9, stands in the adjoining pasture.

The sound of a whetstone on a scythe blade.

The gravestones, each marked "Serbian Soldier," reveal a chronology of violence:

1959-1994
1969-1992
1968-1992
1967-1992
1965-1992
1949-1992
1967-1992
1937-1994
1965-1992
1967-1992
1941-1992
1945-1992
1972-1993
1972-1993
1973-1993

There are nearly 100 graves. One of every 200 citizens of Višegrad. One of every 100 Serbs of Višegrad. Where are the Muslims buried?

Each stone bears an image of the deceased. One young man stands in a suit and plays an accordion. Another, wearing dark glasses, sits spread-eagled on a stone. The man born in 1949, my birth year, wears a military sweater, a sheepskin hat, camo pants, a web belt holding a handgun and grenades, a vest with a dozen pockets, and boots. A heavy metal cross hangs from a chain around his neck.

Most of the graves have a glass of brandy and a cup of coffee next to the stone.

A young man wearing a sleeveless t-shirt enters the cemetery, walks to a grave, kisses the image on the stone, lights a candle, places it in a tin housing, crosses himself, and leaves the cemetery.

I walk back down to the river. Sorrowful for the dead men (and two women). Angry at the nationalist spectacle of the Serbian Soldier.

◷ VIŠEGRAD, 1 JUNE 1998 // 1:30 AM

I'm sitting in my room in the Hotel Višegrad, looking out onto the Drina and its Turkish bridge, still lit by floodlamps. The bridge's eleven arches are reflected in the silky black river. A nightingale calls from across the river. I've never heard a nightingale; but it can be nothing else. Unmistakable. It calls again, and then again. It's indescribably romantic. I'm alone in my room.

From the terrace below, there is an occasional burst of laughter from Peter, Zlatko, Thomas, and Žarko, who are still talking with the two women from the OSCE, the younger one from Spain, the older from France. We argued for hours about the role of organizations like theirs in Yugoslavia. At one point, I hauled out *The Bridge on the Drina* and read the passage about the Muslim's angry self-reliance after an Austrian pulled the nail holding his ear to the bridge.

"So you don't think the Austrian should have pulled out the nail?" asked the soft-spoken woman from Spain.

"I don't think the Austrians should have been outside of Austria in the first place," I answered, happy to be conversing in my native tongue.

"How long have you been in Yugoslavia?" Peter asked the French woman.

"For a year-and-a-half," she answered.

"Do you speak Serbo-Croatian?" Peter asked.

"No," she answered. "I've been too busy to learn. The first town I was in was under attack for nine months. I worked through an interpreter."

"You are here to tell the people how to run their country and you don't understand their language!" Peter exclaimed. "You can't bother to learn their language?"

"Who are you?" the woman asked. "What are you doing here? What gives you the moral right to judge what I'm doing?"

"We're here as tourists," Peter answered. "We order food and stay in hotels and help the local economy. But mainly we don't tell them what they ought to do."

"You're being silly," the woman said. "Who are you really?"

"Just visitors," Peter said. "You should go home."

"I'm doing important work here," the woman countered.

"Go home," Peter said.

"Fuck you," the woman said.

"Go home."

"Fuck you."

The night air had chilled, and the French woman was shivering. Peter took his coat from the back of his chair and draped it around her shoulders. "There," he said, "that will help."

"Fuck you," she said, and pulled the coat around herself.

◯ BELGRADE, 3 JUNE 1999

My brother John's birthday. He would have been 47 today.

Peter and Zlatko and I sit at a table in front of the Hotel Moskva. Silence for the most part. A few desultory comments. The theater director Mladen Materić joins us. Peter and Zlatko rise. It's time for Peter to get a cab to the airport, for Zlatko to return to his parents' farm in Porodin for a few days. Hugs all around. And then they are gone.

Mladen and I sit and talk.

Basketball is our first topic. The Utah Jazz, naturally. Krešimir Čosić the great Yugoslav star who played for Brigham Young University where I was a student and then returned to coach the Yugoslav national team. And Mladen's son who is currently playing for the University of Alabama Birmingham.

He is interested in my views on Peter's play, *The Hour We Knew Nothing of One Another*, which he'll produce in Žarko's translation. "What about the war?" I ask him.

"The Serbs," Mladen says, "are affected by a laziness that can be a moral force. The Croatians organized celebrities, artists, and sports heroes to support their new state. Tudjman had two basketball stars by his side when he planted the Croatian flag in Knin. But the Serbs, for whatever reason, organized nothing. That is good in principle, but wasn't helpful in shaping world opinion."

Mladen pulls a couple of big books from a bag. He shows me photos of Bogomil gravestones and talks about that Bosnian place where religions, cultures, languages intersect, about the cultural fault lines that brought the Bogomils and then the Turks.

We exchange addresses. I promise to send articles about Peter's play. And we say good-bye.

The 13th day of student protests. Bright sunshine. Rock music blares from the square in front of the Plato bookstore. Students sit around tables, stand around talking. A couple of students unroll a banner. On corners all along the main pedestrian street stand groups of policemen. Or they buy ice cream. Or, as the day stretches on, they sit at restaurant tables under sunscreens.

Near the Hotel Moskva, Gypsy children play naked in a fountain.

In the newspaper *Danas*, part 16 of the series *The Road to Dayton*, Ričard Holbruk's book in translation.

Žarko and I sit under big plane trees, drink lemonade, and write.
A young man with a knitted cap approaches and offers vegetarian
cookbooks for sale.

"Is it possible to be a Serb and a vegetarian?" I ask.

"Yes," he says. "We are opening a vegetarian restaurant near here
in less than a week."

"Who is we?"

"Members of the Hare Krishna community," he answers.

"Did you know," he asks, "that of all languages Serbian has the
most Sanskrit words? One professor found 1,500 of them. Another
3,000. Which makes Serbian the closest to the pure original language."

"Is that good?" I ask. "What do you think about the war in
Kosovo?"

"It's Mafia controlled," he says. "The Albanian Mafia lives by
selling drugs, and they are driving the Serbs out. The Freemasons are
involved as well, continuing the work they began in Bosnia."

"That's bullshit," I counter. "I wrote a book about Freemasonry.
You're parroting the old conspiracy theory. People explain their
economic downturns, their civil wars, their shocking lack of control,
by dusting off *The Protocols of the Elders of Zion*. In El Salvador it
became a bestseller, as it is here. But it's a patent fake."

"No," he says, "it's true. The American dollar has a Masonic sign
on the back."

"Yes, it does. The design is by Benjamin Franklin, who found
Freemasonry a fine vehicle for enlightened international cooperation."

"No! Many of the Freemasons are doctors. They arranged to get
Tito into a hospital where they could kill him. There are hospitals all
over Europe where doctors kill people. Forty-five percent of all the
world leaders are connected to the Mafia."

"I used to work as an industrial designer," he says in conclusion.
"But now I live a life devoted to spiritual pursuits like selling books.
To give people the truth is a fine thing."

The afternoon heat builds. The policemen disperse.

English-language graffiti on a wall:

FUCK THE SISTEM/POLICE/SLOBODU.

✐ BELGRADE, 4 JUNE 1998

I've been reading Andrić again. By means of the epic sweep of the novel, by evoking the timelessness of the bridge while narrating the individual tragedies and achievements of the people living in and around Višegrad, Andrić rises above the crushing events and gives a reassuring sense of continuation, of meaning.

For example: The two men beheaded by Turks made insecure by Serbian insurrection. These were simple men, almost fools. They had nothing to do with the events. But by accident, they were the first to confront the guards in the new blockhouse constructed on the bridge.

As readers, we feel the injustice. But this is not Zola's "J'accuse!"

Why not?

Because it is written long after the fact. The novelist will not, cannot change the events of the past.

Injustices are forgotten. War gives way to peace. Destruction fades into prosperity. The epic perspective reassures us.

A generation from now, Vižegrad, Goražde, and Foča will be populated by people who haven't witnessed atrocities, who haven't fled from killers, who haven't killed.

Of course, there's the other side of the epic vision. Inevitably, peace and prosperity are followed by war. It has been so in Bosnia (and where not?) for 500 years. Why should, how could the pattern change?

❧

I meet Žarko in front of the Hotel Moskva, and in the midday heat we make our way to the basement offices of Stubovi Kulture, formerly Vreme Knjige, the publishing house of our book: *Ponavljanje – Repetitions.*

Photos of all the authors published by Stubovi Kulture adorn the walls: Bruce Chatwin, Joseph Conrad, Anthony Burgess, Dragan Velikić, Danilo Kiš, Žarko, and myself.

Žarko introduces me to the publisher, Predrag Marković, a small man with a long, full beard and intense black eyes, and to Gojko Božović, editor for literature, a thin man who looks like he's about 15.

"Pleased to meet you," says the publisher. "You look just like your photo."

"What did you think I would look like?" I ask.

"All this time we've thought you were a fiction made up by Žarko for narrative purposes," the publisher explains.

"There may be some truth to that," I say. "Žarko tells me you are an author as well as a publisher."

"Yes," he says. "But I've run into a problem. Last year, our house was named the best publisher in Yugoslavia, and now Gojko tells me we're too good to publish my work."

Žarko describes our new project, a co-authored book with the title "Translation." "I'll look forward to it," the publisher says.

We walk on through the sweltering city. Žarko wants to introduce me to the poet Srba Mitrović "He was the librarian at our gymnasium in Zemun," Žarko explains. He told us what books to read. We met with him weekly for discussions. Several of us from that class became writers. With our encouragement, he began to publish his poems. He has won several major prizes.

The retired librarian and active poet lives several floors up in an aged but once splendid apartment house. The elevator rises reluctantly through an open iron-work cage and delivers us to a landing where a short, solid, bald man dressed in half-slippers, shorts, and a purple cotton shirt greets us.

On the table in the front room, a game of solitaire is laid out next to a tabloid newspaper with a naked woman on the cover.

The poet introduces me to Milan Djordjević, a younger man, bearded, slight, with whom he has translated English and American poetry.

We sit, four translators, around the table. The poet brings out a bottle of amber-colored rakija. A black oak cross floats in the aged brandy. Žarko proclaims the smooth-biting liquid a wonder of the art.

The poet's bald head glistens with sweat. Behind thick glasses, his eyes shine brightly. "It was at this table," he says, "that Milan Djordjević and I translated John Berryman."

Djordjević remembers the table heaped with dictionaries and grows ecstatic as he describes the quantities of rakija imbibed in the process.

Žarko asks if we can't see the poet's study. It is a spacious room, or was once spacious. Lined with books floor to ceiling, a bed tucked into one corner, a big desk into another, the room is navigable only by means of a pathway snaking through piles of books and boxes. "Here," the poet points out, "is my unmade bed. There, my desk. There my literary prize. And hanging from the bookshelf, my pants."

Back at the front-room table, I ask about the other persons we have seen in the apartment, several of whom are watching TV in a closed-off end of the front room.

Refugees, the poet says, relatives, three families of them, Serb refugees from Bosnia.

Žarko mentions our trip along the Drina River. The poet says an acquaintance of his recently ran into trouble there, a Serb who had owned an inn in Goražda before the war. Emboldened by the agreements in Dayton, he drove back to see what was left. He parked his car and went in. Having a drink with several people he had known, he heard glass crashing outside. He went out and found his car being demolished. The crowd grabbed him and might have demolished him as well if SFOR soldiers hadn't appeared on the scene.

He opens the newspaper with the naked woman and shows us a photo of the man.

"I was in the United States last month," he says. "I went to Minnesota to visit a family member at the Mayo Clinic. While I was at the clinic, I had an examination. The doctor told me I had several physical problems, that I drink too much, that I eat too much, and that I don't exercise enough. I told him that far from being physical problems, those were signs of a good life. The real reason I went to Minnesota, however, was to find the bridge John Berryman jumped from. I asked several people which bridge it was, but none of them had heard of Berryman."

We exchange books. The poet receives Žarko's and my *Ponavljanja (Repetitions)*, which I inscribe "from one translator to another." I receive *Snapshots for a Panorama (From the Abyss)*, published in 1996 in the Cyrillic alphabet.

In my hotel room, I turn to Mitrovic's shortest poem, open my dictionary, and without benefit of grammar, "translate" each word:

VILLAGE NEAR BRATUNAC, BOSNIA, 1992

Destroyed [celac – ?]
hill/mountain trunk/chest receive:
whole/safe village.

The botched attempt reminds me of my inadequacy as a translator of experience into the English language, of the impossibility of this book

I'm sitting in a tiny patch of shade on the wall of the Kalemegdan. A small hawk, light brown with black and white speckling and a grey band near its rump hunts along the hill till it sweeps out of sight behind a stone tower. Seconds later it's back, chased by a black-and-grey raven. The raven seems quicker, but the hawk is adept at swerving out of the way at the last second. Suddenly the hawk turns on the raven. A second raven sweeps into the fight and the hawk gives up the battlefield.

A lizard flits across the sunny stone wall. Below me, in the newly mown grass, a pheasant hen and two chicks. The hawk floats along the hill again, just below the pheasants. From behind the tower, a furious raven rejoins the skirmish. The brown-grey pheasant moves warily, pecking now and then at the ground. Her chicks bob in and out of the long grass at the side of the field.

Ọ Cologne, 10 June 1998

The German word for misery, "Elend," means, in its root sense, "in a foreign country."

Žarko and I walk through a park in Cologne. We see a handsome young couple standing in an embrace. A young man and a boy kick a soccer ball back and forth. Just past them, facing the street but nicely tucked back into the park, stands an apartment house with a discrete sign on the front: Halfway House for Asylum Seekers. At the moment, Germany is home for somewhere near 350,000 refugees from Bosnia, more than the number who have taken refuge in all other countries combined.

"I was walking past here one day," Žarko says, "and a little boy asked me, in German, for a Mark. Why do you want a Mark?" I asked him. "To buy ice cream," he said. I thought he might be a Bosnian refugee, so I asked him in Serbo-Croatian where he was from. He was surprised, but then answered with the name of a Bosnian town. "Where are you from?" he asked in our language. "From Serbia," I said. "Then I don't want your Mark," he said.

Dear Žarko,

I taught Primary, or Sunday School today, the class you visited when you were here four years ago. Do you remember? This is the class I must teach or lose my professorship at the church university. The assigned lesson was about Joshua and the battle of Jericho. I remembered the story vaguely from my own childhood Sunday School, the part about the circling army and the shouts and the city's wall that falls down. What I didn't remember was God's command that was fulfilled as Joshua and his army "utterly destroyed all that was in the city, both man and woman, young and old, and ox, and sheep, and ass, with the edge of the sword." Joshua went on to the city of Ai, all of whose inhabitants he killed, men and women, and then he burned it "and made it a heap for ever, even a desolation unto this day." Next was the city of Hazor: "There was not any left to breathe: and he burnt Hazor with fire. . . . So Joshua took the whole land, according to all that the Lord said unto Moses; and Joshua gave it for an inheritance unto Israel according to their divisions by their tribes. And the land rested from war."

The lesson manual suggested that I emphasize how the Lord blesses those who follow his orders exactly.

After our trip, I could not teach that lesson. After our trip, many things will be different.

Activity in the Mormon Church? Working at a Mormon university? Continuing a Mormon marriage?

Time will tell.

Dear Žarko,

Last night I bought a novel by Steve Tesich, the Serbian-American screenwriter Slobodan said was from Bajina Bašta (although Tesich's sister Nadja writes that her brother "Steve (Stojan) . . . was born and raised in Užice." The book has just been published, although Tesich died of a heart attack in 1996.

Karoo is a hilarious tragedy set in New York and Los Angeles in 1991. The book has nothing whatsoever to do with Yugoslavia or the war there except, perhaps, indirectly:

The kids continued their game of siege and resiege, but shortly after Leila's departure I could tell that things were beginning to wind down. Battle fatigue was spreading through the ranks. The bloodcurdling cries of the invaders and the defiant screams of the defenders were losing some of their earlier conviction. And then it was over. They all knew it. They wandered away in little groups, in various directions, much like a disbanded army of adults might have done after a war: a little weary, a little bored, but not at all eager for the rigors of peace that they knew awaited them at home.

Žarko, this novel is a masterpiece of personal despair. While burning with the sharply focused political anger he reveals elsewhere, Tesich has written a moving personal account of love and talent and alcoholism and failed humanity.

"Elsewhere" is a series of essays aimed at the media, in particular *The New York Times*. Look for the essays on the Internet and you'll find the following quotations:

> Genocide is a natural phenomenon, in harmony with the societal and mythologically divine nature. Genocide is not only permitted, it is recommended, even commanded by the word of the Almighty, whenever it is useful for the survival or the restoration of the kingdom of the chosen nation, or for the preservation or spreading of its one and only correct faith.

> There can be no peace or co-existence between Islamic faith and non-Islamic faith and institutions . . . . The Islamic movement must and can take power as soon as it is morally and numerically strong enough, not only to destroy the non-Islamic power, but to build up a new Islamic one . . . .

The first quotation is from Croatian President Franjo Tudjman's *Wastelands of Historical Reality* (had he been reading about Joshua?), the second from Muslim Bosnian President Alija Izetbegović's "Islamic Declaration." Why, Tesich asks, have these two men been "embraced by the western media as victims and martyrs for the cause of freedom"?

And now, Dear Žarko, "your" Yugoslavia has beaten "my" United States 1:0. "Your" Mijatović came out of the game only 31 minutes from the beginning. "My" Radosavljević, born in "your" country, entered the game at 58 minutes. "Your" team was dressed in red socks, white shorts, and blue jerseys. "My" team was in white with red and blue trim.

"Sam," I said to my eleven-year-old son, "Žarko's team is playing the U.S. team." "Who are you going for?" he asked me. "For Žarko's team," I said. "Traitor," he said.

I am a worse traitor than he knows.

I don't like the American team. Their coach is a little dictator with bad judgment. There is bad blood among the players. And there is my nagging distaste for the economic power and moral self-righteousness "my" country "projects" around the globe.

But as I sat there watching "your" team play "my" team, in spite of two weeks in Belgrade and in the Republika Srpska, contrary to what I know rationally, I tried to pick out which of "your" players were killers. When the game got rough, I thought: They have the advantage, their training on the battlefield, their work for Arkan, has made the violence of this game nothing for them.

Where, Žarko, do these racist impulses come from? After all I've done to combat them? After everyone I've met? Everything I've seen?

Yesterday morning, before discovering that racist black hole in my moral character, I read the following from a 1996 decision by the Russian Judicial Chamber for "Information Disputes": "In the pamphlet 'Hand Grenade at Croats,' Limonov (Savenko) writes that the Croats are 'an exceptionally savage people.' His wish is that 'their children be born without fingers.'"

This Russian poet turned fascist politician, this resident of "my" country for five years, this "bad boy" of Russian literature, his fame based in part on his daring obscenities (which I don't mind, by the way—this is not a puritanical tirade on my part), this man of hatred writes the reprehensible thoughts my subconscious nurtures.

Is there a difference between us?

✏ PROVO, UTAH, 29 JUNE 1998

Žarko. Yesterday, Bora Milutinović's Nigerian team fell 4:1 to the

Danish team: "The biggest upset of the 1998 World Cup." I listened as he spoke with reporters after the game in a combination of Spanish, English, and Serbian and who knows what other languages. A walking abbreviated multilingual dictionary.

At this moment, one p.m. "my" time, "your" team is playing the team from the Netherlands.

But I'm not in the mood for sports this afternoon.

First, the news this morning that Slavko Dokmanović, awaiting the verdict in his war crimes trial at the Hague, hanged himself on the hinge of the door to his cell last night.

Second, I read this morning the June 27, 1996 indictment of the International Criminal Tribunal for the Former Yugoslavia against eight men from Foča charging gang rape, torture, and enslavement of Muslim women. Here are some excerpts:

> The city and municipality of Foča are located south-east of Sarajevo . . . . According to the 1991 census, the population of Foča consisting of 40,513 persons was 51.6 percent Muslim, 45.3 percent Serbian and 3.1 percent others. . . .

> Muslim women, children and the elderly were detained in houses, apartments and motels in the town of Foča or in surrounding villages, or at short and long-term detention centers such as Buk Bijela, Foča High School, and Partizan Sports Hall, respectively. Many of the detained women were subjected to humiliating and degrading conditions of life, to brutal beatings and to sexual assaults, including rapes . . . .

> Dragan Gagović, in his capacity as chief of police, was the person in charge of the detention and the release of female Muslim detainees in Foča . . . . On or around 17 July 1992, Dragan Gagović personally raped one of the women who, on the previous day, had complained about the incidences of sexual assaults . . . .

> The same night, after Janko Janjić returned the women to Partizan, Dragoljijb Kunarać(?) took the same three women to the Hotel Zelengora. [One woman] refused to go with him and he kicked her and dragged her out. At Hotel Zelengora, [this latter woman] was placed in a separate room and both Dragoljijb Kunarać and Zoran Vuković raped her. Both per-

petrators told her that she would now give birth to Serb babies.

This 24-page document describes dozens of such incidents, several of them taking place in the very Hotel Zelengora where we spent the night.
I see only black.

⟁ PROVO, UTAH, 30 JUNE 1998

Dear Žarko,
Bad news from the World Cup: Holland over Yugoslavia. We've seen the last of Predrag Mijatović, although his teammates for Real Madrid, Clarence Seedorf of Holland and Davor Šuker of Croatia, will continue.

⟁ PROVO, UTAH, 4 JULY 1998

Dear Žarko,
It's our independence day. My neighbors display American flags in their front yards. There was a big parade this morning in Provo. And tonight there will be fireworks.
Independence.
This afternoon, when the American TV announcers introduced the Croatian team for its game against Germany, they talked about a proud nation, independent for seven years. This game is enormously important for Croatia, the announcers explained. Just being in the quarterfinals means they have advanced beyond their enemy Yugoslavia. Croatia is a poor nation, they explained. The Croatian president, Tudjman, they added, is present today at the game. This would be a remarkable victory for a country of 4 million people. To put that in perspective, the announcers pointed out that in Germany there are 6 million athletes registered as soccer players. But there is no bad blood between these nations, the announcers continued. When Croatia declared its independence seven years ago, Germany immediately recognized the new country.
And thus, duly informed, we Americans cheered on the poor, newly and courageously independent tiny country against its powerhouse friend Germany.
As you know, Croatia won the game 3:0.

Dear Žarko,

I'm embarrassed to report that the U.S. Senate passed a resolution on Friday recommending that the International War Crimes Tribunal for the former Yugoslavia in the Hague bring Slobodan Milošević to trial. The resolution accuses Milošević of "the deaths of hundreds of thousands, the torture and rape of tens of thousands and the forced displacement of nearly 300,000" in Bosnia. Žarko, you know how much I despise your President. You know I would like to see him made responsible for his actions. But the resolution is false. False in its one-sidedness, its incompleteness.

And Tudjman? And Izetbegović?

What's wrong with these idiots? "My" idiots, I mean.

In the same issue of the *New York Times* that reported the Senate story, there was a piece on Kosovo Albanians who killed 20 Serb soldiers yesterday as they took over the town of Orahovac. Arresting Milošević, patriotic Senators, isn't going to make this problem go away.

I am rereading your Nobel Prize winner, Žarko. You gave me a German translation of this book during our student days in Tübingen, but I never dreamed how much I would come to rely on it to interpret my world.

> The notice . . . announced that Her Majesty the Empress Elizabeth had died in Geneva, the victim of a dastardly assassination by an Italian anarchist, Lucchieni . . . . When, returning home from work grey with stone-dust and streaked with paint, Maistro-Pero read the announcement, he pulled his hat down over his eyes and feverishly bit on the thin pipe which was always between his teeth. He explained to the more serious and respected citizens whom he met that he, although an Italian, had nothing in common with this Lucchieni and his dastardly crime.[37]

Žarko, my serious and respected friend, although I am an American, I have nothing in common with these Senators and their dastardly crime.

---

[37] Andrić, *The Bridge on the Drina*, 200.

⌀ PROVO, UTAH, 15 OCTOBER 1998

Dear Žarko,

Newspaper reports today say that police officers have closed down the offices of two of Belgrade's major newspapers: *Danas* and *Dnevni Telegraph*. What caught my eye was the justification spoken in phrases Mormon university officials have been using to denounce our fight for academic freedom: "Reports have spread fear, panic and defeatism while undermining the people's readiness to safeguard the territorial integrity and sovereignty of the country."

Why, my friend, do authoritarian regimes, yours and mine, think they can control thinking? Don't they read history? Don't they question their own motives? Don't they blush?

Here's the answer to the latter question, again in the exact words my self-righteous academic officers have used in the press, spoken in the Yugoslav version by the Minister of Information, Alexander Vučic: "I am proud of what I've done. I wish there were more condemnations. They show that we were right."

I must find a new job!

⌀ PROVO, UTAH, 9 JANUARY 1999

Dear Žarko,

Today French Stabilization Force (SFOR) troops killed Dragan Gagović, former police chief of Foča. He had five children in his car. The soldiers shot him when he drove the car at them.

"This event was significant," the BBC's Jim Fish declared, "because of the area . . . Foča is a notoriously secretive and sinister place . . . where very few people, certainly no Muslims, dare to go."

Žarko, I wish there were a hell so the rapist Gagović could rot there alongside the verbal rapist Jim Fish. The latter is wielding the language of war, justifying any and every action against those furtive and left-handed Serbs.

Just when I need a hell, however, I find that I've lost my faith.

⌀ PROVO, UTAH, 13 JANUARY 1999

Žarko,

Proof today, again, of how Jim Fish and colleagues pollute our minds.

I have read and translated Peter's meticulously dialectical work. I have read your fanciful and subversive texts in translation. I'm a professional literary critic. I have traveled in Yugoslavia. I know a few Serbs. And yet, over the last few days, while Slobodon Milošević has continued his "provocations" and "games," while he refuses to listen to "reason and truth," while he won't heel to NATO ultimatums, while NATO leaders make these points and threaten to bomb Yugoslavia, I have found myself drifting into thought patterns shared by most of my fellow Americans and Europeans, I have been swayed, sentence by sentence, story by story, by NATO press agents and by U.S. government officials, and suddenly, after days and weeks of tension in the HEADLINES, I shouted: Bomb the son-of-a-bitch!

"The son-of-a-bitch," of course, translates into Yugoslavian civilians. Into friends in Bajina Bašta. Into your mother.

What are we doing with our writing, my friend? What is Peter doing? What is Thomas doing? What are a few words, a few little books, in the face of THE PRESS?

✐ PROVO, UTAH, 19 MARCH 1999

Here comes the war, Žarko, like a freight train—timetable published in the *New York Times*:

> President Clinton prepared congressional leaders today for what one senator called a "robust and serious" bombing campaign against the Serbs that would soon put American military lives in danger. The U.S. Embassy in Belgrade was being evacuated.

✐ PROVO, UTAH, 22 MARCH 1999

Headline in yesterday's *Salt Lake Tribune*: "Murderous Serbs Defy U.S. Ultimatum." The language of war, the language that causes war, the war that is language. Halfway through the piece, unconsciously calling the headline's murderous stupidity into question, the author noted that, "In Priština on Sunday, four Serb police officers were gunned down as their four patrol cars were ambushed."

Dear Žarko,

At 3 a.m. this morning in Belgrade the radio station B92 was shut down by state "security forces."

B-52s have taken off from their bases in England and are approaching Yugoslavia, to start bombing as night falls.

The justification? Here are portions of Bill Clinton's speech [24 March 1999] to the nation, his version of the history underlying and justifying NATO bombing:

> By acting now, we are upholding our values, protecting our interests, and advancing the cause of peace. Tonight I want to speak with you about the tragedy in Kosovo and why it matters to America that we work with our allies to end it.
>
> First, let me explain what it is that we are responding to. Kosovo is a province of Serbia, in the middle of southeastern Europe and about 160 miles east of Italy. That's less than the distance between Washington and New York, and only about 70 miles north of Greece.
>
> Its people are mostly ethnic Albanian and mostly Muslim.
>
> In 1989 Serbia's leader Slobodan Milosevic, the same leader who started the wars in Bosnia and Croatia, and moved against Slovenia in the last decade, stripped Kosovo of the constitutional autonomy its people enjoyed, thus denying them their right to speak their language, run their schools, shape their daily lives. For years, Kosovars struggled peacefully to get their rights back. When President Milosevic sent his troops and police to crush them, the struggle grew violent.

I'm beyond words, Žarko, I can't catch my breath. Let me have Andrić speak for me, as so often before:

> Only then began the real persecution of the Serbs and all those connected with them. The people were divided into the persecuted and those who persecuted them. That wild beast, which lives in man and does not dare to show itself until the barriers of law and custom have been removed, was now set

free. The signal was given, the barriers were down. As has so often happened in the history of man, permission was tacitly granted for acts of violence and plunder, even for murder, if they were carried out in the name of higher interests, according to established rules, and against a limited number of men of a particular type and belief.[38]

⌒ Provo, Utah, 26 March 1999

Dear Žarko,

No mention in the papers of last week's report by the International War Crimes Tribunal indicting Croatian generals for war crimes committed when they "ethnically cleansed" 100,000 Serbs from the Krajine using weapons supplied by the U.S. and employing tactics taught them by U.S. generals.

"Murderous Serbs" my ass!

⌒ Provo, Utah, 28 March 1999

Dear Žarko,

Sunday morning. Sunny and quiet. In Utah.

NATO planes bombed a "military target" in Zemun yesterday. Ten months after we sat on the barge on the Danube and talked with Pera about his propaganda film.

I'm listening to a live broadcast from Radio B92. The station's broadcasting facilities have been shut down, but over the Internet they are still a presence. I click on an image of the Trg Republike and call up a video clip of the square shot two days ago with a hand-held camera: celebrators streaming around the equestrian statue, the museum, the theater; some pedestrians, a few cars, a bus. I strain to catch sight of you and me and the boy who thought you were a poet. I look for Djinjić. I search for your mother. Is that the woman who issued our visas? There's the poet carrying a volume of Berryman. Pera motors past in his boat. Slobodan has driven to Belgrade from Bajina Bašta. He waves at Olga and Milica. Peter sits by the fountain sketching. The sunlight reflects off his boots.

We're all wearing targets. We're all smiling.

Yesterday my son Ben came up from where he was watching TV to tell me that a stealth fighter had been shot down near Belgrade.

---

[38] Andrić, *The Bridge on the Drina*, 282.

"Good," I said.

✑ PROVO, UTAH, 29 MARCH 1999

Dear Žarko,
On U.S. TV today, when asked whether NATO could win a
ground offensive against Yugoslavia, a former U.S.
general said it would be easy: "We would simply attack across the northern plains
with our tanks like the Nazis did."

✑ PROVO, UTAH, 30 MARCH 1999

Dear Žarko,
I could have listened to the English version of the B92 news, but
today I was in no mood to hear English. Here are my notes (the spell-
ing is obviously my own):

Television
Priština
Yugoslavia
International
Dobro jutro
NATO
DANAS
Slobodan Milošević . . . Primakov
Situation
Slobodan Milošević
Organization
Information
Aggression
Ljudi
Central Beograd
Katastrofe
Informatia
National
NATO
Yugoslavia
Serbia
Beograd
Instilatia

Interventia
Beograd
Polizia
Apotheka
Katastrophe
Ruski
Boris Jelzin
Milliarde Dollera
Ljudi
Beograd
Radio B92
Radio Bajina Bašta
Radio Kraljevo
Radio Užica
Radio Kotor

Not much of a story. But catastrophe, intervention, police, NA-TO, aggression, and Belgrade, shoulder to shoulder in the same report can't be good.

            ✍ PROVO, UTAH, 31 MARCH 1999

Word from Žarko that his mother's apartment is 400 meters from a new NATO target.
    Peter went to Belgrade yesterday. Solidarity.

            ✍ PROVO, UTAH, 5 APRIL 1999

Zemun hit again last night. More bridges bombed.
    The bridge on the Drina?

            ✍ PROVO, UTAH, 6 APRIL 1999

Graffiti on a Serbian wall: "Columbus—damn your curiosity!" Billboard in a city as yet untouched by NATO bombs: "What's wrong with us?"
    Žarko, I like your fellow Serbs more and more. They remind me of you, of your wit, of your imagination, of your indomitable opposition to authority.

◯ PROVO, UTAH, 12 APRIL 1999

"The bastards attacked the train," he said through an interpreter. "Now go away. I don't want to hear English anymore." How will I ever travel in Yugoslavia again?

◯ PROVO, UTAH, 15 APRIL 1999

Dear Žarko,
Tax day. Before midnight I'll mail the $2,000 I still owe in federal income taxes. It's never a pleasant task, but tonight, I'll send the check with a bitter heart. My money will buy, however indirectly, part of an anti-personnel bomb that will parachute down into a column of Serb or Albanian refugees, a section of a rocket that will destroy a passenger train on a bridge, or the tail fin of a cruise missile that will strike the center of Belgrade.
"Who bombed our bridge?" the doctor/mayor asked. "I did," I'll have to say.

◯ COLOGNE, GERMANY, 1 MAY 1999

Dear Scott,
I am lucky to still be alive.
Last night the "NATO criminals" bombed the long-since empty Yugoslav Army Command Center. It is just 400 meters from my mother's apartment. Poor woman. It was horrible. Several dead and many wounded. Rubble and dust (with uranium) everywhere. By the way, that's the street where you and I were doused by a car running through a puddle. According to a friend of mine, the street is impassible, even by pedestrians.
Bill Clinton is coming to Cologne. I would like to assassinate him. (By the way, that's exactly how it was in Sarajevo 1914 when Gavrillo Prinzip killed Ferdinand.)
That's how one becomes a terrorist.
I'm ashamed to live in a democracy.
I still didn't get the jazz cassettes featuring your son Tom. I haven't listened to music for 39 days.

Žarko

◯

Goddamit, Žarko, you frighten me. When my mind starts whirling like this, when I panic, when I'm sinking into blackness, my impulse is to throw bombs—or to tell jokes.

A Serb meets an American and as they talk the Serb cuts the American short with the observation that while the Serbs have a history that goes back for thousands of years, the Americans have no history to speak of. That may be, the American replies, but unlike us, you Serbs now have no geography.

A Serb is fishing and catches a golden fish. I will grant you three wishes, the fish says. For my first wish, the Serb says, I would like to have Bill Clinton as my father. Done, says the fish. For my second wish, the Serb continues, I'd like Madeline Albright as my mother. Done, the fish says. And for my third wish, the Serb says, I wish I were an orphan.

✐ Salt Lake City Airport, 4 June 1999

Dear Žarko,

My brother John's birthday yesterday. Had he not contracted AIDS, he would have been 48. As you know, John's death loosed some of my moorings, undermined some of my certainties, stimulated new certainties. Our trip along the Drina River was a similar experience for me. I'm not the same person I was before traveling in your country.

Yesterday I signed papers resigning from Brigham Young University. For eleven years, I worked for an increasingly coercive church, for a church that hated my brother and his kind. As the regulations tightened, I found ways to subvert requirements I had complied with for years. Forced to pay tithing, ten percent of my earnings, I quit paying all but a token. Forced to comply with dietary laws I had obeyed all my life, I began to imbibe. Forced to state my allegiance, I decided I had no allegiance.

Imagine requiring an annual "ecclesiastical endorsement" for all professors at a university. A churchman deciding my academic fate on the basis of perceived orthodoxy! But you know this pattern. I walked with you among demonstrating students from the University of Belgrade.

This fall I'll be a professor of philosophy and humanities at Utah Valley State College. A step toward a life I can construct on my own terms.

✑ VIENNA, AUSTRIA, 5 JUNE 1999

Žarko,

I have checked into the Pension Falstaff, just around the corner from Sigmund Freud's rooms in the Berggaße.

From the train into town I saw a hawk hanging over a hops field lined with brilliant red poppies and blue flax. Like a sleek NATO jet over a fruitful Yugoslav landscape.

While waiting for you and Anne to arrive, I'll work on my translation of Peter's *Voyage by Dugout, The Play of the Film of the War*, whose premiere in the Burgtheater we are gathering to witness.

✑ VIENNA, AUSTRIA, 6 JUNE 1999

Žarko,

This afternoon I walked down to the Danube. The bridges here have not been bombed. The Danube still flows toward Belgrade. And the Serbs I meet in Vienna are dealing with their stress the same way I do: by telling jokes: Madeline Albright gives the Serbs an ultimatum: love or war! They take one look at her and decide on war.

Ducks fly overhead, sharp-winged and heavy bodied. A white swan flies toward the bridge, skimming the water, its neck impossibly long. The big bird swoops up over the bridge and then dives to continue downstream. Large raven-like birds with grey-brown heads, backs, and chests and black wings and tails, birds I first saw in Belgrade, beg for crumbs from picknicking families. Lime trees are blossoming, as are wild roses.

Later, in the city center, I stumble onto a Sunday-evening demonstration against NATO and for Yugoslavia. "NATO—fascistik, NATO—fascistik!" the crowd of maybe 3,000 chants. I donate 200 Schillings to a humanitarian group and they give me a blue, white, and red Serbian flag in return. A Vienna policeman, pistol in his belt, leans against a post studying a book with the title: *Learn Greek.*

Back in my room, unable to sleep, I turn to my translation. I wish you were here Žarko, to compare notes. Peter's prose is not easy to reproduce, nor are the word-images. How, for instance, did you translate "Fertigsatzpisse"? Pissing your finished, your modular sentences? Sentential piss?

At 10:30 I watch a pre-premiere report on Peter done for Austrian TV (ÖRF2). Peter's crime, the reporter and his commentators agree, is that he is a "Serbenfreund," a friend of the Serbs. Not good to be a friend of the enemy. Peter should have known better. It's an old story: Jap lover, Kraut lover, Jew lover, Nigger lover, Serb lover. I turn off the sentential piss and turn back to Peter's play. Before midnight I'm out of paper. I write across the face of my travel itinerary. I fill margins. By 1 a.m., having exhausted all possibilities, I look through the cupboards and drawers in my room. The drawer of the night table opens to a Gideon Bible, in the back of which are ten blank pages. I decide the hand of God has provided and rip them out and continue translating till first light.

✐ VIENNA, AUSTRIA, 7 JUNE 1999

Elections this week for the European Parliament. Posters for the FPÖ, Freedom Party of Austria, advertise its clean-cut, right-wing, xenophobic leader Jörg Haider, and proclaim that EUROPE NEEDS CONTROL. It doesn't say control over what, but the subtext is law and order, control over the foreigners who represent chaos, control over those who are different, control over people like my brother John.

How is it that I, who would like to see those controlled who exploit the planet and pollute the earth but who wants less control over individuals, how is it that I ended up working for a repressive religious institution whose Republican leaders and guiding principles require more control over individuals and less over exploitative corporations, more control of those who are different and less control over those who devastate the environment?

✐ VIENNA, 9 JUNE 1999 // BEFORE MIDNIGHT, ŽARKO'S BIRTHDAY

I ought to go to bed, but I'm still reeling from the events of the day.

Several hours ago NATO and the Yugoslav Parliament came to some kind of agreement ending the bombing after 78 days.

And, I'm just back from the world premiere of Peter's *The Play of the Film of the War*, directed by Claus Peymann. I've never attended the world premiere of a play of this magnitude; and I've seldom been this moved, this challenged, by a work of art.

Peter has filmmakers John Ford and Luis Buñuel in a Serbian town ten years after the war trying to decide how to make a film of the war. Characters who appear before the directors tell conflicting and complex stories as the play feels its way to questions about war and its aftermath. The really bad guys of the play, three "Internationals" who know all the answers, who dictate all the terms, who can think only in absolutes, appear on the stage as follows: "Three mountain bike riders, preceded by the sound of squealing brakes, burst through the swinging door, covered with mud clear up to their helmets. They race through the hall, between tables and chairs, perilously close to the people sitting there. 'Where are we?' the First International asks. 'Don't know,' the second answers. 'Not a clue,' the third says."

American and European moralists, functionaries with no hint of self-irony or humor, absolutists who run the world because of their economic power—these sorry excuses for human beings were depicted this evening as mountain bike riders.

"Žarko," I said, "Don't you ever tell Peter I ride a mountain bike."

"No," he whispered, "I'd never do that."

The play drew on several incidents from our trip, including when Peter put his coat around the shoulders of the OSCE woman in Višegrad. After the performance, flushed with enthusiasm and insight, I told Peter how well he had integrated that real event into an imaginative play.

"Dr. Scott," he chided. "Always the professor."

✎ COLOGNE, GERMANY, 11 JUNE 1999

Driving through the night from Vienna to Cologne, through heavy rain, slowed repeatedly by construction for the ultra-fast train, Anne sleeping in the back, I risked a question I had been thinking since our Drina trip: "Žarko, you know how I feel about Yugoslavia. You know where my heart is. Please don't take this question wrong. What do you think about the killings and rapes and ethnic cleansing done by your fellow Serbs?"

Žarko pointed out that the Albanians didn't flee Kosovo until NATO began bombing.

This was what I feared.

Žarko began to develop a half-baked theory about American financial interests in Yugoslavia and the need to bomb the country into a new economic dependency.

The muscles tightened behind my ears. "Žarko, Žarko," I said. "What about Serb atrocities? What do you think about Serb atrocities?"

Žarko began a disjointed story about Milošević being in power for so long and the hundreds of thousands of Serb refugees from the Krajine.

In the rainy darkness, traveling swiftly along the Autobahn, I slipped toward despair.

And, Žarko said, the paramilitary killers and rapists and arsonists who are Serbs ought to be raped and burned and killed.

My scalp muscles relaxed. I remembered Žarko's response when Slobodan Milošević spoke at the Kosovo Polje a decade ago. In contrast to the politician's nationalist ranting, Žarko wrote an account of mundane Serbs and Albanians, of human beings in troubled times. I remembered the gentle rationality and determined cosmopolitanism of that text. How could I have doubted my friend?

✍ COLOGNE, GERMANY, 16 JUNE 1999

I'm walking from Žarko's and Anne's apartment into the city center this morning, a pleasant stroll along the Rhine River. Long narrow barges ease their loads of coal up the river. A woman riding a rickety bike along the bank is followed by a frantically galloping short-legged dachshund cursing the invention of the wheel.

There are police everywhere: police on horses, police tending surly rottweilers, police sitting on the tops of buildings with sniper rifles, police in marked and unmarked cars, police on mountain bikes. It's the G-8 economic summit in Cologne this weekend, and the presidents need protection.

From Žarko? No, he's a verbal assassin. They'll have to ban his books.

It looks like the newspapers have exacted revenge for my friend. When Bill Clinton arrived here last night, the first thing he did was go to dinner in Cologne's old town, washing the sausage down with a local light beer, a Kölsch. Leaving the restaurant, hoping to make a good impression on the locals á la John Kennedy in Berlin, he stopped and didn't tell the crowd of gawkers "Ich bin ein Kölner," but "Ich bin ein Kölsch." The headlines are three inches high: "Ich bin ein Kölsch!"

In the evening we stroll back into town. "What does the word 'nazdravie' mean?" I ask Žarko. It's at the end of the article on the Duško Goykovich in the *Penguin Guide to Jazz on CD*, after a review of the 1995 "Bebop City" that ends with the comment that "these must have been difficult years for Goykovich as his old country tore itself apart."

"It means something like 'take care' or 'Gesundheit,'" Žarko answers.

We listened to Goykovich's two-disc set called "Balkan Blue," the first disc called "A Night in Skopje," recorded in 1994, and the second one a composition Goykovich originally called "Sketches of Yugoslavia," but that was renamed "Balkan Blues," the liner notes say, "because in the course of political changes Yugoslavia had ceased to exist."

"Goykovich was a national hero," Žarko says. "When I was growing up in Belgrade in the 1960s and 1970s, there was an annual Belgrade version of the Newport Jazz Festival, and when Goykovich came one year with Woody Herman, we were in seventh heaven. I also heard Louis Armstrong, the Oscar Peterson trio with Ella Fitzgerald, Art Farmer, Charles Mingus, the MJQ, Gary Burton, Bill Evans, Gil Evans, and Miles Davis with his 'Bitches Brew' band. I heard Dave Brubeck and Paul Desmond, and there must have been others as well. The concerts were held in a 5000-seat hall, always sold out. We loved the music; and we also loved the influence from the West. Since the Second World War we had felt close to our allies Great Britain and the United States, and the jazz reminded us of that. So when those two countries started bombing Belgrade this March, fifty-eight years after the Germans bombed Belgrade in 1941, it was confusing to most of us."

But now the bombing has stopped, and Cologne's "Balkan Forum," headed by Dužan Milosević (a formerly innocuous name), is sponsoring a jazz night in the Litho Restaurant. It's a noisy, smoke-filled place, seating a hundred people at most. Black-and-white photos decorate the walls, and a short-haired dog begs for scraps. Featured tonight is the Nicolas Simion Quintet, with Simion, a broad-chested, black-bearded Romanian, on tenor sax, a young and talented flugelhorn player whose name I didn't catch, and a rhythm section of stubble-faced, slack-jawed Mihal Farcas (Romanian) on drums, Macedonian Martin Gjakonovski (who appears with Dusko Goykovich on "A Night in Skopje") on bass, and the quick-fingered German Norbert Scholly on guitar.

I sit with Dušan and Anne and Žarko at a tiny table tucked into the armpit of the bandstand. By the time the evening is over the table is buried under a dozen beer and wine glasses, two bags of tobacco, three packs of cigarette paper, a pack of cigarettes, two overflowing ashtrays, a tape recorder, a pack of batteries, a sketch pad for the snakey haired house artist, assorted pens and pencils, Simion's soprano case, a candle, a dozen CD's for sale, and loose cash for the CDs that have sold.

Sketch by Benno Alfred Maria Türke

The crowd of Serbs, Croats, Bosnians, Bulgarians, Romanians, Hungarians, Germans, and at least one American warms quickly to the quintet. In his freely ranging solos Simion leaves no doubt about his debt to Ornette Coleman. Simion's tunes also hint at the oriental scales and rhythms of Balkan folk music, songs like "Geamparale," based on a Romanian wedding dance in 9/8 time (reminiscent of Dave Brubeck's "Blue Rondo a la Turk"—or better said, Brubeck's tune, as its title suggests, is reminiscent of music from the Balkans).

Back home, Žarko calls his mother. Scott Abbott is here, he tells her. Tell him, she replies, that we still like him.

○ PROVO, UTAH, 22 NOVEMBER 1999

Dear Žarko,

James Lyon, Director of the Crisis Intervention Center in Sarajevo, spoke today at Utah Valley State College. He emphasized the point in the Dayton Peace Accord requiring that all refugees be allowed to return home. I told him about the Serb refugees from Sarajevo who were building an apartment building in Višegrad on a hill overlooking the Drina River. "It was a hopeful sight," I said, "people moving on with their lives."

"I know that building," he said. "It is built on the site of a razed 17th-century mosque."

Goddamit, Žarko, why can't anything be what it seems?

◯ Provo, Utah, 15 February 2000

Dear Žarko,

It's done. The divorce. I've cut my moorings. I'm adrift and nervous as hell. I think I'll be okay, unless the International Monetary Fund or the U.N.'s International Tribunal for the Former Yugoslavia or the Federation of Concerned Mountain Bikers decides to take a hand in molding my character.

Will I find love? Can I love?

Scott

photo by Anne Kister

BIOGRAPHIES

ŽARKO RADAKOVIĆ is the author of several books published in Belgrade, including *Tübingen, Knifer, Ponanvljanje* (*Repetitions*, with Scott Abbott), *Emigracija* (*Emigration*), *Pogled* (*The View*), *Vampiri & Razumni rečnik* (*Vampires & A Reasonable Dictionary*, with Scott Abbott), *Strah od Emigracije* (*Fear of Emigration*), *Era*, and *Knjiga o muzici* (*A Book about Music*, with David Albahari). He has translated more than twenty of Austrian author Peter Handke's books into Serbian and has been traveling companion and translator for Handke during repeated trips to Serbia, Bosnia, Montenegro, and Kosovo. He collaborated on three performances with artist Slobodan Era Milivojević (1971, 1973, and 1974; the 1973 performance, titled "Turtle," is described in the book *Era*). He recorded numerous audio and video interviews with Croatian painter Julije Knifer, edited a special edition of the literary journal *Flugasche* about Knifer, and wrote the book *Knifer*. His recent work with Serbian/German artist Nina Pops includes collaboration on a series of collages that feature manuscript translations of Peter Handke's novel *Bildverlust* (*The Loss of Images*, or *Crossing the Sierra de Gredos*) and Pops' "translations" of the text into images. Radaković edited an edition of the German literary magazine *Nachtcafé* on the theme of Walking, and more recently, with Peter Handke, an edition of the German literary magazine *Schreibheft* on "Literature from Serbia." He has published essays on art, music, and literature. David Albahari described Radaković as "one of the few absolutely isolated, independent, creative personalities of contemporary Serbian prose. . . . He deals with our language like a foreign language in the same way Beckett uses the English language and Handke the German language. . . . I think I will not be wrong when I say that Žarko . . . is the most radical Serbian writer of the present time." He lives in Cologne, Germany.

SCOTT ABBOTT is the author of *Fictions of Freemasonry: Freemasonry and the German Novel* and of two books with Žarko Radaković, *Ponanvljanje (Repetitions)* and *Vampiri & Razumni rečnik (Vampires & A Reasonable Dictionary)*. He was the jazz critic for the *Salt Lake Observer* and co-author, with Sam Rushforth, of the series "Wild Rides, Wild Flowers: Biking and Botanizing the Great Western Trail," which appeared for four years in *Catalyst Magazine* (published as a book by Torrey House Press in 2014). He has translated Peter Handke's *A Journey to the Rivers: Justice for Serbia* (Viking) and Handke's play *Voyage by Dugout, the Play of the Film of the War* (PAJ). A translation of Handke's "To Duration, A Poem" is forthcoming with Cannon, Amsterdam. Abbott has published reviews of books and art in *The Bloomsbury Review, Open Letters Monthly,* and *Catalyst Magazine*. He is Professor of Philosophy and Humanities at Utah Valley University and has published literary-critical articles on Goethe, Schiller, Kleist, Thomas Mann, Rilke, Grass, and Handke. With Lyn Bennett, he is working on a book about how barbed wire was given meaning in late 19th-century advertising and then in literature of the twentieth and twenty-first centuries ("It was a nun they say invented barbed wire": James Joyce, *Ulysses*). For a book to be called "On Standing," he is analyzing the metaphor of standing in literature and philosophy (Herder, Humboldt, Schopenhauer, Heidegger, and Derrida; Goncharov and Dostoevsky; Kleist and Döblin; Rilke and Knausgaard; Faulkner and Morrison; and in the poetry of Dickinson, Eliot, Norris, Jarman, Hass, and Ashbery). He lives in Woodland Hills, Utah.

We are grateful to Utah Valley University for supporting the translation of *Vampires*.